TO
PLAY THE
FOOL

Also by Laurie R. King

Kate Martinelli novel
A Grave Talent

Mary Russell novel
*The Beekeeper's Apprentice:
On the Segregation of the Queen*

◆

TO
PLAY THE
FOOL

◆

LAURIE R. KING

ST. MARTIN'S PRESS
NEW YORK

m
c. 1

The chapter headings come from G. K. Chesterton's biography of St. Francis of Assisi (Garden City, N.Y.: Doubleday, 1924).

The passage quoted on page 128 and the reference on page 105 to the modern Irish community of Fools are to be found in John Saward, *Perfect Fools*, Oxford: Oxford University Press, 1980.

Library of Congress Cataloging-in-Publication Data

King, Laurie R.
    To play the fool / Laurie R. King.
      p. cm.
    "A Thomas Dunne book."
    ISBN 0-312-11907-0
    I. Title.
    PS3561.I4813T6   1995
    813'.54—dc20   94-40981
                                          CIP

First edition: February 1995
10 9 8 7 6 5 4 3 2 1

For the aptly named
Nathanael Wayland,
Anglo-Saxon trickster
and the only man in the Bible
to crack a joke.

It would be idle to deny that the cities of San Francisco and Berkeley, the University of California, and the Graduate Theological Union (*in aeternum floreant*) do actually exist and possess a certain degree of similarity to their equivalents within the pages of this book. It is therefore the more necessary to reassure the reader that although the institutions do stand in brick and glass, the individuals, be they seminarians, deans, police officers, or citizens of the streets, as well as the modern international Fools movement as described herein, are but figments of the writer's imagination.

Except perhaps one.

This fellow's wise enough to play the fool,
And to do that well craves a kind of wit:
He must observe their mood on whom he jests,
The quality of persons, and the time;
And like the haggard, check at every feather
That comes before his eye. This is a practice
As full of labour as a wise man's art . . .
—William Shakespeare
Twelfth Night

TO
PLAY THE
FOOL

◆

ONE

◆

Brother Fire

The fog lay close over San Francisco the morning the homeless gathered in the park to cremate Theophilus.

Brother Erasmus had chosen the site, the small baseball diamond in the western half of Golden Gate Park. Only one or two of the men and women who came together recognized the macabre irony in the site's location, which adjoined the barbecue pits, and wondered if Brother Erasmus had done it deliberately. It was his style, to be sure.

The first of the park's residents to wake that gray and dripping January morning was Harry. His awakening was abrupt as always, more a matter of being launched from sleep by the ghosts in his head than it was a true waking up. One moment he was snoring peacefully; the next he snorted, and then there was a brief struggle with the terrifying confines of the bedroll before he flung it off and scrambled heavily upright to crash in blind panic through the shrubs. After half a dozen steps his brain began to make its connections, and after three more he stopped, bent over double to cough for a while, and then turned back to his bed beneath the rhododendrons. He methodically loaded his duffel bag with the possessions too valuable to risk leaving behind—the photograph of his wife and their long-dead son taken in 1959, one small worn book, a rosary, the warm woolen blanket some kind person had left (he was certain) for him, folded on their front steps—and began to close the duffel bag, then stopped, pulled it open again, and worked a hand far, far down into it. Eventually his fingers closed on the texture they sought, and he pulled out a necktie, a wadded length of grubby silk with an eye-bruising pattern that had been popular in the sixties. He draped it around the back of his neck, adjusted the the ends in front, and began the tricky loop-and-through knot with hands composed of ten thumbs. The third time the slippery fabric escaped his grasp, he cursed, then looked around guiltily. Putting an expression of improbable piety onto his face, he returned to the long-unused motions. The fifth try did it. He pulled the tie snug against the outside collars of the two shirts he wore, then after a moment of thought bent again to the duffel bag. This time he did not have to dig any farther than his forearm before encountering the comb, as orange as the tie and almost as old. He ran the uneven teeth through his thin hair, smoothed the result down with spit-wet palms, straightened his wrinkled tie with the panache of an investment banker, and pulled the top of the duffel bag shut.

Harry took a final look around his cavelike shelter beneath the shrubbery, swung the bag over his right shoulder, and pushed his way back out into the clearing. He paused only to pick up the three dead branches he had leaned against the tree the night before; then, branches upraised in his left hand, he turned west, deeper into the park.

Scotty was awake now, too, thanks to Harry's convulsive coughing fit 150 feet away. Scotty was not an early riser. He lay for some time, listening through a stupor of sleep and booze to the preparations of his neighbor. Finally Harry left, and the silence of dripping fog and cars on Fulton Street lulled him back toward sleep.

But Theophilus was your friend, he told himself in disgust; the least you can do is say good-bye to him. His hand in its fingerless glove crept out from the layers of cardboard and cloth he was swaddled in, closed on the neck of the bottle that lay beside his head, and drew it back in. The mound that was Scotty writhed about for a moment; gurgles were followed by silence; finally came a great weary sigh. Scotty evolved from the mound, scratched his scalp and beard thoroughly, drank the last of the cheap wine against the chill of the morning, and then with a great heaving and crashing hauled his grocery cart out of the undergrowth.

Scotty did not bother with self-beautification, just set his weight against what had once been a Safeway trolley and headed west. However, he walked with his eyes on the ground, occasionally stopping and bending down stiffly to pick up pieces of wood, which he then arranged on top of his other possessions. He seemed to prefer small pieces, but he had a sizable armful by the time he reached the baseball diamond.

As he went under the Nineteenth Avenue overpass, which was already humming with the early bridge traffic, Scotty was joined by Hat. Hat did not greet him—not aloud, at any rate—but nodded in his amiable way and fell in at Scotty's side. Hat

3

almost never spoke; in fact, he had received his name only because of the headgear he always wore. Brother Erasmus might know his real name—Harry had once said that he'd seen the two men in deep conversation—but no one else did. Hat migrated about the city. For the last few weeks, he had taken to sleeping near the Stow Lake boathouse. Today's hat was a jaunty tweed number complete with feather, rescued from a bin outside a health-food store; it was marred only by three small moth holes and a scorch mark along the back brim. He also wore a Vietnam-era army backpack slung over his shoulder. In his right hand he held a red nylon gym bag that he'd found one night in an alley. (He had discarded most of the burglary tools it contained as being too heavy, though the cash it held had been useful.) In his left hand he clutched the pale splintery slats of a broken-up fruit crate. His waist-length white beard had been neatly brushed and he wore a cheery yellow primrose, liberated from a park flowerbed the previous afternoon, in his lapel.

From across the park the homeless came, moved by a force most of them could neither have understood nor articulated. Had you asked, as the police later did, they could have said only that they came together because Brother Erasmus had asked them to. That good gentleman, though, despite appearing both lucid and palpably willing to help, proved as impossible to communicate with as if he had spoken a New Guinean dialect.

And so, despite their lack of understanding, they came: Sondra from the Haight, wearing her best velvet; Ellis from Potrero Street, muttering and shaking his head (an indication more of synapse damage than of disapproval); Wilhemena from her habitual residence near the Queen Wilhemena Tulip Garden; her neighbor Doc from the southern windmill; the newlyweds Tomás and Esmerelda from their home beneath the

4

bridge near the tennis court. Through the cultivated wilderness of John McLaren's park they came, to the baseball diamond where Brother Erasmus, John, and the late, lamented Theophilus awaited them. Each one carried some twigs or branches or scraps of wood; all of them tried to assemble before the sky grudgingly lightened into morning; the entire congregation came, each adding his or her wood to the pile Brother Erasmus had made beneath the stiff corpse, and then standing back to await the match.

Of course, there were other people in the park that morning. Cars passed through on Nineteenth Avenue, on Transverse Drive, on JFK Drive, but if they even noticed the park residents drifting through the fog, they thought nothing about it.

Other early users, however, did notice. The spandex-and-Nike-clad runners from the neighboring Richmond and Sunset districts had begun to trickle into the park at first light. Committed runners these, men and women who knew the value of sweat, unlike the mere joggers who would appear later in the day. They thudded along roads and paths, keeping a wary, if automatic, eye out for unsavory types who might beg, or mug, or certainly embarrass. It was actually relatively rare to see one of the homeless up and around at this hour, though they were often to be glimpsed, huddled among their possessions in the undergrowth or, occasionally, upright but apparently comatose.

This morning, though, the natives were restless. Several runners glanced at their chronographs to check that it was indeed their usual time, two or three of them wondered irritably if they were going to have to change where they ran, and some saw the sticks the tatterdemalion figures carried and abruptly shied away to the other side of the road.

The morning's injury (aside from the blow that had downed poor Theophilus—but then, that was from the previous day) happened to a bright young Stanford MBA, a vice president's assistant from the Bank of America. He was halfway through his daily five-mile stint, running easily down Kennedy Drive past the lake, the morning financial news droning through the headphones into his ears and the thought of an ominous meeting in four hour's time looming large in his consciousness, completely unprepared for the apparition of a six-foot-four bearded lunatic crashing out of the bushes with a huge club raised above his head. The MBA stumbled in sheer terror, fell, rolled, struggled to rise, his arms folded to protect his skull—and watched his would-be attacker give him a puzzled glance and finish hauling the eucalyptus bough out from the bushes, then walk away with the butt end of it on his shoulder and the dead leaves swishing noisily and fragrantly behind him.

By the time the trembling jogger had hobbled painfully onto Park Presidio, hitched two rides home, iced his swollen ankle, and telephoned the police, the assembly in the glen was complete: some two dozen homeless men and women, arrayed in a circle around a waist-high heap of twigs and branches, into which was nestled a small stiff body. They were singing the hymn "All Things Bright and Beautiful," painfully out of tune but with enthusiasm, when Brother Erasmus set the match to the pyre.

The headline on the bottom of page one of that afternoon's *Examiner* read: HOMELESS GATHER TO CREMATE BELOVED DOG IN GOLDEN GATE PARK.

◆

Three weeks later, his breath huffing in clouds and the news announcer still jabbering against his unhearing ears, the physically recovered but currently unemployed former Bank of America vice presidential assistant was slogging his disconsolate way alongside Kennedy Drive in the park when, to his instant and unreasoning fury, he was attacked for a second time by a branch-wielding bearded man from the shrubbery. Three weeks of ego deflation blew up like a rage-powered air bag: He instantly took four rapid steps forward and clobbered the unkempt head with the only thing he carried, which happened to be a Walkman stereo. Fortunately for both men, the case collapsed the moment it made contact with the wool cap, but the maddened former bank assistant stood over the terrified and hungover former real estate broker and pummeled away with his crumbling handful of plastic shards and electronic components.

A passing commuter saw them, snatched up her car telephone, and called 911.

Three minutes later, the eyes of the two responding police officers were greeted by the sight of a pair of men seated side by side on the frost-rimed grass: One was shocked, bleeding into his shaggy beard, and even at twenty feet stank of cheap wine and old sweat; the other was clean-shaven, clean-clothed, and wore a pair of two-hundred-dollar running shoes on his feet. Both men were weeping. The runner sat with his knees drawn up and his head buried in his arms; the wino had his arm across the other man's heaving shoulders and was patting awkwardly at the runner's arm in an obvious attempt at reassurance and comfort.

The two police officers never were absolutely certain about what had happened, but they filled out their forms and saw the two partners in adversity safely tucked into the ambulance. Just before the door closed, the female officer thought to ask why the homeless man had been dragging branches out of the woods in the first place.

By the time the two officers pounded up the pathway into the baseball clearing, the oily eucalyptus and redwood in this second funeral pyre had caught and flames were roaring up to the gray sky in great billows of sparks and burning leaves. It was a much larger pile of wood than had been under the small dog Theophilus three weeks earlier, but then, it had to be.

On the top of this pyre lay the body of a man.

♦

TWO

♦

*The Little Brothers lived at the Portiuncula,
without comforts, without possessions, eating
anything they could get and sleeping anyhow on
the ground.*

"God Almighty," muttered Kate Martinelli, "what'll you bet Jon
does a barbecue tonight."

She and Al Hawkin stood watching the medical examiner's men package the body for transport. The typical pugilist's
pose of a burned body was giving the men problems, but they
finally got the fists tucked in and loaded the body onto the van.
The cold air became almost breathable.

"You know," remarked Al, squinting up at a tree, "that's the
first joke I've heard you make in—what, six months?"

"It wasn't a joke."

"It'll pass for one."

"Life has not been funny, Al."

"No," he agreed. "No. How is Lee?"

"She's doing really well. She finally found a wheelchair that's comfortable, and the new physical therapist seems good. She wants to try Lee in a walker in a week or so. Don't mention it, though, if you talk to Lee. She'll want to do it then and there."

"I'll remember."

"Did I tell you she's started seeing clients again?"

"No! Now, that *is* good news."

"Only two of them, and on different days, but it gives her a feeling of real life. It's made a hell of a difference."

"I can imagine. Do you think she'd like a visitor?"

"She always loves to see you, Al."

"I got the impression it tired her out."

"Tires her for that day, cheers her up for the next two. A good trade. Just call before you go; she doesn't deal too well with surprises."

"I'll call. Tomorrow, if I can swing it. I'll take her some flowers."

"Don't do that. Lee hates cut flowers."

"I know. It'll give us something to argue about."

"So thoughtful, Al."

"That's me."

"Well," said Kate, pulling her notebook and pen from a jacket pocket, "back to work."

"Martinelli?" She stopped and turned to look at her partner. "It's good to have you back."

Kate ducked her head in acknowledgment and walked quickly away.

Al Hawkin watched her walk toward the motley congregation of homeless, her spine straight and her attitude as qui-

10

etly self-contained as ever, and found himself wondering why the hell she had come back.

The last months must have seared themselves straight down into the bones of her mind, he reflected, but aside from the increased wariness in her already-wary eyes, she did not show it. Oh, yes—and the white-eyed terror with which she regarded the three newspaper reporters who slouched behind the police tapes.

Last spring the media had seized her with sheer delight, a genuine San Francisco lesbian, a policewoman, whose lover had been shot and left dramatically near death by a sociopath who was out to destroy the world-famous artist Eva Vaughn— the combination of high culture, pathos, and titillation were irresistible, even for serious news media. For a couple of weeks, Kate's squarish face and haunted dark eyes looked out from the pages of supermarket scandal sheets and glossy weekly news journals, and ABC did a half-hour program on homosexuality in the police force.

And while this jamboree was going on, while the hate mail was pouring in and the Hall of Justice switchboard was completely jammed, Kate lived at the hospital, where her lover teetered on the edge of death. It was six weeks before Kate knew Lee would live; another six weeks passed before the doctors voiced a faint hope that she might regain partial sensation and a degree of control below the waist.

At this juncture Hawkin had done something that still gave him cold sweats of guilt when he thought about it: Guided by an honest belief that work would be the best therapy for Kate, he had taken ruthless advantage of her newfound optimism and yanked her back onto the force, into their partnership, and straight into the unparalleled disaster of the Raven Morningstar murder case. And of course, when the case blew up in blood and scandal back in August, the media had been ecstatic to find Kate right in the middle. That she was one of the few out of the cast of dramatic personae not culpable for any fault greater than a lack of precognition mattered not. She was their prize, their Inspector Casey, and she bled publicly for the nation's entertainment.

Why she had not resigned after the Morningstar case, Hawkin could not understand. She hadn't put her gun inside her mouth because Lee needed her; she hadn't had a serious mental breakdown for the same reason. Instead, she had clawed herself into place behind a desk and endured five months of paper shuffling and that special hatred and harassment that a quasimilitary organization reserves for one of their own who has exposed the weakness of the whole. Two weeks ago, pale but calm, she had appeared at Hawkin's desk and informed him that if he still wanted her as his partner, she was available.

He held an enormous respect for this young woman, a feeling he firmly kept from her, and just as firmly demonstrated before others in the department.

However, he still didn't know why the hell she had come back.

♦

At four o'clock that afternoon, across town at the Hall of Justice, the question had not been answered so much as submerged beneath the complexities of the case.

"So," Hawkin stretched out in his chair and tried to rub the tiredness from the back of his neck. The coffee hadn't helped much. "Have you managed to make any sense of this mess?" He might have been referring to the case in general, or to the unruly drift of papers covering the desk's surface, which now included roughly transcribed interviews, printouts of arrest records for the people involved, as well as the records from the earlier dog incident. This last report had been couched in phrases that made clear what the two investigating officers had thought of their odd case, wandering as it did between a recognition of its absurdity and downright sarcasm at the waste of their time. The recorded interview with the dog's owner had been perfunctory and less than helpful, and Hawkin's interview with the officer involved had stopped short of scathing only because he knew that his own reaction would have been much the same as the younger man's.

"A bit, but we have to find this man Erasmus. He organized the cremation of the dog last month, though everyone was quite clear—those who were clear, that is, if you know what I mean—that he wasn't here this time. They seem to have decided that what was good enough for the dog was good enough for the dog's owner. Crime Scene's going back tonight to check the whole area with Luminol, but it looks like one patch of blood that bled slowly and stopped with death rather than blood pouring out from, say, a knife wound. Could have been shot, but Luis, one of the men who found him, said his head looked bashed. And of course we know what happened to every loose stick in the whole damned park. Sorry? Oh, yes, I'll have another cup, thanks.

"Where was I?" Kate thumbed through her notes a moment. "Okay, who found the body. Harry Radovich and Luis Ortiz both claim they saw him first, but they were together, and their stories mesh—though Harry's is a little clearer in the details. They saw his kit abandoned behind a bench at about six P.M., went looking for him, and found him. You saw the place, about three hundred yards from where they tried to burn him this morning. At first they thought he was asleep, lying face-down, slightly tilted onto his right side, under that tree with the branches that touch the ground. They were worried, seeing him lying on the ground just in his clothes, and thought he

13

might be sick, this flu that's going around. So they shook his legs, got no response, pushed their way in and turned him on his back. There was dried blood covering the right side of his head and face, his eyeballs were slightly sunken and dry-looking, the corneas cloudy, his facial skin dark with no blanching under pressure, and he was getting pretty stiff in his upper body."

"A couple of drunks told you all that?" asked Hawkin, turning from the coffee machine to look at her in astonishment.

"Luis was a medic in Vietnam for three years; he knows what a dead body looks like."

"So you think his judgment's good on this?"

"Large grain of salt, but he swears he didn't get truly smashed until after finding the body, and he seems shaky now but sober. His testimony is worth keeping in mind, that's all, until we hear the postmortem results."

"Which probably won't tell us much about time of death unless the stomach contents are good."

"Any idea when they'll do the postmortem?"

"First thing in the morning."

"Good," she said evenly, as if talking about the arrival of a tidy packet of information instead of the participation in an ordeal of burned flesh and the smell of power saws cutting through bone.

"Meanwhile, though," he said, "what are we talking here? Middle-aged alcoholic on a night just above freezing, how many hours to rigor?"

"John didn't drink. They all agree on that. Or use drugs."

"Okay. So assuming they recognize liver mortis when they see it, which I doubt, that'd put it, oh, say some time before noon on Tuesday morning. Just as a guideline to get us started."

14

"I agree, though I'd lean to the later end of that. His body looked on the thin side."

As Hawkin had studiously avoided any close examination of the remains, he couldn't argue.

"Any of them have a last name for him, any ID?" he asked.

"Nope. They just knew him as John."

"Theophilus's owner."

"Who?"

"The dog. Means 'one who loves God,' I think."

"What is this, a mission to the homeless? Lover of God and Brother Erasmus. Batty names." Kate snorted.

"Erasmus was a philosopher, wasn't he? Wrote *The Praise of Folly*. Seventeenth century? Sixteenth?"

"I'll take your word for it. Anyway, this Erasmus is across the Bay somewhere, Berkeley or Oakland, not due back until Sunday, and they were afraid the body would smell, so they didn't wait for him to get back. Just hauled in every scrap of wood they could find, shoved his body on, added a few bottles of various flammable liquids, and lighted it. With prayers, read by Wilhemena and one of the men. Rigor mortis may have been beginning to wear off, by the way, at six this morning. His head was floppy when they moved him onto the woodpile."

"Right. Let's hang on to Harry, Luis, and Wilhemena, at least until we get the postmortem report to give us a cause of death. Charge them with improper disposal of a body, interfering with an investigation, whatever you like. The rest of them can go. And we might as well go, too. There's not much more we can do until the results come in, except find the good Brother Erasmus. You want to do that?"

"Tonight?"

"Tomorrow. I'll take the postmortem."

How interesting, Hawkin thought. I've only worked with

Martinelli for a total of a few weeks, and most of that was months ago, but I can still read her face. She's trying to decide if she should insist on taking the shit job, to prove herself capable. No, can't quite do it. Can't quite admit she's relieved that I took it, either.

Kate was still wrestling with gratitude when Hawkin's phone rang.

"Hawkin," he said, and listened for a minute. "I am." Another longish pause, then: "Sure, bring her up." He hung up and looked at Kate. "There's a homeless woman downstairs, came in with information on the cremation."

♦

THREE

♦

. . . Water his sister, pure and clean and inviolate.

The woman who entered a few minutes later wasn't quite what
Kate had expected. She was quite tidy, for one thing, her graying hair gathered into a snug bun at the nape of her neck; her
eyes darted nervously about, but they were clear, and her spine
was straight. She wore the inevitable eclectic jumble, long skirt
with trouser cuffs underneath, blouse, vest, knitted shawl, and
rings on five fingers, but she wrapped her clothes around her
with dignity and sat without hesitation in the chair Hawkin indicated. Kate turned another chair around to the desk and took
out her pen. Hawkin looked down at the paper he'd just been

given and then up at her, a smile of singular sweetness on his rugged face.

"Your name is Beatrice?" he asked, giving the name two syllables.

"Beatrice," she corrected, giving it the Italian four.

"Any last name?"

"Not for many years."

"What was it then?"

"The men downstairs asked me that, too."

"And you didn't give it to them."

"I was not impressed by the manners of your police department."

"I apologize for them. Their youth does not excuse them." She studied him thoughtfully.

"Forgive them; for they know not what they do. That's what Brother Erasmus would say, I suppose."

"Who is this Brother Erasmus?" he asked her.

"Jankowski."

"Erasmus Jankowski?" Hawkin said, polite but amazed.

"No! I hardly know the man," Beatrice protested. Kate rested her elbow on the desk and pinched the bridge of her nose for a moment. "Well, no, I admit I do know him, as well as anyone you brought in this morning, which isn't saying much."

"It's your last name, then? Beatrice Jankowski?"

"You can see why I gave up the last part."

"Oh, I don't know," said Hawkin, rising to gallantry. "It has a certain ring to it."

"Like a funeral toll," she said expressively. Hawkin abandoned his flirtation.

"What do you know about what happened in Golden Gate Park this morning, Miss—is it Miss Jankowski?"

"Call me Beatrice. I told them they were imbeciles, but

18

even men who fry their brains on cheap wine don't listen to women."

"You tried to dissuade them . . . from the cremation."

"There is a difference between a man and a dog, after all."

"You were there when the dog was cremated—what was it, three or four weeks ago?" Hawkin asked.

"That had a certain beauty," Beatrice said wistfully. "It was appropriate. It was also—well, perhaps not strictly legal, but hardly criminal. Wouldn't you agree?" she asked, and blinked her eyes gently at Al Hawkin. He avoided the question.

"Did you know the dead man?"

"I knew the dog, quite well."

"And the man?"

"Oh dear. He was . . ." For the first time Beatrice Jankowski looked uncomfortable. "You don't really want to know about him."

"I do, you know."

She met his eyes briefly, looked down at her strong fingers with their swollen knuckles, twisting and turning one ring after another, and sighed.

"Yes, I suppose you do. I'd rather talk about the dog."

"Tell us about the dog first, then," Hawkin relented. Relief blossomed on the woman's weathered face and her hands lay still.

"He was a real sweetheart, white, with a black patch over his left eye. His coat looked wiry, but he was actually quite soft, picked up foxtails terribly. John—that's his owner—had to brush him every day. Very intelligent, particularly when you consider the size of his skull. I saw him cross the road once, looking both ways first."

"So how did he die?"

"We . . . They . . . No one saw. He must have made a

mistake crossing the road. John found him, in the morning. He'd hit his head on something."

"Or something had hit him." She nodded. "Or kicked him." Her face contracted slowly and her fingers began to wring each other over and over.

"How did John die?"

"I don't have any idea. I didn't even see him."

"How did you hear about his death?"

"Mouse told me late last night. He was sorting through the bins behind a restaurant on Stanyon Street."

"Which one is Mouse?"

"They call him Mouse because he used to be in computers, before his breakdown. Lovely man. His other name is Richard, I believe."

"Richard Delgadio. Tall black man, hair going gray, short beard?"

"Is that his last name? Delgadio. What a lovely sound."

"What time did he tell you about John's death?"

In answer, the woman pushed her left sleeve up her arm and looked eloquently at the bare wrist.

"Roughly what time, then?" Hawkin asked patiently.

"Time," she mused. "Time takes on rather a different aspect on the streets. However, I do remember that the dress shop was closed, but the bookstore was still open, so that would make it between nine and eleven. Is it of any importance to your investigation?"

"Probably not." Beatrice giggled, and Hawkin gave her a smile. "But you didn't go to the—what did they call it? The cremation?"

"I did not. I told Mouse then and there he was a cretin and a dunderhead, and that he should tell Officer Michaels about John."

"Michaels is one of the local patrolmen?"

20

"He's a hunk."

"Sorry?" Hawkins asked, startled at the unlikely word.

"He is. Gorgeous legs, just the right amount of hair on them. Don't tell him I said anything, though. He might be embarrassed."

Kate thought she recognized the description.

"Is this one of the bicycle patrol officers?" she asked.

"Gorgeous," Beatrice repeated in agreement. Al Hawkin's mouth twitched.

"But you didn't report John's death?" he asked.

"It was not my place."

"You knew they were planning on burning the body first thing in the morning."

"Mouse found a half-empty bottle of paint thinner and asked me if it would burn. And I saw Mr. Lazari at the grocer's giving Doc and Salvatore a couple of old wooden crates. I told him, too."

"Mr. Lazari?"

"Of course not. He's quite sensible."

"You told Doc. That John was dead?"

"Inspector, are you listening to me?"

"I am trying, Ms. Jankowski. Beatrice."

"Ah, you are tired, of course. I apologize for keeping you. No, I told Doc that he and Harry and the rest were a parcel of half-wits and were going to find themselves in trouble. I told them Brother Erasmus would be unhappy. Doc listened; Salvatore didn't. He even had a Bible, although I didn't think much of his choice of readings. Song of Songs is hardly funereal."

"Salvatore had the Bible? So Salvatore led the . . . funeral service."

"I was surprised, too, considering."

"Considering what, Beatrice?"

"Well, you know."

21

"Actually, I don't."

"Oh, of course, how silly of me. You never met the man."

"Salvatore Benito? I spoke with him earlier."

She sat in her chair and gave him a look of sad disappointment.

"Or do you mean John? No, I never met him."

"Lucky old you," she muttered.

"You didn't like John?"

"He did not deserve a dog like Theophilus."

"That surprises me. The others seemed to think he was a nice guy."

"One may smile, and smile, and be a villain. Did Erasmus say that, or did I read it somewhere? Oh dear, I am getting old."

"John was friendly on the surface but not when you got to know him? Is that what you mean?"

"I did not know him," she said firmly. "Unfortunately, he knew me. But he couldn't make me go to his funeral, and now he can't—" She caught herself, looked down at her hands, and twisted her rings before shooting a chagrined glance at the two detectives. "He was not a nice man."

Hawkin leaned back in his chair and studied her.

"He was blackmailing you?" he suggested.

"That's a very ugly word."

"It's an ugly thing."

"I didn't like it, but it wasn't anything nasty. Maybe a wee bit nasty," she amended. "Just a sort of encouragement, to make me do things I otherwise might not have."

"Such as?"

"They were such big shops, they could afford to lose a bit to pilfering."

"He had you shoplifting for him?"

Her head came up and she flushed in anger.

"Inspector! How could you think that of me? I would

never! There's a world of difference between actually doing something like that and just not . . . tattling."

"I see. You witnessed John shoplifting and he made you keep silent," Hawkin translated.

"After that he would show me things he'd taken. He knew I didn't like it, that it made me . . . uncomfortable."

"Did he blackmail others?"

"It wasn't really blackmail," she protested. "He never wanted anything. It was just a sort of . . . control thing. He liked to see people squirm."

"Who were these others?"

"I've only known him for two years."

"Their names?" he asked gently.

"I . . . don't know for sure. I wondered, because there were a couple of men he seemed friendly with who suddenly seemed to be uncomfortable around him and then moved away. One of them was named Maguire—I think that was his last name—and then last summer a pleasant little Chinese man named Chin."

"Any who didn't move away?"

"Well, I . . ."

"Salvatore, perhaps?"

"It did seem very odd, him conducting the funeral like that, when he's never been all that close to Brother Erasmus."

"Was John? Close to Brother Erasmus, I mean?"

"He thought he was."

"But you felt Brother Erasmus was keeping some distance?" Kate was very glad that Al seemed to be following this woman's erratic line of thought, more like a random series of stepping-stones than a clear path.

"Brother Erasmus has no friends."

"But John thought he was Erasmus's friend?" Hawkin persisted.

"Undoubtedly. He always steps in when Brother Erasmus is away. Stepped."

"Do you think John was blackmailing Erasmus?"

"I don't think that is actually his name."

"John? Or Erasmus?"

"Why, both, come to think of it."

"Was John blackmailing Brother Erasmus?"

"Brother Erasmus isn't the sort to be blackmailed."

"Do you think John was trying?"

"Oh, Inspector, you are so pushy!"

"That's my job, Beatrice."

"You're as bad as John was, in a way, though much nicer with it, not so sort of slimy."

"Do you think—"

"I don't know!" she burst out unhappily. "Yes, all right, it seemed an unlikely friendship, partnership, liaison, what have you. But Brother Erasmus is not the sort to submit to overt blackmail."

"But covert blackmail?" Hawkin seized on her word.

"I . . . I wondered. There was a sort of—oh, how to describe it?—a manipulative intimacy about John's attitude toward Erasmus, and in turn Erasmus—Brother Erasmus—seemed to be . . . I don't know. Watching him, maybe. Yes, I suppose that's it. John would kind of sidle up to Erasmus as if they shared a great secret, and Erasmus would draw himself up and, without actually stepping back, seem to be stopping himself from moving away."

Considering the source, it was a strikingly lucid picture of a complex relationship, and Kate felt she knew quite a bit about both of the men involved. She continued with the motions of note-taking until Hawkin finally broke the silence.

"Tell me about the man Erasmus."

"You haven't met him yet?"

"Not that I know of."

"Oh, you'd know it if you had. He's a fool!" she said proudly, varying her terms of derision to include a monosyllable.

"He's a sort of informal leader of the homeless people around Golden Gate Park?"

"Only for things like the funeral."

"John's funeral?"

"I told you, Inspector, he wasn't there. He brought us together, said words over Theophilus, and lighted the pyre. Today's lunacy would never have happened on a Sunday or Monday, but instead those morons Harry and Salvatore and Doc—and Wilhemena! God, she's the worst of them—decided they could say words as well as he could. I should have insisted, I know," she admitted sadly. "There's not a one of them playing with a full deck."

"And Brother Erasmus is a bad as the others, you said."

"I never!" she said indignantly.

"But you did. You called him a fool."

"A fool, certainly."

"But the others are fools, too?" asked Hawkin. He spoke with the caution of a man feeling for a way in the dark, but his words were ill-chosen, and Beatrice went rigid, her eyes narrowing in a rapid reassessment of Inspector Al Hawkin.

"They most certainly are not. They haven't any sense at all."

Kate gave up. The woman's occasional appearance of rationality was obviously misleading. Even Hawkin looked lost.

"I think we should talk with your Brother Erasmus," he said finally.

"I'm sure he'll straighten things out for you," Beatrice agreed. "Although you might find it difficult to talk with him."

"Why is that?"

"I told you, he's a fool."

"But he sounds fairly sensible to me."

"Of course. Some of them are."

"Some of whom?"

"Fools, of course."

Kate was perversely gratified to see that finally Al was beginning to grit his teeth. She'd begun to think she was out of practice.

"And where is this foolish Brother now?" he growled.

"I told you, it's Wednesday. He'll be on Holy Hill."

"Holy Hill? Do you mean Mt. Davidson?" There was a cross on top of that knob, where pilgrims gathered every year for Easter sunrise services.

"I don't think so," Beatrice said doubtfully. "Isn't that in San Francisco? This one is across the bay."

"Do you mean 'Holy Hill' in Berkeley, Ms. Jankowski?" Kate asked suddenly.

"That sounds right. There's a school there, in Berkeley, isn't there?" The flagship of the University of California fleet, demoted to a mere "school" status, thought Kate with a smile.

"Yes, there's a school in Berkeley."

"Brother Erasmus is in Berkeley every Wednesday, Ms.— Beatrice?" continued Hawkin. "Just Wednesday?"

"Of course not. He leaves here on Tuesday and is back on Saturday. Although usually he doesn't come to the Park until Sunday morning, when he conducts services, which is the excuse those idiots used to cremate John right away. They said he'd stink; personally, I think the weather's been too cold."

"Good. Well, thank you for your help, Ms. Jankowski. We'll need to talk with you again in a day or so. Where can we find you?"

"Ah. Now that's a good question. On Friday night I am usually at a coffeehouse on Haight Street, a place called Sentient Beans. Some very nice young people run it. They allow me to use their washing machine in exchange for drawings."

"Drawings?"

"I'm an artist. Or I was an artist—I never know which to say. My nerves went, but my hand is still steady enough. I do portraits of the customers sometimes while my clothes are being cleaned—I do so enjoy the luxury of clean clothes, I will admit. And a bath—I use the one upstairs at the coffeehouse on Fridays, and occasionally during the first part of the week the man who runs the jewelers on the next street lets me use his shower—if he doesn't have any customers. But I'm never far from that area if you want to find me. It's my home, and the people know me. It's safer that way, you know."

"Yes," agreed Hawkin thoughtfully. "Unlike some of the gentlemen in this case, you are certainly no fool."

"I told you," she said with a degree of impatience, "they are not fools. But then," she reflected sadly, "neither am I. I'm afraid I haven't enough strength of character."

FOUR

And as he stared at the word "fool" written in luminous letters before him, the word itself began to shine and change.

When Beatrice Jankowski had gone, Kate and Al sat for a long minute, staring at each other across his desk.

"Al," said Kate, "did that woman have a short in the system or was she just speaking another language?"

"I feel half-drunk," he said in wonder, and rubbed his stubbled face vigorously. "I need some air. Come on."

Kate scrabbled her notes together into her shoulder bag, snatched up her coat, and caught up with Al at the elevators, where he stood with his foot in the door, irritating the other passengers, who included three high-priced lawyers and an assistant DA. The door closed and they began to descend. The four suits resumed their discussion, which seemed to involve a plea bargain, and suddenly Hawkin held his hand up.

"Fool!" he exclaimed. The lawyer in front of him, who in a bad year earned five times Hawkin's salary, started to bristle, but Al wasn't seeing him; he turned to Kate intently. "The way she used the word *fool*," he said. "It meant something to her, other than just an insulting term."

Kate thought back over the woman's words. "You're right. It's as if she thought of the word as being capitalized."

"Damn. Oh well, we can find her Friday night at the coffee place, if we want." The doors opened onto the ground floor and Kate followed him outside, where he stood breathing in great lungfuls of the pollution from the freeway overhead. Kate tried to breathe shallowly, if at all, and was suddenly very aware of the trials of the long day.

"You'll go to Berkeley tomorrow morning, then," said Al. "I've been in touch with the department there, letting them know you'll be waltzing across their turf. If you need to make an arrest, call them for backup. I doubt that you will, though," he added. "Erasmus sounds a peaceable sort. Better take a departmental car, though. You do know where this Holy Hill is?"

"If it's the same place, it's what they call the area above the Cal campus, where there's a bunch of seminaries and church schools."

"Sounds like a reasonable shot. I'll take the postmortem, and we'll talk when you get back."

Right." It was a good time to leave, but she lingered, enjoying the sensation of being back in her own world. The nightmare of the last year was not about to fade under two weeks' worth of cold reality, but she did feel she had achieved some small distance. It was a good feeling. "Al," she said on impulse, "come home for a drink. Or coffee, or dinner. Or even just a breath of real air."

"No, I can't. You haven't warned Lee."

"Oh hell, a little surprise will do her good. Unless—do you have something planned for tonight?"

"Not tonight."

"Still seeing Jani?"

"Still seeing Jani."

"She's a fine person, Al."

"She is. She was happy to hear you're back in harness, sent her greeting. Invited you for dinner, as soon as Lee's up to the drive."

"She might enjoy that. Ask her yourself, tonight."

"You're sure?"

"I'm sure."

"Okay. One drink and a brief conversation with Lee, and if that damned houseboy of yours is cooking a barbecue, I'll break his neck."

♦

Hawkin did not stay to dinner, and as Jon was experimenting with lentils, he escaped with his neck intact. After Hawkin left, Kate settled Lee at the table, which was set for two, and went into the kitchen. She peered past Jon's shoulder at the pot on the stove, plucked a piece of sausage out, receiving a slap from the wooden spoon, and put the meat in her mouth.

"Are you not eating, or am I?" she asked Jon.

"Since you're here, I'm going out."

"You're leaving me phone numbers?"

He turned to look at her. "Why on earth do you need phone numbers? You're not a teenaged baby-sitter."

"Jon," she said with exaggerated patience, "I am back on active duty. I explained to you last month what this would mean. I am no longer shuffling papers from eight to five. I may be called out at any time, and I do not want Lee left alone for hours and hours. I need all of your phone numbers."

"But I don't know them," he cried. "I mean, what if I decide to go somewhere?"

"Report in. Damn it Jon, you know it isn't good for her to be alone for any length of time."

"All right, all right, all right. I'll give you phone numbers. But don't you think it's time we entered the twentieth century and got me a beeper?"

"Good idea. Get one tomorrow."

"How chic. Everyone will think I'm a doctor. I think I'll be an obstetrician. Terribly exotic, and it'll save me from having to look at strange growths and aches on strangers that I'd rather not know about. Now for heaven's sake, quit jabbering and take those plates in. I have to go do my hair."

Kate obediently took the plates, served herself and Lee, and then bent her head and wolfed the lentil-and-sausage cassoulet. Whatever Jon's shortcomings (and she'd had her doubts from the very beginning, even before the day they had passed in the hallway and he had paused to say, "Look, dearie, it isn't every man gets to change his shrink's diapers. I mean, what would Papa Sigmund say? Too Freudian"), the man could cook.

Kate helped herself to a second serving and started in more slowly.

"Did you eat today?" Lee asked.

"I think so. There were sandwiches at some point, but it was a while ago. Jon, this is gorgeous," she said as he came in from the recently converted basement apartment. "Will you marry me?"

"You just want me to work for nothing, I know you macho types," he said with an exaggerated simper and held out a piece of paper. "Here is my every possible phone number, plus a few unlikelies. And I've also put down the numbers of Karin and Wade, in case you've lost them. Karin can come anytime; Wade, up until six in the morning."

"What about Phyllis?"

"She's in N'Orleans this week, y'all," he drawled. "Playin' with the bubbas and all them good ol' boys, hot damn."

"Have a good time, Jon," said Lee.

"You too, darlin'."

The house seemed to expand when he left, and suddenly, unexpectedly, Kate was aware of a touch, just a faint brush of unease at being alone with Lee. She wondered at it, wondered if Lee felt it, and decided that she couldn't have or she would say something.

"I feel like my mother has just left me alone in the house with a girlfriend," Lee said.

"I was just thinking how quiet it was."

Without taking her eyes from Kate's, Lee reached down and freed the brakes on her chair, backed and maneuvered to where Kate sat, laid her hand on the back of Kate's neck, and kissed her, long and slow. She then backed away again and returned to her place, leaving Kate flushed, short of breath, and laughing.

"Necking while Mom's away," Kate commented.

"Different from having her in the next room."

"I'm sure Jon would love it if you started calling him Mom."

"You still don't like him, do you?"

"I like him well enough." That Kate detested having any person other than Lee in the house, no matter how easy to live with, was a fact both unavoidable and best not talked about.

"You don't trust him."

"With you, with the house, I believe he is a thoroughly responsible and trustworthy person," Kate said carefully. "He is

32

absolutely ideal as a caregiver for you, and I think we're very, very lucky to have him. If there's anything about him I don't trust, it's his motives. He's a blessing from heaven, he works cheap, he even knows when to disappear, but I can't help having a niggling suspicion that we're going to have to pay for it somehow in the end."

"Transference with a vengeance," Lee agreed. "Every therapist's nightmare, a client who gets his foot in the door. However, I think Jon Sampson's a much more balanced individual than he appears. He plays up the 'patient turned powerful doctor' role in order to defuse it, and he is aware that one of his motives in taking the job was his lingering guilt at having a part, however minor, in my being shot. He's clearly focused both on his sense of responsibility for what happened to me and on how invalid the guilt is, and he's working on it. It's a complex relationship, but I still don't think I was wrong to allow it."

"You're probably right. I just get suspicious when someone wants to ingratiate himself." Kate paused, remembering Beatrice Jankowski's similar description of the dead man John. Odd, the coincidence in names, although come to think of it Jon's name had been chosen to replace the hated Marvin his parents had blessed him with. Though what was to say John was not an alias, as well? Beatrice thought so. Another thing to ask Brother Erasmus tomorrow, if she found him. She put the forkful in her mouth and looked up, to see Lee gazing at her with an odd, crooked smile on her face.

"What?"

"You really are back into it, aren't you?" Lee said.

"Back into what?"

"You know what I'm talking about. You were suddenly miles away, thinking about the case."

"Was I? Sorry. Funny, Al said pretty much the same thing

today. I guess you're right. This case is different. It's . . . interesting. Could you push the salad over here?"

Silence, and the sounds of fork and plate, and then Lee spoke, deliberately.

"For a while there, I thought you might quit."

"What, resign? From the department?"

"You've been hanging by a thread for months, and I got the distinct impression that going back into partnership with Al was a final trial to prove to yourself how much you hated the job."

"I don't hate the job."

"Kate, you've been a basket case. You'd hate any job that did that to you."

"Don't exaggerate."

"It's true. You've been a classic example of posttraumatic stress syndrome. I'm not saying without reason, sweetheart. I mean, I know you're Superwoman, but even a Woman of Steel can develop metal fatigue."

"I've just been tired. I've been working too hard."

"Bullshit," Lee said politely. "You've spent months doing nothing but type reports and worry about me. You've been through hell, Kate. First the man Lewis and then, when you got your feet under you again, the Morningstar case steamrolled over you."

"So what do you want me to say?" Kate demanded. "That I'm not quitting? Okay, I'm not quitting. We can't afford it, for one thing. We'd starve if I went private." Which, she realized belatedly, revealed that she'd at least considered it, a point that Lee did not miss.

"You know full well that with your reputation in the city, if you went into private investigations, within a year you'd be making twice what you do now."

"Not twice," Kate protested feebly.

34

"Damn near. So don't use salary as an excuse."

Anger did not sit well on a face so carved by pain's lines as Lee's face was, and the sight made Kate rise up in wretchedness and despair.

"You want me to quit? I'll quit. I've told you that before, but you have to say it. All right, I thought if I hated the job enough, I'd want to resign on my own, and that would make you happy. But I didn't. All I hated was being away from my job. I will quit if you ask me, Lee, but if you don't, all I can say is, I'm a cop. I am a cop."

Lee's features slowly relaxed and the lines lessened, until she was smiling at Kate.

"Your resignation would not make me happy, sweetheart. I've never much liked your job, and now it just plain frightens me, but I don't want you to quit. You are a cop, Kate, and I love you."

◆

FIVE

◆

Le Jongleur de Dieu

The sun came out while Kate was driving across the Bay Bridge the next morning, and the hills behind Berkeley and Oakland were green with the winter rains. The departmental unmarked car had something funny about its front end, so rather than wrestle it through the side streets, Kate stayed on the crowded freeway, got off at University Avenue, and drove straight up toward the University of California's oldest campus, squatting on the hill at the head of the broad, straight avenue like an ill-tempered concrete toad. At the last possible instant, Kate avoided being swallowed by her alma mater and veered left, then right on the road that followed the north perimeter. Between university buildings on the right and converted Victorians and apartments on the left, she drove until she came to a cluster of shops on a side street and one of the main pedestrian entrances to the campus, a continuation of Telegraph Avenue on the opposite side. She turned up this street away from the University of California, moving cautiously among the crowds of casually earnest students and suicidal bicyclists, and in two hundred yards found herself in a different world. As she had remembered, the university crowds seemed miraculously to vanish, leaving only the serious-minded graduate schools of divinity and theology and eternal truths.

There were also more parking spaces. She fought the car into one, fed the meter, and then walked back down the hill to indulge in a few minutes of nostalgia. The Chinese restaurant was still there, and the pizza-and-beer joint in whose courtyard, in another lifetime, Lee the graduate student had oh so casually brushed against the arm of Kate the junior-year student, Kate the unhappy, Kate the unquestioningly hetero, leaving a tantalizing and only half-conscious question that would crop up at inconvenient moments until it was finally resolved almost two years later: Yes, Lee had meant it.

The espresso bars and the doughnut shop, the scruffy bookstore and the art-film theater, shops selling clothes and pens and backpacks, all crowded into one short block. Browsing the windows in bittersweet pleasure, Kate's attention was caught by a display of unusual jewelry made of some small scraps of odd iridescent plastic. She went to the shop and bought the hair combs, a pair of extravagant multicolored swirling shapes, the blue of which matched the color of Lee's eyes. The woman wrapped the box in a glossy midnight paper and Kate dropped it into her coat pocket.

She turned briskly uphill, crossed the street that brought an end to commerce, and walked up another block to the sign for a Catholic school she had noticed while cruising for a parking space: Surely the Catholics would know.

As she reached for the door, it opened and a brown-robed monk came out.

"Excuse me," she said, stepping back, "I wonder if you can tell me where I might find the Graduate Theological Union?" Sketchy research the night before had brought her as far as the name, and indeed, the monk nodded, gestured that she should follow him back to the street, and once there pointed to a brick building a couple of doors up, smiling all the while. She thanked him; he nodded and crossed the street, still smiling. A vow of silence, perhaps? Kate speculated.

The ground floor of the building proved to be an airy oak-floored bookstore. The customer ahead of her was just finishing her purchase of three heavy black tomes with squiggly gilt writing on the back covers. When she turned away with her bag, Kate saw that she was wearing a clerical collar on her blue shirt, an odd sight to someone raised a Roman Catholic.

At the register, Kate showed her police identification and explained her presence.

"I'm looking for a man in connection with an investigation. He's a homeless man in San Francisco who apparently comes over to this part of Berkeley regularly. How do I find the head of your security personnel?"

The man and woman looked at each other doubtfully.

"Is he a student here?" the woman asked.

"I doubt it."

"Or a professor—no, he wouldn't be, would he? Gee, I don't know how you'd find him."

"Don't you have some kind of campus police?"

"We don't actually have a campus, per se," the young man explained. "In fact, you could say that there's actually no such

38

thing as the GTU. It's an administrative entity more than anything else. Each of the schools is self-contained, you see. We're just this building. Or actually, they're upstairs. We're just the bookstore. If you want to talk with someone in administration, you could take the elevator upstairs."

"And how many schools are there?"

"Nine. And of course the affiliated groups, Buddhist Studies, the Orthodox Institute; most of them have separate buildings."

"What about a student center?"

"All the seminaries have their own."

Kate thought for a minute. "If someone came over here regularly, where would he go?"

"That depends on what he's coming for," the young man said helpfully. Another customer arrived with a stack of books, mostly paperbacks. These titles were in English, but as foreign as the gilt squiggles had been. What was—or were—hermeneutics? Or semeiology?

"I don't know what he's coming for. All I know is that he comes over on Tuesday and returns to San Francisco before Sunday. Look, this is not a part of Berkeley that gets a lot of homeless men. Surely he'd be conspicuous."

"What does he look like?"

"Six foot two, approximately seventy years old, short salt-and-pepper hair, clipped beard, Caucasian but tan, a deep voice."

"Brother Erasmus!" said a voice from the back of the store. Kate turned and saw another woman wearing a clerical collar, this shirt a natural oatmeal color.

"You know him?" Kate asked.

"Everyone knows him."

"I don't," said the young man.

39

"Sure you do," said the woman (priest?). "She means the monk who preaches and sings in the courtyard over at CDSP. I've seen you there."

"Oh, *him*. But he's not homeless."

"Do you know where he lives?" Kate asked.

"Of course not, but he can't be homeless. I mean, he's clean, and he doesn't carry things or have a shopping cart or anything."

"Right," said Kate. "Where is CDSP?"

"Just across the street," the man said.

"I'll take you if you want to wait a minute," said the woman. (Priestess? Reverend Mother? What the hell did you call her, anyway? wondered Kate.) She waited while the woman rang up her purchases, and Kate glanced at these titles, then looked again with interest: *Living in the Lap of the Goddess; Texts of Terror; Jesus Acted Up: A Gay and Lesbian Manifesto.* Well, well.

"Thanks, Tina," she said to the cashier.

"Have a good one, Rosalyn."

Kate followed her out the door and down the wide steps. On the sidewalk the woman stopped and turned to study Kate.

"I know you, don't I?" she asked, uncertain. Kate became suddenly wary.

"Oh, I don't live around here."

"I know that. What is your name?"

There was no avoiding it. "Kate Martinelli."

"I do know you. Oh, of course, you're Lee Cooper's part-ner. Casey, isn't it? We met briefly at a forum at Glide Memorial a couple of years ago. Rosalyn Hall." She held out her hand and Kate shook it. "You won't remember me, especially in this"—she stuck a finger into her collar and wiggled it—"and with my hair longer. I was into spikes then."

"Sorry," Kate said, though she did remember the forum on

40

community violence and vaguely recalled a woman minister. She relaxed slightly. "I go by Kate now," she added. "I grew out of Casey."

"Amazing how nicknames haunt you, isn't it? My mother still calls me Rosie. Tell me, how is Lee? I heard about it, of course. It's one of those situations where you feel you should do something, but to intrude seems ghoulish."

"She's doing okay. And I don't think it would be intrusive. Actually, she's lost a lot of friends in the last months. People feel uncomfortable around wheelchairs and catheters and the threat of paralysis."

"I hadn't thought of that. I'll try to find some excuse to go see her. Something professional, maybe. Her profession, I mean. Is she working?"

"She just started up again, and that would be ideal, if you need an excuse."

"Fine. I'm glad I stumbled into you, Kate. I've got to get myself together for a lecture, but we'll meet again. Oh—stupid of me. Brother Erasmus. I'll show you where he holds forth."

They crossed the tree-lined curve of street with its sodden drifts of rotting leaves and winter-bare branches and went through an opening in the brick wall into a broad courtyard, at the far side of which were doors into two buildings and, between them, steps climbing up to more buildings. Rosalyn went to the doors on the right, and Kate found herself in a long, dimly lighted and sunken room with a bunch of tables, some of them occupied by men and women with paper cups of coffee.

"This is the refectory," said Rosalyn. "The coffee isn't too bad, if you want a cup. And that's where Brother Erasmus usually is." She nodded toward the opposite windows, which looked out on another, smaller courtyard, this one grassy and with bare trees, green shrubs, and a forlorn-looking fountain playing by itself in a rectangular pond. Rosalyn glanced at her watch. "He may be in the chapel. I'll take you there, and then I have to run."

Across the refectory, out the doors at the corner of the grassy space, and up another flight of stairs, more brick and glass buildings in front of them—the place was a warren, Kate thought, built on a hillside. Up more stairs, more buildings rising up, and then suddenly confronted with what could indeed only be a chapel. Rosalyn opened the door silently and they slipped in.

"That's Erasmus," she murmured, nodding her head toward the front. "In the second pew from the front on the right-hand side. He's sitting next to Dean Gardner," she added with a smile, then left.

It was a small building, simple and calm. The pews were well filled, Kate thought, for a weekday morning. There were two priests near the altar, and a woman at the lectern reading aloud earnestly from the Bible. Kate chose a back pew, sat one space from the aisle, and listened to the service.

She hadn't even thought to ask what kind of church this was. She knew that each school in the Graduate Theological Union was run by a different church, or an order within a church—the first building with the silent but friendly monk, for example, had been the Franciscan school. However, Church Divinity School of the Pacific could be anything. The service going on in the front was vaguely like the familiar Catholic Mass, but she imagined that most churches would at least be similar. Rosalyn, she thought she remembered, had belonged to a small, largely gay and lesbian denomination, but it surely could not be the possessor of a grand setup like this.

She looked at the books of various sizes and colors in the holder in front of her. The first one she pulled out was a Bible, which didn't help much. The next one she tried was a small limp volume, its onionskin pages covered with Greek writing and a sprinkling of English headings such as "The ministry of John the Baptist" and "The five thousand fed." That went back into the holder, too. At this point, the man next to her took pity on the poor heathen. He handed her a book, put his finger to the page to guide her reading, and smiled in encouragement.

She studied the page for a minute, which seemed to offer alternate choices for prayers, and then flipped to the front of the book: The Book of Common Prayer didn't tell her much, but farther down the title page she came across the key words *Episcopal Church.* So Brother Erasmus, homeless advocate and adviser, traveled across the Bay every week to say his prayers with the church that, if she remembered the joke right, served a vintage port as its sacramental wine. And furthermore, he seemed quite chummy here. Look at him seated next to the dean, two gray heads, one in need of a haircut and above a set of shoulders in a ratty tweed jacket, the other hair cropped short above some black garment that looked both elegant and clerical, both of them—

Everyone stood up. Kate nearly dropped the prayer book, then rose belatedly to her feet. There was a reading and a brief hymn, for which she had to flip back thirty pages in the prayer book, after which came a familiar prayer called the Apostles' Creed, forty pages ahead of the hymn. Then everyone kneeled down to recite an unfamiliar version of the Lord's Prayer.

After the "Amen" some people sat, although others stayed on their knees; Kate compromised by perching on the edge of her pew. Her view of Erasmus, partial before, was now limited to the top of his head, and it would not be improved short of sitting on her neighbor's lap. The important thing was not to let him leave, and she could see him well enough to prevent that. She glanced through her prayer book, looking up regularly at the shaggy graying head in the second pew. She learned that The Book of Common Prayer had been ratified on October 16, 1789; that the saint's day for Mary Magdalene was July 22 and that of the martyrs of New Guinea, 1942, was September 2.

There was a shuffle and everyone stood up again with books in their hands, but not the book Kate held. Fortunately, the hymnal was clearly marked on its cover, so she traded the two books, found the page by looking over her neighbor's arm, and joined the hymn in time for the final verse. When they sat, it was time again for the prayer book, but at that point Kate decided the hell with it and just sat in an attitude of what she hoped looked like pious attentiveness.

More words from the altar, response from the congregation, another hymn, a final blessing, and then everyone was rising and chattering in release. Kate stayed in her pew, allowing the people on the inside to push past her until the two men she had been watching hove into view, and she realized that she had made a profound mistake: The unkempt graying head belonging to the ratty tweed turned out to be that of a much younger, shorter, and beardless man. Brother Erasmus, on the other hand, was wearing an immaculate black cassock that swept from shoulders to feet in an elegant arc, broken only by the white rectangle of a clerical collar at his throat. Brother Erasmus was dressed as a priest.

She tore her eyes from him and studied the altar as he went past, his head down, listening to something the dean was saying. She turned to follow them out, noticing Brother Erasmus do two interesting things. First, an older woman wearing rather too much makeup hesitated as if to speak to him. Without breaking stride, he reached out his left hand, fixed it gently to the woman's cheek in a gesture of intimacy and comfort, and took it away again. The woman turned away, beaming; the dean kept talking; a gold ring had gleamed dully from the fourth finger of the Brother's hand. Then, as they reached the doors to go out, Erasmus took a step to one side and reached out for a tall stick that stood against the wall. Outside in the sun, Kate could see that it was a gleaming wooden staff. Its finial had been carved to resemble a man's head, with a bit of ribbon, colorless and frayed with age, around its throat. The stick was almost precisely the same height as the man, who did not so much lean on it as caress it, stroke it, and welcome it as a part of his body—a part temporarily removed.

Kate looked at the fist-sized knob on top of the heavy stick and found herself wondering if the postmortem now going on across the bay would find that the man John had been killed by a blow to the head.

A part of the congregation now dispersed, most of them touching Erasmus somehow—a handshake, a pat on the back, a brief squeeze of his elbow—before leaving. The dean was one of them, and he added a brief wave as he walked off, fingers raised at waist level before his arm dropped to his side.

Erasmus himself, surrounded by fifteen or twenty of his fellow worshipers, moved off and down the steps Kate and Rosalyn had come up, which led to the grassy courtyard and the adjoining refectory. Kate trailed behind. She had to see the dean, who she assumed was the man in authority here, but first she needed to be certain that Erasmus would not leave the area.

However, he planted his staff into the damp turf with an attitude of permanence and then stood, his hands thrust deep into pockets let into the side of his cassock, eyes focused at his feet, while people drifted onto the grass, standing about or leaning against the walls, all of them expectant. It occurred to Kate that she had not yet seen him utter a word, but these people were obviously waiting for him to do so, with half smiles on their lips and sparkles of anticipation in their eyes.

Silence fell. Brother Erasmus raised his head, took his hands from his pockets and held them out, palms up, closed his eyes, and opened his mouth to sing. In a shining baritone the words of the Psalm sung by the congregation a short time before rang out and reverberated against the brick and the glass: "Praise the Lord! For it is good to sing praises to our God. The Lord builds up Jerusalem, he gathers the outcasts of Israel," he sang joyously. "The Lord lifts up the downtrodden, he casts the wicked to the ground." And then he stopped, as abruptly as if a hand had seized his throat.

For a very long time, Brother Erasmus did not speak. The smiles began to fade; people began to glance at one another and fidget. Then, unexpectedly, the man in the priest's robe sank slowly to his knees, and when he lifted his face, there were tears leaking from his closed eyelids, running down his weathered cheeks, and dripping from his beard. A shudder of shock ran through the assembly. Two or three people took a step forward; several more took a step back. Erasmus began to speak in a deep and melodious voice that had the faintest trace of an English accent, more a rhythm than an accent. At the moment, it was also hoarse with emotion.

"O Lord, rebuke me not in thy anger, nor chasten me in thy wrath! For thy arrows have sunk into me, and thy hand has come down on me. There is no soundness in my flesh because of thy indignation; there is no health in my bones because of my sin." His beautiful voice paused to draw a breath that was more like a groan, and the noise seemed to find an echo in the electrified audience. Whatever they had been expecting, it was not this. "My wounds grow foul and fester because of my foolishness, I am utterly bowed down and prostrate; all the day I go about in mourning."

It was something biblical, Kate could tell, but with little relation to the readings she had heard in the chapel half an hour earlier; those cool tones had been nothing like this.

"My loins are filled with burning, and there is no soundness in my flesh. I am utterly spent and crushed; I groan because of the tumult in my heart." The young man standing next to Kate did moan, deep in his throat. Nearby, a thin young woman began openly to weep. "I am like a deaf man, I do not hear, like a dumb man who does not open his mouth. Yea, I am like a man who does not hear, and in whose mouth are no rebukes." He paused again, eyes still shut, swallowed, and finished in an almost inaudible voice. "Do not forsake me, O Lord. O my God, be not far from me."

He bent forward until his forehead touched the grass, held the position for a moment, then knelt back onto his heels again. His eyes opened and he smiled a smile of such utter sweetness that Kate was instantly aware that Brother Erasmus was not altogether normal. Disappointment and relief hit her at the same moment and dispelled the spookiness of the scene she'd just watched: Probably a third of San Francisco's homeless population had some form of mental illness. Erasmus was obviously one of them, and very likely he had cracked John across the head because a voice had told him to, or John had angered him, or just because John had happened to be there. No mystery.

This cold splash of sobriety had not hit the others; they still stood around him enthralled. Kate heard feet on the cement steps and turned, to see the dean coming down. He nodded at her politely, and then he saw the tableau beyond.

"What's happened?" he asked. Before Kate could attempt an explanation, another man, one of the group from the chapel, turned and answered in a low voice.

"He recited Psalm Thirty-eight, making it very . . . personal. I've never seen him like this, Philip. It's very—"

"Wait," commanded the dean. Erasmus was speaking again.

"I am a fool," he said conversationally, and scrambled to

47

his feet, bending to brush off the knees of his cassock. For some reason, this phrase, an echo of Beatrice Jankowski's cryptic judgment, seemed abruptly to defuse the tension in the crowd. The weeping young woman pulled a tissue from her pocket, blew her nose, and raised her head in shaky anticipation. There were two people with pen and notebook in hand, Kate noticed. Was this to be an open-air lecture? Erasmus had both hands in the pockets of the garment again, and when he pulled them out, there were objects clutched in them—a small book, a little silver plate—which his left hand began to toss high into the air, one after another, rhythmically—juggling! He was juggling, four, five objects now in a circle, and he began to talk.

"It is actually reported that there is immorality among you," he declared fiercely, glaring at a figure Kate had noticed earlier, a tiny wrinkled woman in the modern nun's dress, plain brown, with a modified wimple. She blushed and giggled nervously as his gaze traveled on to the man behind her. "I wrote to you in my letter not to associate with immoral men. Not to associate with an idolater, reviler, drunkard, or robber. Not even to eat with such a one. Drive out the wicked person from among you! Do not be deceived, neither the immoral, nor idolaters, nor adulterers, nor homosexuals, nor thieves, nor the greedy, nor drunkards, nor revilers, nor robbers will inherit the kingdom of God."

Oh Christ, thought Kate in disgust, he's just another end-of-the-world, repent-and-be-saved loony. Why the hell are these people listening to this crock of shit?

Erasmus had turned his attention to the things he was juggling, looking at them with a clown's amazement at the cleverness of inanimate objects. He allowed each of them, one after another, to come to a rest in his right hand, paused, holding them for a moment, and then began to toss them back into the air with that right hand, reversing the circle. When he spoke again, his voice was neither hoarse with suffering nor fierce with condemnation, but gentle, thoughtful.

"After this he went out, and saw a tax collector, named Levi, sitting at the tax office, and he said to him, 'Follow me.' And he left everything, and rose and followed him. And Levi made him a great feast, in his house, and there was a large company of tax collectors and others sitting at the table with them. And when the Pharisees saw this, they said to his disciples, 'Why does your teacher eat and drink with tax collectors and sinners?' And Jesus answered them, 'Those who are well have no need of a physician, but those who are sick.' "

There were seven objects in the air now, different sizes and weights but perfectly, effortlessly maintaining their places in the rising and falling arcs of the circle. Again, Erasmus studied them with the openmouthed admiration of a child, and then suddenly the objects leaving his right hand did not land in the left but flew wildly through the air to be caught by onlookers. The small red book with a wide green rubber band holding it closed was caught by the young woman who had cried, the silver plate by the older man who had spoken to the dean, a palm-sized plastic zip bag by a scruffy young man with lank blond hair. A gray plastic film container hit a tall black woman on the shoulder, and then the last thing left his hand, something shiny that flashed at Kate and she automatically put out a hand to catch it: a child's toy police badge, the silver paint chipped. She jerked her head up and looked into Erasmus's dark and smiling eyes.

"I think that God had exhibited us apostles as last of all, like men sentenced to death, because we have become a spectacle to the world, to angels and to men. We are fools, for Christ's sake, but you—you are wise in Christ," he said slyly. "We are weak, but you are strong. You are held in honor, but we in disrepute. To the present hour we hunger and thirst, we are ill-clad and buffeted and homeless, and we labor, working with our own hands." Leaving the staff upright in the grass, he held out his rough hands before him and moved slowly forward, toward the dean and Kate at his side. "When reviled we bless, when persecuted we endure. We are the refuse of the world, the offscouring of all things. I urge you, be imitators of me. The kingdom of God does not consist in talk but in power." He was very close now, and he was facing not the dean, but Kate. "What do you wish?" he said, and stretched out his hands to her, cupped together, his elbows in and his wrists touching: the position for receiving handcuffs.

♦

SIX

♦

The whole point of St. Francis of Assisi is that he certainly was ascetical and he certainly was not gloomy.

Kate stared for several seconds at the thin pale wrists with their fringe of black and gray hairs before the automatic cop reflex of *never react* kicked in. She calmly took the toy star, reached up to pin it onto the chest of the black cassock, and patted it. The beard split in a grin of white teeth.

"Our feelings we with difficulty smother, when constabulary duty's to be done," he commented, then turned to the dean. "Blessed are you poor, for yours is the kingdom of God," he said, cocking his head expectantly. The dean frowned for a moment, then his face cleared and he laughed.

"I agree, I'm feeling particularly blessed myself. Omelette or Chinese?"

"O Jerusalem, Jerusalem, killing the prophets and stoning those who are sent to you," Erasmus said inexplicably. He then looked pointedly first at Kate, then back at the dean, who in response turned to extend his hand to her.

"I'm sorry. Philip Gardner. I'm the dean of this school. Are you a friend of the Brother here?" he asked.

"Not yet," replied Kate somewhat grimly. "I would like to speak with both you and Brother Erasmus. Privately," she added, although the people around her had obviously picked up some signal to indicate the end of the—performance? lecture?—and were beginning to move away, up the stairs and across the lawn, most of them clapping the oblivious Erasmus on the arm or back as they went.

"Right. Sure. Have you had breakfast yet? Or lunch? We were just going for something."

"I had a late breakfast," she lied.

"Coffee, then. I hope you don't mind if we eat, you heard the good Brother say he was hungry."

Kate had heard no such thing, but now was not the time to quibble. The courtyard was emptying, the wet moss-choked lawn surrounded by brick walls looking cold and bleak. Kate took out her identification folder and held it open in front of Erasmus.

"Inspector Kate Martinelli, SFPD. We're investigating a death that occurred Tuesday in Golden Gate Park. The man seems to have been one of the homeless who live around the park, and we were told that you might know more about him than the others did. You are the man they call Brother Erasmus, are you not?"

The man turned his back on Kate and went to the tree, pulled his staff out of the turf, came back, and, curling his right

52

hand around the wood at jaw level, leaned into it. She took this as an affirmative answer.

"Were you aware that there was a death in the park?" she asked. Silently he moved the staff to his left side and dug around with his right hand in the cassock's pocket, coming out with a much-folded square of newspaper. He handed it to Kate. It was the front page of that morning's *Chronicle*, whose lower right corner (continued on the back page) told all the details that had been released, including the man's first name, the cremation attempt, and even a paragraph on the cremation of Theophilus last month.

"You knew the man?"

"He was not the Light, but came to bear witness to the Light."

"Sir, just answer the question, please."

"Er, Inspector?" interrupted the dean. "Could I have a word?" He led her aside, under a bare tree. She kept one eye on Erasmus, but the man merely pulled a small book with a light green cover out of his pocket, propped himself against his staff, and began to read. "Perhaps I ought to explain something before you go any further. Brother Erasmus does not speak in what you might call a normal conversational mode. He may not be able to answer your questions."

"He was doing well enough talking to all those people. There's only one of me."

"But he wasn't talking. He recites. Everything he says is a quotation."

Kate took her eyes from the monk and looked at the dean.

"Well then, he can just quote the information I want."

"It's not that simple. If the answers to your questions were contained in the Bible or the Church Fathers or Shakespeare or a couple dozen other places, he could give you answers. But a direct question is very difficult. Look, you heard me ask him if he wanted omelette or Chinese food for breakfast, or lunch, whatever you call it this time of day."

"He didn't answer you."

"But he did. He gave me the first part of a quote from Matthew's Gospel, which ends, 'even as a hen gathers her chicks under her wings.' Hen: egg. He wants an omelette."

"But all that . . . speech he gave."

"All quotations. First Corinthians, Luke, Matthew. And a bit of Gilbert and Sullivan to you—that's a first."

"Why does he talk like that?"

"I don't know. I just know he never speaks freely. I suspect he carries a fair amount of suffering around with him. Perhaps it's his way of dealing with it."

"Would you say that he is mentally disturbed?"

"No more than I am. Probably less, since he doesn't have any administrative jobs hung around his neck. No, but seriously, he's not delusional, doesn't think he's Jesus. He never mutters and mumbles to invisible beings. He's always cooperative and helpful. He reacts and understands even if he doesn't always answer in a way people can understand. The board here discussed his presence—this is not public property, you know, so in effect he has been invited. He stimulates discussion and thought, the students enjoy his stream-of-consciousness talks, and frankly I find him great fun. I love asking him direct questions, just to see how he answers. It's a game, for both of us."

Oh, right lots of fun, thought Kate: prospecting the off-the-wall remarks of a religious fanatic in hopes of finding nuggets of sense. Well, since he enjoyed it: "I wonder if I could ask you to stay with me, then, while I talk with him. You can be my translator."

"I'd be happy to, but I'm leading a seminar in an hour, so could we do it while we eat?"

"No problem."

In the café down the road, the air was thick with the smells of cooking eggs and hot cheese and coffee, the clatter of crockery and voices, the essence of a morning café in a university town. Erasmus stepped inside behind the dean, then circled behind the door and propped his staff up in the corner before following the dean to a table next to the window. Kate, behind both of them, noticed the easy familiarity of both men with the place and its patrons, the way they collected and distributed nods.

The waitress knew them, too, and automatically brought two mugs of coffee along with the menus. Erasmus paused in the act of sitting down and rose up again to his full height. After she had put down the coffee and distributed menus, he reached out, took hold of her heavily ringed hand, and, looking into her eyes, black with makeup, declaimed in full rotundity of voice, "The sweet small clumsy feet of April came into the ragged meadow of my soul."

The waitress blushed scarlet up into the roots of her emerald colored hair and began to giggle uncontrollably. She managed to find out from Kate that yes, coffee would be fine, then took her giggles off to the kitchen.

The dean looked sideways at Kate. "Her name is April," he said, more as an apology than an explanation.

Kate let them study their menus. The dean did so perfunctorily, then dropped it onto the table. Brother Erasmus read through it thoroughly, as if to memorize it and recite it at a later time, although when April returned with a third mug, he did not recite. When the dean had given his order, Erasmus placed his finger on the menu and April looked over his shoulder, wrote it down on her pad, and looked to Kate for her order. Kate shook her head, and the woman left. No question: The man could communicate when he wanted to. Let's see how much he wants to, she said to herself.

55

"They call you Erasmus, I understand," she said to him. He looked at her with his gentle dark, eyes but said nothing. "Is that your real name?"

"Whatever the man called every living creature, that was its name," he said, after a brief pause.

"That's a quote?" she said.

"From Genesis," contributed the dean. "Er, the Bible."

"Fine, I'll call you Erasmus if you like, but I do need to know your real name."

"That which we call a rose, by any other name would smell as sweet."

"Shakespeare," murmured the dean.

"Right. Okay. We'll come back to names later. You saw the article this morning that one of the homeless men who lives around Golden Gate Park died and that some of his friends there attempted to cremate him. I think the article said his name, as well?"

"He was not the Light," said Erasmus with a nod.

"You told me that before."

"Er, Inspector? That phrase is used in the New Testament about John the Baptist," said the dean. "Was this man's name John?"

"It was. Did you know John?" she asked Erasmus. Again, there was a short delay before he answered, as if he needed to consult some inner oracle.

"A fellow of infinite jest," he said dryly.

"Would you take it that means yes?" she asked the dean.

"Probably."

"This is going to be such a fun report to write up," she grumbled, and took the mug of coffee from the waitress, poured cream in it, and took a sip. "Sir, can you tell me where you were on Tuesday morning?"

56

Erasmus smiled at her patiently, tore open a packet of sugar, and stirred it into his own cup.

"Does that mean you don't remember, or you won't tell me?"

He put the cup to his lips.

"It may simply mean that he can't think of a quote that fits the answer," suggested the dean. Erasmus smiled at him with an air of approval.

"Did you know the man they called John?" she persisted.

"I knew him, Horatio," he said clearly and without hesitation.

Thank God, one answer anyway, thought Kate. I'll just have to choose my questions to fit a classical tag line.

"Do you know his last name?"

Erasmus thought for a moment, then resumed his drinking. With a regretful air?

"Do you know where he came from?"

Erasmus began to hum some vaguely familiar tune.

"Do you know where he stayed?" There was no answer. "What he did? Who his close friends were?"

Erasmus looked at his cup.

"Why do you do this?" Kate threw her spoon down in irritation. "You're perfectly capable of answering my questions."

Erasmus raised his eyes and studied her. His eyes were remarkably eloquent, compassionate now, but Kate could make no use of that kind of answer. Suddenly he leaned forward, held his hand out in an attitude of pleading, and began to speak.

"I am a fool," he pronounced. "And thus I clothe my naked villainy with odd old ends stolen forth of holy writ, and seem a saint when most I play the devil. Vanity of vanities, saith the Preacher, all is vanity. A man's pride shall bring him low," he said forcefully, and his eyes searched her face—for what? Un-

57

derstanding? Judgment? Whatever it was, he did not find it, and he turned to the dean. "A man's pride," he said pleading, "shall bring him low," but the dean gave him no more satisfaction than Kate had. He turned back to her, the muscles of his face rigid with some powerful but unidentifiable emotion. He swallowed and his voice went husky. "Then David made a covenant with Jonathan, because he loved him as his own soul. Would God I had died for thee, O Absalom, my son, my son. Behold, I am vile. What shall I answer thee? A fool's mouth is his destruction." Seeing nothing but confusion in his audience, he sat back with a thump and forced a weak smile of apology. "I am a very foolish fond old man, forescore and upward, not an hour more or less, and to deal plainly, I fear I am not in my perfect mind."

While we're talking quotations, thought Kate, how about "crazy like a fox"? They were interrupted by the waitress bringing two plates, and Kate instantly regretted not ordering something to eat. She half-expected Erasmus to say a prayer, or at least bow his head over his food, but instead he calmly spread his napkin onto his lap and began to eat.

"So," she said, "you cannot tell me anything about the man John?" She did not hold out much hope for an answer, but he surprised her.

"A back-friend, a shoulder-clapper," he said promptly, his face going hard. "The words of his mouth were smoother than butter, but war was in his heart. His words were softer than oil, yet they were drawn swords." He took a forkful of food and chewed it thoughtfully for a moment, then added, "Choked with ambition of the meaner sort. His heart is as firm as a stone, yea—as hard as a piece of nether millstone." He returned to his omelette.

"You don't say. Your friend Beatrice would certainly agree with that."

Erasmus's stern features relaxed. "Her voice was ever soft,

58

gentle, and low—an excellent thing in a woman."

"Do you know how John died?"

He paused briefly.

"Can a man take fire in his bosom, and his clothes not be burned?" He began to butter a piece of toast. *"Mors ultima ratio."*

" 'Death is the final accounting,' " translated the dean sotto voce, around a mouthful of eggs and cheese and chili peppers.

"And John had much to account for?" Kate suggested. She did not know whether or not to take the first part of his statement as an assertion that John had actually died by fire—something to be explored later.

"Forbear to judge, for we are sinners all. Close up his eyes and draw the curtain close, and let us all to meditation."

"That's fine for some," answered Kate. "However, it's my job to find how he died and if someone hurried him on his way. Even an obnoxious sinner has a right to die in his own time."

Erasmus surprised her again, by smiling hugely.

"O tiger's heart wrapped in a woman's hide!" he boomed into the startled restaurant. The dean stifled a laugh, but Kate refused to be distracted. She looked him in the eye and bit off her words.

"Do you know anything about John's death?"

The seriousness of her questions, what they meant for the man on the pyre and all involved with him, seemed suddenly to reach the figure in the cassock. Erasmus studied the food on his plate as if searching for an answer there, and when he did not find it, he brought his left hand up and laid it flat on the table, studying the worn gold ring that encircled one finger. Gradually his mobile features took on the same appearance they had shown when he had knelt on the ground to declare his abject inadequacies. He was not far from tears. "The voice of your brother's blood is crying to me from the ground," he whispered finally. The dean choked on a piece of food, shot a brief glance

59

at Kate, and then, despite the half-full plate in front of him, he looked at his watch and began to make a business of catching April's attention. Kate ignored him, staring at Erasmus, who seemed mesmerized by the gold on his hand.

"Erasmus, do you know how he died?" she said quietly.

The man took a long breath, exhaled, and then looked up at her. "Am I my brother's keeper?"

The dean stood up so rapidly, his chair nearly went over. He looked from Kate to Erasmus helplessly, and when the bill was placed in his hand by the passing waitress, he could only throw up his arms and go pay it.

"Erasmus," Kate began evenly, "you have the right to remain silent."

◆

SEVEN

◆

He was, among other things, emphatically what we call a character.

Kate closed the back door of the departmental car and turned to the unhappy man standing beside her on the sidewalk.

"Is this really necessary?" he said, more as a plea than a protest.

"You heard what he said back there. Even I know the Bible well enough to remember that 'Am I my brother's keeper?' is how Cain answers the accusation that he killed Abel. Which, if I remember rightly, he did. That comes very near to being a confession, the way Brother Erasmus talks. You can't argue with that," she pointed out, though in fact he was not.

"The man's mixed up, but he's not violent, never harmful.

You can't arrest him on the basis of biblical passages."

Kate was not about to go into the technicalities of precisely what constitutes an arrest, particularly in a fuzzy situation like this one. Still, she had to tell him something. "I haven't actually arrested him. I read him his rights because at that point he changed status, from being a witness to being a potential suspect. He is not in handcuffs; he is with me voluntarily."

"What will you do with him?"

"As you heard me tell him, I'll take him back to the City, interview him, and then we'll either let him go or, if information received during the interview demands, we'll arrest him. Personally, I doubt that will happen, at least not today."

"I'd like to be informed," he said with authority.

"Certainly." Kate retrieved a card from her shoulder bag and handed it to him. "I have a few questions I need to ask, if you don't mind."

"I did promise to take this seminar."

"Ten minutes," said Kate, knowing that if he'd eaten the abandoned breakfast, he would have taken at least that. "How long have you known Brother Erasmus?"

"He's been coming here for a little over a year now."

"And you didn't know him before?"

"No."

"Have you any idea what his real name might be?"

"No, I don't. It might actually be Erasmus, have you considered that?"

Kate ignored the dean's sarcasm. She was used to that reaction to police questions. "What about where he might have come from?"

"I'm sorry, Inspector, but no. I don't know anything about him."

"Can you narrow it down, when he first appeared?"

"Let's see," said the dean. He stood thinking for a while, oblivious of the curious looks they were receiving from young passersby with backpacks and books. "I was on sabbatical two years ago, and I came back in August, eighteen months ago. Erasmus appeared in the middle of that term—say October. He's come regularly as clockwork ever since—during term time, I mean. Last summer and during breaks and intercession, he shows up from time to time."

"How does he get here?"

"The last few months, one of our students who lives in San Francisco has brought him."

"I'd like the student's name, address, and phone number."

"I suppose I could give that information to you. I'll have to check and see if there's a problem."

"This is an official murder investigation," said Kate sternly, hoping the postmortem hadn't found a heart attack or liver failure.

"I know that. I'll call you with the information."

"I'd appreciate that, sir. What can you tell me about his movements here? When does he come; when does he go; where does he sleep; does he have any particular friends here?"

"Well, he sleeps in one of the guest rooms."

"That's very . . . generous of you," commented Kate, wondering how the other guests felt about it.

"It's only been for the last few weeks." The dean seemed suddenly to become aware that the subject of their conversation was sitting practically at their feet, albeit behind the car window, and he moved away across the sidewalk and lowered his voice. "Back in the first part of November, he showed up one Tuesday in bad shape. He looked to me like he'd been beaten up—his lip was swollen and split; one eye was puffy; he had a bandage on his ear—a real mess, and, well, shocking, see-

63

ing that kind of damage, especially to an old man. It wasn't fresh, probably three or four days old, though he was obviously in some pain, but he was still just carrying on. However, he was in no condition to sleep out, so we got together and put him into a hotel for the next three nights."

"We?"

"Some of the other professors and I passed the hat. The next week, he was better, but it was raining, so we did it again, and then the third week he seemed to have made other arrangements. It wasn't until the fourth week that we discovered the dorm had formed a conspiracy and had him sleeping in their rooms the nights he was here."

"Which nights are those?"

"Tuesday, Wednesday, and Thursday, usually."

"So you just gave him a room?"

"Not exactly. I mean, we did, but only after a tremendous number of meetings and discussions, and student petitions. The students themselves did it, pointing out gently but firmly that to collect funds for Thanksgiving meals and preach Christmas sermons on the theme 'no room at the inn' and then to lock the gates against an individual who by that time was a part of the community was perhaps not operating on Christian principles. They did it very well, too. Not once did they even use the word *hypocrisy*, which I thought was very mature of them—have you ever noticed how students love that word? Anyway, to make a long story short, we presented the case to the board and they agreed to a trial period of two months. That's nearly at an end now, and I expect it'll be renewed."

He saw the polite disbelief on her face, so he strung the explanation out a bit further. "Yes, it was more complicated than that, insurance and security and all that. But what won them over was Erasmus himself. He has . . . it's difficult to explain, but I suppose there's such an air of sweetness around him, even administrators feel it."

Kate decided to let it go for the time being. "You said he comes on Tuesdays."

"Yes. The young man he rides with is an M.Div. student." (Whatever that is, thought Kate.) "He has an afternoon class at three, I think, or three-thirty—a seminar on pastoral theology, but he may come over earlier and work in the library, I see him there quite a bit. He has a couple of kids, so it's hard for him to work at home."

"Did you see him this Tuesday? Or Erasmus?"

"I had meetings pretty much all day. I didn't see anyone but university bureaucrats."

"And when does he usually leave Berkeley?"

"Berkeley as a whole, I can't vouch for, but we rarely see him after Friday morning."

"You don't know how he leaves?"

"No."

"What about friends here? Does he have any particularly close relationships with students or professors, or with any of the street people?"

"Joel, the young man who brings him over on Tuesdays, is probably the student closest to Erasmus. I suppose I'm his best friend among the faculty. I wouldn't know about the homeless, or anyone out of the GTU area, for that matter. Look, Inspector Martinelli, I have to go."

"Just one thing. I'd appreciate it if you could write down for me where those quotes he used today come from."

"*All* of them?"

"Whatever you can remember."

"Why? Surely you can't consider them evidence?"

"I don't know what they are, and I don't know that I will

want them. But I do know that if it turns out I need them in two or three weeks, you won't remember more than a handful. Right?"

"Probably not. Okay, I'll do my best. And I'll be talking to you. Um, . . . can I say good-bye to him?"

Kate opened the back door of the cruiser and Dean Gardner bent down, holding his hand out to Erasmus.

"So long, old friend," he said. "Sorry you'll miss dinner tonight, I hope we'll see you next week. You remember my phone number?" Erasmus just smiled and let go of the hand. "Well, call me if you need anything." He stepped back and allowed Kate to slam the door, her mind busy with the image of Erasmus in a telephone booth. Why was that so completely incongruous?

She told the dean she would talk with him soon, got in behind the wheel, and drove away from Berkeley's holy hill.

◆

Kate kept her eyes firmly on the road, for Berkeley had long been a haven for the mad cyclist and the blithe wheelchair-bound, although on this occasion it was a turbaned Sikh climbing out of a BMW convertible who nearly came to grief under her wheels. She did not glance at the passenger behind the wire grid until they were on the freeway, passing the mud-flat sculptures, but when she did, she found him sitting peacefully, displaying none of the signs of the guilty killer apprehended: He was not asleep; he was not aggressive; he was not talking nonstop. He met her eye calmly.

"The driving is like the driving of Jehu the son of Nimshi, for he drives furiously," he commented.

"Yeah, well, if you don't dodge around a bit, you get mowed down." Glancing over her left shoulder, she slipped over two lanes and then slid back between two trucks and into the turnoff for the Bay Bridge. Once through the toll booths, she looked again at Erasmus, who again met her eyes in the mirror. She had been dreading the drive, fearing the mindless recitations and the inevitable stink of the wine-sozzled unwashed, but he smelled only of warm earth, and his silence was somehow restful. He shifted slightly to ease his cramped position beside the long staff that had barely fit in, and the toy star she had pinned to his chest caught the light.

"How did you know I was a cop?" she asked.

"I have heard of thee by the hearing of the ear, but now my eye sees thee."

"That doesn't explain how you recognized me."

He answered only with a small and apologetic shrug. Perhaps, she realized some time later, it was one of those places where exact quotes were unavailable.

"Do you mean you saw my picture somewhere?" she tried.

"The morning stars sang together," he said gently. Right: the Morningstar case. Really great when even the homeless had your face memorized from papers salvaged out of the trash cans, she reflected bitterly, and wrenched the car's wheel across to the exit for the Hall of Justice. She drove around to the prisoners' entrance and let him out, wrestled with his long staff and the small gym bag the dean had fetched from the room Erasmus stayed in, and began to lead him to the doors. Erasmus stopped, a large and immovable object, and looked down at her from his great height. His eyes were worried, but not, Kate thought, because of what might happen in this building. Rather, he searched her face as if for an answer.

"Weeping may endure for a night," he said finally, "but joy comes in the morning."

"Thanks for sharing that; now, in you go." He pulled his elbow away from her hand and turned as if to seize her shoulders. She took a quick step back, and he did not pursue, but bent his entire upper body toward her.

"It is a good thing to escape death, but it is no great pleasure to bring death to a friend."

"What are you—"

"Faithful are the wounds of a friend. What is a friend? One soul in two bodies." The intensity with which he was trying to get his message across was almost painful.

"Are you talking about John?" she asked.

To her dismay, he straightened and with both fists pounded on his head, once, twice in frustration. Two uniformed patrolmen walking toward the building stopped.

"Need some help, Inspector Martinelli?" the older one said, warily eyeing the tall, graying priest in the distinguished black robe with the child's badge pinned to one shoulder. Erasmus paid him no attention but flung out a hand to her in appeal.

"I have heard of thee by the hearing of the ear," he repeated, nearly shouting. Then immediately, as if the one arose from the other, exclaimed, "These vile guns. The wounds of a friend."

Kate felt her face stiffen as the sense of his peculiar method of communication hit home: He was not talking about the man John; he meant Lee. He saw her comprehension, and his face relaxed into the loving concern of a kindly uncle, but there was no way Kate was going to accept his sympathy. She cursed bitterly under her breath and seized his elbow again, propelling him past the patrol officers and through the doors. There was no escape, no relaxing; she was not even allowed to perform the simplest tasks of her job without the constant reminder that everyone and his dog knew who and what and where she was. She would have preferred to have her nude photograph on the front pages—at least that would have required a degree of imagination on the part of the voyeurs. Instead of that, even the looniest of the park-bench homeless knew everything about her, had followed her exploits like some goddamned soap opera.

She stabbed her finger on the elevator button and stood staring straight ahead, not looking at the man beside her whose whole being radiated a patient understanding that was in itself infuriating. They stepped inside the elevator along with four or five others and the door closed. They went up, the others got off at the second floor, and when the elevator had resumed, Erasmus spoke to her.

"A fool's mouth is his destruction," he said, sounding apologetic. "Let there be no strife, I pray thee, between me and thee."

Kate tried hard to hang on to her anger, but she could feel it begin to dissipate, shredding itself against the monumental calm of the old man in the priest's robe. She sighed.

"No, Erasmus, I'm not angry. Hell, I'm a public servant; I have no right to a private life, anyway." The elevator stopped and the door opened. Kate gestured with the carved end of the staff. "Down there. I'll see if my partner is here."

She parked Erasmus at a desk and went in search of Al Hawkin. There were no signs of recent habitation in his office, and the secretary said no, she hadn't seen him yet, so Kate phoned down to the morgue to find out when he would be through. She waited while the woman went to find out, but instead of a female voice, Al himself came on the line.

"What's up, Martinelli?"

"I didn't mean you should come to the phone, I just wanted to know how much longer you'd be."

"Just finished."

"What did he find?"

"Fractured skull—compression, not from the heat. Somebody whacked him. It's ours." Not just an illegal body disposal

69

case, then, but murder. Kate eyed the hefty staff that she had left leaning on the wall behind Hawkin's desk, wondering if she was going to have to bag it as evidence.

"There's a fair amount of stuff for the lab, of course," he said, "but there were no other overt signs."

"Any chance of lifting fingerprints?"

"Two of the fingers have a bit of skin left, might give partials if we're lucky. And there were no teeth to x-ray, and no dentures, though the doc said he's been wearing them until recently. Is that what you're phoning about?"

"No. I have Brother Erasmus here; you said you'd like to be in on the interview."

"I would, yes. Have you had lunch?"

How the man could think of food with the stench of the autopsy still in his nose . . .

"No. You're going for a sandwich? Bring one for the good brother, too. He didn't eat much of his breakfast."

"I'll be there as soon as I've changed." He hung up. In the months since she'd been on active homicide duty, Kate had forgotten Al's almost ritual cleansing after witnessing an autopsy. The smell was pervasive and tenacious, clinging to hair and clothes, and after the first couple of times she, too, had made a point of taking along a change of clothes and some lemon-scented shampoo.

Kate went back to Erasmus. He was sitting where she'd left him, the small green book open in his left hand, his right arm tucked up against his chest, with the fist curled into the line of his jaw. It was a peculiar position, and Kate stood studying him for a moment until it came to her: That was how he had stood on the seminary lawn, with the right side of his body wrapped around the tall staff. Except now there was no staff inside the fist.

70

"What's that you're reading?" she asked. He closed it and held it out to her.

APOSTOLIC FATHERS
I
Translated by Kirsopp Lake

She opened it curiously. The first thing she noticed was that it was a library book, property of the Graduate Theological Union Library. It was divided up into chapters titled "Clement," "Ignatius to Polycarp," "The Didache." In the text of the book, the left-hand page was in Greek, which Kate recognized but could not read, with the right-hand page its English translation. Erasmus, she thought, had been reading the left side of the book. Kate read a few lines, which had to do with repenting, salvation, seeking God, and fleeing evil, then closed the book and let it fall open again, something she'd once seen Hawkin do, although she supposed it wouldn't mean much in a library book. She read aloud: " 'Wherefore, brethren, let us forsake our sojourning in this world, and do the will of him who called us.' " She let the pages flip and sort themselves out, finding: " 'Let us also be imitators of those who went about "in the skins of goats and sheep." ' Yes, I've seen a few of those downtown lately." She let the book fall shut and handed it back to him. "It's going to be about half an hour before we can get started. Sorry about that. Do you want something to drink? Coffee? A toilet?" At her last word, he stood up with an air of expectation. She escorted him down the hall, brought him back, and left him at the desk with his *Apostolic Fathers* while she retreated to Hawkin's office, keeping one eye on Erasmus.

It was closer to forty-five minutes before Hawkin arrived—his hair still damp—smelling faintly of lemons and strongly of onions from the pair of white bags he dropped on her desk.

"I didn't know if your religious fanatic was a vegetarian, so I got him cheese." Kate waited while Al dug the sandwiches out and handed her one, then she picked up a packet of french fries and a can of Coke and took them to Erasmus.

"Just another ten minutes," she told him. "There's cheese and avocado in that; hope that's all right."

"My mouth shall show forth thy praise," he replied gravely.

"Er . . . you're welcome."

She went back and found Hawkin halfway through his sandwich.

"What are you grinning at?" he said somewhat indistinctly.

"I've dealt with nuts before," she told him, "but nobody quite like Erasmus. Is this that chicken salad with the almonds and orange things? Great." The french fries were thick and crisp, and for several minutes the only noises to come from Hawkin's desk were the sounds of food being inhaled.

"So," said Hawkin eventually, "tell me about our friend down the hall."

"Well, he's going to be an interesting interview. He speaks only in quotations—the Bible, Shakespeare, that kind of thing—so of course there're a lot a direct questions he can't answer."

"Is he coherent?"

"Yes, in a roundabout sort of way. There's usually a kind of key idea in his quote that answers whatever question you've asked, but sometimes you have to dig for it. He usually hesitates before he speaks, to think about what he's going to say, I guess. Some questions he just doesn't answer at all; others, he answers with body language or facial expressions. When he really wants you to understand, though, he just keeps at it until

72

he's sure you've got whatever it is he's driving at."

"Interview by inference," Hawkin grumbled. "How the hell can we transcribe a whole session filled with shrugs and eloquent silences?"

"It might not be so bad. The problem is interpreting the meaning of his words. For example, it looks like he's confessed to John's murder, but I may have misunderstood him."

"Explain."

Kate told him what had happened in the restaurant. "And Dean Gardner agreed that to have Erasmus using the words of a biblical murderer could be taken as an admission of guilt. So I read him his rights and brought him here." Kate decided it wasn't necessary to mention the little scene outside.

Hawkin shook his head and then began to laugh. "As you say, it's nice to have a variety of nuts to choose from." He drained his Coke and swept the rubbish into the wastepaper basket. "Let's go see what sense we can shake loose from the holy man."

◆

EIGHT

◆

. . . A camaraderie actually founded on courtesy.

At home, sitting at the dinner table, Kate asked a question.

"Do you know anything about fools?"

Lee finished chewing her mouthful of lasagna and swallowed.

"It's not a clinically recognized category of mental illness, if that's what you're asking. Far too widespread."

"Not this kind of fool. This one thinks of himself as some kind of prophet, spouting the Bible."

"You mean a Fool?" Lee said in surprise, her emphasis placing a capital letter on it. "As in Holy Fool?"

"As in," Kate agreed.

"How on earth did you find one of those?"

"He's connected with that cremation in the park. Seems to be a sort of friend or maybe spiritual leader, if that isn't too farfetched, to the street people in the area."

"That would make sense, I suppose."

"So what do you know about fools?"

Kate watched Lee take another forkful while she thought.

"Not an awful lot, off the top of my head. It's a Jungian archetype, of course, a way of counteracting the tendency of social and religious groups to become concretized. The Trickster is a combination of subtle wisdom and profound stupidity, a person both divine and animalistic." She pinched off another square of lasagna with the edge of her fork, ate it. "Many of the most influential reforms, certainly in religious history, have been made by people who fit the description of fools. St. Francis, for example, was a classic fool: He was the son of a wealthy family, who suddenly decided it wasn't enough, so he gave it all away and went to live on the streets, preaching simplicity. Let's see. In the Middle Ages, the court fool was the only one who could speak the truth to the king. Clowns are a degenerated form of fool. Charlie Chaplin used traces of Trickster behavior. I don't know, Kate, I'd have to do some research on it." She chewed for a while longer, on the food and on the idea. "You know, I vaguely remember this guy at a conference, years and years ago, in the Berkeley days maybe, who presented himself as a fool. A very deliberate and self-conscious evocation of the archetypal figure—it must have been a Jungian conference, come to think of it, one of those weekend things sponsored by UC Extension or the Jung Institute."

"Do you remember anything about him?"

"Not really. Tall fellow, had a beard, I think. White. Him, I mean, not the beard—he was young, not more than about thirty."

"You're sure about the age?"

"Kate, love, this was—what, fifteen years ago? All I remember is that he was taller than I was, hairy but neat, wearing motley and carrying this skinny little cane with an ugly carving on it, and trying hard to project an aura of wisdom and self-confidence, although I think at the time I was not impressed. I picture him as uncomfortable, and I think I wondered if he felt silly. Memory is too unreliable to be sure, but I'm fairly sure if he'd been much older I would have been even more struck by his lack of self-assurance. I take it your fool is too old."

"He is. I'd say he's a very healthy seventy, seventy-five."

"No, I don't think the man I remember could have been anywhere near fifty. Is there no way of finding out who he is?"

"We're making inquiries, but so far everything's negative. Nobody knows where he came from; he was not carrying any ID. He won't tell us anything."

"He doesn't talk?"

"Oh, he talks. Just doesn't always make sense. He speaks in phrases taken from someplace—the Bible, Shakespeare, things like that."

"*Everything* he says?"

"So far as I can see. I don't know, of course; I'm just a Catholic, and everyone knows Catholics don't read their Bible. But I've been told that." She explained about Dean Philip Gardner and the Graduate Theological Union. "He says they're quotes, and I'll take his word for it. They're definitely not straight speech."

"How strange."

"You'd say that isn't standard behavior for a fool?"

"I don't know that there is such a thing as standard behavior among fools," replied Lee, "rules of behavior being almost a contradiction in terms. Still, I wouldn't have thought that speaking only in quotations was completely consistent with

76

being a fool. In fact, I'd have said fools would be the last people to constrict themselves in that way. Spontaneity would be their hallmark, clever wordplay, and a definite, um, suppleness in mind and body. Two things that I possess not, at the moment. I'd have to make a deliberate effort and research the topic before I could give you more than a superficial idea, I'm afraid."

"It's not superficial, and you're doing fine. It's very helpful, especially knowing there was a fool in the woodwork ten or fifteen years ago, even if it's a different man. Would you like to look into it for me, see if you can find out who he was, or maybe find someone like him?"

"For you, or for the department?"

"I suppose it would be for me. I doubt they'd pay you a consultancy fee, if that's what you're asking."

"It isn't that. I'm just . . . I don't know."

"What is it, sweetheart?" Kate could see that Lee was troubled but couldn't understand why.

"Oh nothing. No, I guess it is something," said the therapist. "I just don't know how I feel about getting involved in another case."

"Oh God, then don't, hon." She took Lee's hand from the table, kissed it, held it tightly. "I don't want you to touch any of my cases; I don't want them to touch you. The question of who fools are or were is of no earthly importance; I can't imagine it has the slightest relevance to the case. This man who calls himself Brother Erasmus, he interests me, that's all. I don't know what to make of him and I was curious about what you might know." She did not add, And I thought it might interest you, give you a project that was challenging but not strenuous. Think again, Kate. The last and only time Lee had been involved with one of her lover's cases, she'd ended up with a bullet tearing through two of her vertebrae and a multiple murderer dead on her living room floor, ten feet from where they were now sitting. A lack of enthusiasm for future involvement was not only understandable, it was to be encouraged.

"It was a bad idea, hon. Forget it." She gave Lee's hand a squeeze and let it go, but Lee did not immediately resume her meal, and Kate kicked herself for her stupidity.

"It's not a bad idea," Lee said slowly. "When I said I don't know how I feel about it, I meant just that: I don't know. I think I'm expecting to feel apprehension, but I honestly don't know if I am. If anything, there's an absence of emotional overtones, just a vague interest, intellectual almost. Perhaps the apprehension is so strong that I'm blocking it. There's a degree—What are you laughing at?"

Kate wasn't laughing, but she was grinning widely. "God, you sound like a therapist, Lee."

"What are you talking about?" she demanded. "I am a therapist."

"I know," Kate said, loving her, loving the surge of affection and exasperation and normality that had hit her, and then she really was laughing, and Lee with her. When it had washed on, Lee picked up her fork again and continued where they had left off.

"If it's just for you, I'd be happy to see what I can do. Jon has the modem up and running; this would be a good exercise in learning how to use it in research."

"If you want to, if you have the time, I'd appreciate it. But I want it kept on a purely theoretical level. If you find someone, I don't want you talking to them, even through the computer. I don't want your identity out there at all. The last thing we want is the press standing in our petunias and looking in our windows, and the case is colorful enough already without you getting involved."

"Actually, I think Jon dug out the petunias and put in some sweet peas, but I agree. Newspaper reporters know how to use

78

computer nets better than I do. Now, tell me more about this fool of yours."

Dinner progressed with the story of Erasmus, told as entertainment, with the dark moment of the cremation and the possible confession downplayed and the conversation in the parking lot behind the Hall of Justice omitted altogether.

Jon came into the kitchen just as Kate was putting on the coffee. He raised his eyebrows at the plates in the sink.

"Aren't you a clever girl, then?" he murmured.

"What do you mean?"

"She hasn't eaten that much in a month," he said, and then in a normal volume added, "Well, toodles, ducks, I'll be seein' ya. Dr. Samson has his beeper on, so buzz me if you have to go out. *Arrivederci,* Leo," he called.

"Have a good time, Jon," she called from the living room, and the door opened and shut behind him.

Kate loaded the dishwasher, put the leftovers in the refrigerator, and took the coffee back into the living room. The television was on and Lee was on the sofa, slightly flushed from the effort of clambering from the wheelchair. Kate stood and looked down at her, smiling.

"You look gorgeous," she said.

"Tamara came today and gave me a cut and a shampoo. You should let her do yours; she's pretty good."

"It's not your hair. It's you."

"Poor Kate, going blind from all the paperwork. Come and sit down for a while. There's an old Maggie Smith movie on Channel Nine." Lee had a thing for Maggie Smith.

"The chair's a better place if you're going to watch TV. You'll get a stiff neck sitting here."

"I thought maybe if I sat here I could tempt you away from your paperwork. Then I can lean on you and I won't get a stiff neck."

79

Kate put both cups on the table and obediently inserted herself behind Lee, who leaned into the circle of her left arm. The movie had just started. They drank their coffee. Kate began to find the warm smell of Lee's curly yellow hair distracting.

"Did your mother pronounce it *dahl-ya* or *day-li-ya?*" asked Lee suddenly.

"What?"

"Those hideous flowers," said Lee, gesturing at the screen with her cup. "English people tend to use three syllables, but I always thought there were two. I should check in the dictionary," said the scholar.

"Do you want me to go get it for you?" asked Kate, her face buried in Lee's hair. Her left hand, having migrated from the back of the sofa, was pressed flat against Lee's stomach, her forefinger bent and gently circling the rim of one of Lee's buttons.

"Not just now." Lee slowly finished her coffee. Kate's was going cold. "Don't you love it, a woman with bright red hair wearing that color of red? Only Maggie Smith could pull it off."

"I'm jealous of Maggie Smith," muttered Kate happily.

They never did see the end of the movie.

♦

Murder cases not solved within two or three days tend to drag on into weeks, and this was no exception. The fourth and fifth days passed without any startling revelations. Kate and Al Hawkin had agreed that Brother Erasmus was not likely to run, so after Thursday's fruitless question-and-statement session he was handed back his staff and allowed to walk back out into the city of Saint Francis. Kate, rather to her surprise, found herself making a detour from a Sunday morning shopping trip to drive slowly through Golden Gate Park, where eventually she came across Erasmus, dressed like a tramp and walking along the road in the midst of a group of street people. The raggle-taggle congregation might have been from another world compared to the group of his admirers in Berkeley, except for one thing: on these faces was an identical look, a blend of pleasure, awe, and love.

Hawkin saw him once, too, although his sighting was accidental, when he passed Erasmus on his way home from work one afternoon. Erasmus was not wearing his cassock then, either, but a pair of jeans and a multicolored wool jacket. He was sitting in the winter sun on a low brick wall, reading a small green book and eating an ice cream cone.

The millstones of justice continued to grind. Their John Doe's lab work showed no signs of alcohol, drugs, or even nicotine and indicated that his last meal had been a large piece of beefsteak, green beans, and baked potatoes at least six hours before his death. Death had been due to a blow with a blunt object to the right side of the skull, which, judging from the angle, had been delivered by a right-handed person standing behind the victim as he sat on the stump a few feet from where Harry and Luis had found his body. Death had been by no means instantaneous, although unconsciousness would have been.

John had bled slowly, both internally and onto the ground, for as much as an hour before his heart stopped.

There was one other piece of possible evidence, which Hawkin interpreted as sinister, though Kate privately reserved judgment; twenty feet from the body, at the foot of a tree, had been found a lone cigarette stub that had been pinched off, not ground out. Oddly, though, the drift of ashes on the ground around the tree was considerably more than could be made from one cigarette. The crime scene investigator estimated that five to eight cigarettes could have produced that quantity of ash. There was another, smaller pile of ash just in front of the stump. In three places at the site were found boot prints, none of them complete, but together an indication that a pair of size nine men's heeled boots, not cowboy boots but similar, had been there within a day of the time John had died.

When the lab results were in, Al had Kate drive him across town to the park. He stood within the fluttering yellow tapes marking the crime scene and stared at the ground.

He said deliberately, "I think a man wearing a pair of those expensive men's boots that make you two inches taller stood here and talked with John, smoked a cigarette, walked around, picked up something—baseball bat, tree branch, nightstick—and hit John with it as hard as he could. John collapsed but didn't die, and the man dragged him away from the stump and under the bush so he was invisible. He then stood behind that tree over there, smoking cigarettes—which he pinched off and put in his pocket, except the one he dropped—and watching John die. Cold-blooded, deliberate, smoking and watching."

"I can't see this as a pleasure killing," objected Kate.

"No. Too casual, no ritual. And he didn't come in close to watch; it was more just waiting. He wanted John dead, didn't mind if he suffered, but didn't want to be too close. Could have been simply caution—he could get away more easily from over there if someone came down the road, couldn't he?"

"You think he had a car along one of the streets outside the park?"

"Let's get some posters up, see if anyone noticed something. Funny, though, about the cigarettes."

"What about them?"

"Why did he pinch them all and take them?"

"To leave nothing behind. He watches too much television, thinks we can find him from a fingerprint on paper. Or just didn't want us to know he was here."

"Why not knock the ashes out into the cellophane wrapper, then? I've done that myself, smoking on a tidy front porch. And why didn't he worry about his footprints? They're at least as distinctive as his smoking habit."

"Maybe the TV programs he watches only deal with fingerprints. That could also be why he waited for the man to die instead of bashing him again—he wasn't necessarily cold-blooded, just afraid of getting blood on his clothing. With the single hit, he was probably clean, but multiple blows would increase the risk of contamination."

"You have an answer for everything, Martinelli. How about this one: What kind of man habitually pinches his cigarettes out rather than smashing them?"

"You're the smoker, Al. You were, anyway. *I* don't know. Someone showing macho? Like striking a match with your thumbnail to show how tough you are. Someone about to put the butt in his pocket and wanting to make sure it didn't light his pocket on fire?"

"You're probably right," he said absently.

"Okay, Al. What kind of man would *you* say habitually pinches off his smokes? And why do you think it's habitual?"

"Because he went through at least six or eight of them without once forgetting and putting it out against the tree or under his foot. Pretty calculating for a guy standing there smoking nervously, waiting for a friend to die."

"Friend?"

"Acquaintance at least. And you may be right about the reason for the habit. Or it could be he's a man who doesn't mind a bit of ash but doesn't want to toss a burning butt onto the ground. Someone who works around flammable things, maybe. Or someone concerned with the litter. Groundskeepers rarely toss away their cigarettes, knowing they'll have to clean them up."

"So, we have a short, vain groundskeeper in expensive boots who is friends with a homeless man who doesn't smoke, drink, or do drugs, bashes him on the head, and stands around being tidy until the homeless man dies."

"Yep, that's about it," said Hawkin.

"I like it." Kate nodded and followed Hawkin to the car. "Sure, that is a doable theory. Let's give it to the DA and just arrest every gardener in the city, starting with the park workers. Get a bus and shovel them in."

"You'll take care of it, won't you?" asked Hawkin. "I have a date with Jani tonight."

"No problem. Drag 'em in, beat 'em up, get a confession, be home for dinner."

"I knew I could count on you, Martinelli."

♦

NINE

♦

The way to build a church is to build it.

Six days, seven days. Lee came up with some references and sent Jon in several directions to pick them up and request more from the university's interlibrary loan service. She began to read and digest, in between physical therapy, a trip to the doctor's, the lengthy preparation for and exhaustion following an appointment with one of her two clients, and sleep. Dean Gardner phoned Kate every day, even though Erasmus had been released, until finally, to get rid of him, Kate gave him the same research assignment she'd given Lee: Find me someone who knows what a Fool is.

Kate didn't quite know why she was interested, though she did know that it had more to do with the enigma that was Erasmus than with the investigation into John's murder. She mentioned her by-proxy academic investigations to Hawkin only in a passing way; he, in turn, nodded and told her to let him know if anything came up.

♦

Nine days after the murder, eight days after the cremation, the first faint hairline crack appeared in the case, although Kate did not at first recognize it as such. She was mostly annoyed.

"Dean Gardner, I do not have any news for you. I haven't even seen Erasmus since—oh, he is? Of course, it's Thursday." Erasmus had been told not to leave San Francisco, but somehow she wasn't surprised that he was following his usual rounds. "Is everything all right?"

"Oh yes, he seems in good spirits. The reason I called is that I have some suggestions for that question you put to me. Do you have a pencil?"

"Go ahead."

"The first name is Danny Yamaguchi. Danny is a woman, a professor of Religious Studies at Stanford. Her specialty is cults; she should know if there is a Fool's movement. Second is Rabbi Shlomo Bauer. He's a GTU visiting professor this semester; his field is Jewish/Christian relations in Russia from the seventeenth century to the present. And third is a Dr. Whitlaw, who teaches at one of the redbrick universities in England and is over here on a sabbatical. I don't know her, but I was told that she's something of an expert on modern religious movements." He then gave Kate telephone numbers for Yamaguchi and Bauer, explaining, "Dr. Whitlaw is staying with friends in San Francisco, but I couldn't come up with her number. The only one I have at the moment seems to be an answering machine.

I'm sure I'll have a number for you in a few days, and I know she's coming to lecture here the end of next week, but do you want the machine's number?"

"Might as well." She wrote it down, thanked him, and prepared to hang up, when he interrupted her.

"I also have that list of passages Erasmus was quoting. Shall I send it to you?"

Actually, Kate had forgotten about it. "That would be helpful. Just send it to the address I left with you."

"There was just one odd thing—it struck me when I was thinking about that conversation. One of his passages was wrong. That's never happened before, not that I've ever caught. Remember when he was getting so worked up about something and cited David's lament over his son Absalom? Before that he said, 'David made a covenant with Jonathan, because he loved him as his own soul.' I'm sure he said it in that order. In fact, I was aware of it at the time because it's wrong. It's Jonathan who makes the covenant with David."

"Does that matter?"

"I don't know. I mean, it would in the biblical context, but I don't know if it was only a slip. I just wanted to mention it, because it was unusual."

Kate thanked him, reassured him yet again that she would phone if there was news, and firmly said good-bye. She dutifully wrote the information down, then went out to pick up Al Hawkin so they could tie up the interviews of the people who lived in houses facing Golden Gate Park, on the slim chance they might have noticed, and remembered, the booted man nine days before. The inquiries had to be made, but she was not too surprised when the slim chance had faded into nothingness by the end of the day.

That night she took out her notebook and phoned the three numbers. At the first, a tremulous voice with limited English informed Kate that her granddaughter was away until Tuesday and then hung up. There was no answer at Rabbi Bauer's number. The number for Dr. Whitlaw was indeed an answering machine, which rattled at her in a woman's rushed voice: "You've reached the Drs. Franklin answering service, please leave your name, number, and a brief description of what you need and we'll try to get back to you." That last qualified offer was none too encouraging, but Kate left her name, without any identifying rank, her home number, and the message that she needed to reach Dr. Whitlaw and would the recipients of the message please phone back, whether or not they were able to pass the message on to Dr. Whitlaw, thank you.

When she hung up, she found Lee looking at her, forehead wrinkled in thought. "Was that something to do with your fool case?"

"A rather thin lead to finding an expert, yes. Nobody home."

"I just wondered, because a couple of the names sounded familiar—Yamaguchi and Whitlow."

"Whitlaw."

"Was it? It might not be the same person. Those were a couple of the names I've come up with. Jon's requested a book for me that was edited by a Whitlow or Whitlaw . . . on the Fools movement of the twentieth century."

"You don't have anything yet?"

"Do you want to go up and get the folders and I'll look? It's on my desk next to the computer, a manila folder labeled 'Fools.' "

It was there. Kate came back downstairs with it and handed it to Lee, who opened it on her lap and started sorting through the pages.

"Oh, I meant to mention," she said without looking up

from the file, "Jon has a friend whose brother installs those stairway lifts in peoples' houses; he said he'd do it for cost plus labor. The only problem would be that when we want to tear it out, it'll leave marks on the woodwork. What do you think?"

It was fortunate that Lee was busy with her papers and did not look up—fortunate, or deliberate. Kate felt her face stiffen in an impossible mixture of shock and relief and despair: This was the first time Lee had admitted that her time in the wheelchair might not be brief. The first time, that is, since the early months of complete paraplegia, when suicide had seemed to Lee a real option. Kate turned and walked out of the room, looked about for an excuse, saw the coffee machine, poured herself a second cup, although she hadn't drunk her first yet, and took it back into the living room.

"Any idea what it would cost?" she said evenly.

"It would still be a lot, several thousand dollars, but there's an extended-payment program, and they buy it back when you're finished with it. I don't really mind going up and down on my butt. Actually, it's good exercise, but it is slow. I just thought it would save you and Jon a few hundred trips a week up and down, fetching things for me."

Anything that could increase Lee's sense of independence was to be snatched at, and Kate's face was firmly in line when Lee looked up, a paper in her hand.

"Anyway, it's something to think about. Here's that printout. D. Yamaguchi, Stanford, and E. Whitlaw—you're right, it *is* Whitlaw—Nottingham, England. You said she's here?"

"Dean Gardner thought she was visiting friends in the city."

"The titles of her articles and the one book look like what you need. I should have some of them Monday or Tuesday, if you want to look through them before you see her."

"Good idea. If she calls and I'm not here, see if you can get a real phone number or an address from her. Want another coffee?"

"No, this is fine. Could you stick that tape into the machine for me?"

Kate obediently fed the indicated videotape into the mouth of the player, turned on the television, and, while she was waiting for the sound to come up, looked at the box: *The Pirates of Penzance.*

"Another heavy intellectual evening, I see," she said, grinned at Lee's embarrassment, and went off to do the dishes. Lee thought Gilbert and Sullivan hilarious; Kate would have preferred the Saturday-morning cartoons.

After a while, she heard Jon's voice above those of the cavorting sailors. A minute later, he came into the kitchen, dressed in his mauve velour dressing gown, and took two glasses and a squat bottle out of the drinks cupboard.

"We really must have a crystal decanter," he complained, pouring out a thick red-brown liquid. "Would you like a glass?"

"What is it?"

"Port, my dear. I thought it might be fun to reintroduce gout as a fashionable disease."

"No thanks. Say, Jon? Just now Lee said something about installing a lift on the stairs. Do you know anything about that?"

"Yes, well, I thought it might not be a bad idea."

"I agree. I suggested it three or four months ago and she nearly bit my head off."

"Did she? Well, times change. I admit I did bitch—a small bitch, a gentle bitch—about the state of my knees on those stairs. And, er, I also pointed out that she could probably deduct the depreciated cost of it as a business expense, now she's

90

working again." Jon studied his fingernails for a moment and then looked up through his eyelashes at her—difficult to do, as he was four inches taller than she. Kate began reluctantly to grin, shaking her head.

"By God, you're a sly one. And she fell for it. I'd never have believed it." He laughed and whisked the glasses off the counter. "Jon?" He turned in the doorway. "Good work. Thanks." He nodded, then went to join Lee in front of the television.

An hour later, Linda Ronstadt was bouncing around a moonlit garden in her nightie, flirting with her pirate, when the phone rang. Kate picked it up in the kitchen, where she had retreated with a stack of unread newspapers.

"Martinelli."

"This is Professor Eve Whitlaw, returning your call." The voice was low, calm, and English.

"Yes, Dr. Whitlaw, thank you for phoning. I am the—"

"Is that pirates?"

"Sorry?"

"The music you're listening to. It is, yes. Not perhaps their best, but it has a few delicious moments. You were saying."

"Er, yes. I am Inspector Kate Martinelli of the San Francisco Police Department. We are investigating a murder that occurred recently in Golden Gate Park. The reason I am calling you is that one of the persons involved refers to himself as a 'fool,' and I was told by the dean of the Church Divinity School of the Pacific over in Berkeley that you might be able to tell me exactly what this man means when he uses that description." By the time Kate reached the end of this convuluted request, she was feeling something of a fool herself, and the sensation was reinforced by the long and ringing silence on the other end of the line.

"Dr. Whit—"

"You've arrested a Fool for murder?" the English voice said incredulously.

"He is not under arrest. At most, he's a weak suspect. However, he's a problem to us because it's very difficult to understand what he's doing here. The interviews we've held have been . . . unsatisfactory."

The deep voice chuckled. "I can imagine. He answers your questions, but his answers are, shall we say, ambiguous. Even enigmatic."

"Thank God," Kate burst out. "You do understand."

"I wouldn't go so far as to say that, but I may be able to throw a bit of light into your darkness. When may I meet this fool of yours?"

"You want to meet him?"

"My dear young woman, would you ask a paleontologist if she would care to meet a dinosaur? Of course I must meet him. Is he in jail?"

"No, at the moment he's in Berkeley. He will be back in San Francisco by Saturday, I think, and I could put my hands on him by Sunday. Perhaps we could arrange a meeting on Monday?"

"Not until then? Ah well, it can't be helped, I suppose. However, my dear, if you lose him, I shall find it very hard." There was a thread of steel beneath the jovial words, and Kate had a vivid picture of an elderly teacher she'd once had, a nun who used to punish tardiness and forgotten homework with an astonishingly painful rap on the skull with a thimble.

"I'll try not to lose him," she said. "But I wonder if before then you and I could meet."

"A brief tutorial might well be in order. Tomorrow will be difficult; the entire afternoon is rather solidly booked. Let me look at my diary. Hmm. I do have a space in the early afternoon. What about one—no, shall we say twelve-thirty?"

Dr. Whitlaw gave Kate an address in Noe Valley and the house telephone number, wished her enjoyment of the remainder of *Pirates,* and hung up. Kate obediently poured herself a tiny glass of the syrupy port and went out to sit between Lee and Jon on the sofa, watching the equally syrupy ending of the operetta.

♦

TEN

♦

When Francis came forth from his cave of vision,
he was wearing the same word "fool" as a feather
in his cap; as a crest or even a crown.

At under five and a half feet with shoes on, Kate was not often
given the chance to feel tall, except in a room full of kids. In
fact, when the door opened, she thought for a moment that she
was faced with a child. It was the impression of an instant's
glance, though, because no sooner had the door begun to open
than it caught forcibly on the chain and slammed shut in her
face. The chain rattled, the door opened again, more fully this
time, and the person standing there, colorful and gray-haired
and of a height surely not far from dwarfism, was not a child,
but a woman of about sixty.

"Doctor Whitlaw?" Kate asked uncertainly.

"Professor, actually. You're Inspector Martinelli. Come in."

Kate stepped inside while the woman reached up to fasten the chain.

"I was told that I must always bolt and chain the doors in this city. I live in a village, where a crime wave is the neighbor's son stealing a handbag from the backseat of a car. I'm forever forgetting that I've put the chain on; I nearly took my nose off the other day. Come in here and sit down, and tell me what I can do for you. Will you take a cup of tea?"

She had a lovely voice. On the phone it had sounded gruff, but in person it was only surprisingly deep, and the accent that had sounded English became something other than the posh tones of most actors and the occasional foreign correspondent on the news. Her accent had depth rather than smoothness, flavor rather than sophistication, and made her sound as if she could tell a sly joke, if the opportunity arose. Kate couldn't remember the last time she'd drunk tea, but she accepted.

They sat at a round, claw-foot, polished oak table, between a cheerful pine kitchen and a living room bursting with gloriously happy plants, tropical-print fabrics, and African sculpture. Professor Whitlaw brought another cup from the kitchen (using a step stool to reach the cupboard) and poured from a dark brown teapot so new that it still had the price sticker on the handle. She added milk without asking, put a sugar bowl, spoon, and plate of boring-looking cookies in front of Kate, and sat back in her chair, her feet dangling.

"This is a very pleasant place," Kate offered.

"Do you think so? It belongs to friends of my niece, two pediatricians who are away for the month, so I'm house-sitting. Actually, I am beginning to find its unremitting cheerfulness oppressive, particularly in the mornings. I come out in my dressing gown and expect to hear parrots and monkeys. Fortunately, I don't have to care for the jungle. They have a sort of indoor gardener who comes twice a week to water and prune—a good thing, because if I was responsible, they would come back to a desert. You wish to talk about the Fools movement."

"Er, yes. Or about one particular fool, really." Kate explained at length what she knew about Erasmus, his relationships with the homeless and the seminary, and his apparent unwillingness or inability to speak other than by way of quotations. She then gave a very general picture of the murder and investigation, ending up with: "So you see, the man must be treated as a suspect; he has no alibi, no identification, no past, no nothing. The only thing he has said about himself that sounds in the least bit personal is that he thinks of himself as a fool. Now, he could just be saying that, or he may be referring to this organization or movement or whatever it is. Dean Gardner thought there was a chance he might be, so he referred me to you."

"You are catching at straws."

"I suppose so."

"And even if he is a remnant of the Fools movement, it may have nothing to do with the man's death."

"That's very possible."

"But you are hoping nonetheless to understand the differences between the cultivated lunacy of Foolishness and the inadvertent insanity of a murderer."

"Well, I guess. Actually, I was hoping that if he had been a member of this . . . movement, there might be records, or someone who might know who Erasmus is."

"The Fools movement was short-lived, and fairly comprehensively dispersed. It was also never the sort of thing to have any formalized membership—that would have been seen as oxymoronic. If you will pardon the pun." She chuckled, and

Kate smiled politely, not having the faintest idea what the woman was talking about. "What you require," she continued, sounding every bit the academic, "is background information. However, as I told you over the telephone, my day is fairly full. I'm afraid that I've loaned out my only copies of the book I edited on the subject, but may I suggest that I give you a couple of papers and you come back and talk with me when you've had a chance to digest them? This evening or tomorrow, or whenever."

Without waiting for Kate to agree, she slid down from her chair and went out of the room and through a doorway on the other side of the hall. When Kate reached the door, she found Professor Whitlaw with her head in a filing cabinet. She laid three manila folders on the desk, opened the first two, and took out some papers, leaving a stapled sheaf of papers in each one. The third one, she hesitated over, then opened it and began to sift through the contents thoughtfully.

The doorbell rang. Professor Whitlaw glanced at her wrist in surprise, thumbed through two or three more sheets of paper in the file, and then snapped it shut and handed it to Kate along with the other two folders.

"I don't have photocopies of the loose material," she said, "and it would be very inconvenient if you lost it. But if one cannot trust a policewoman, whom can one trust? Give me a ring when you've had a chance to formulate some questions. The next two nights are good for me."

The professor remembered the chain this time. Kate changed places on the doorstep with an anemic young man wearing a skullcap and went to do her assignment.

◆

"What are you doing home?" demanded Jon. "Did you get fired?"

97

"The teacher gave me homework. Ooh, *love* your outfit, Jonnie." It was quite fetching—a lacy apron over his Balinese sarong and nothing else—as he leaned on the table, making a pie crust on the marble pastry board, the rolling pin in his hand and a smudge of flour on one cheekbone. It always surprised Kate to see how muscular Jon was, for all his languid act. She wiggled her fingers at him and went looking for Lee.

Her voice answered Kate from upstairs, and Kate followed it to the room they used as a study. Lee was in her upstairs wheelchair at the computer terminal. A scattering of notepads and a long-dry coffee cup bore witness to a lengthy session.

"Hi there," Lee said. "I didn't expect to see you so soon."

"I'm obviously getting too predictable in my old age," complained Kate. "You and Jon can plan your orgies around my absences. I had some reading to do and it's too noisy at work," she explained, waving the folders. "Look, I don't know if you want to go on with your search. Dr. Whitlaw—Professor Whitlaw—is a real find, and if you're getting tired . . ."

"Oh, I'm not working on your stuff. This is something else." Feeling both piqued and amused at her sensation of being abandoned, Kate went to look over Lee's shoulder at the screen, which was displaying a graph.

"What is it?"

"I had an interesting visit this morning from a woman I worked with on a project two or three years ago; she said she'd seen you in Berkeley recently."

"Rosalyn something?" Kate tossed the folders onto a table and sat down.

"Hall. She's putting together a grant proposal for a mental-health program targeting homeless women, wondered if I might help with it. Remember that paper I gave at the Glide conference? She wants me to update it so she can use it as an appendix. I was just reviewing it, seeing how much I'd have to rewrite the thing. I don't know, though; my brain seems to have forgotten how to think."

"You and me both, babe. It looks like you've been at it for quite a while."

Lee picked up on the question behind the statement. "I did most of this earlier. I had a long session with Petra; she thinks the tone in my right leg is improving. And then I had a rest, so I thought I'd work for a while longer."

They talked for a while about gluteus and abdominal and trapezius muscles, about spasms and recovery and tone, the things that until a month ago had formed their entire lives, until Lee had seemed to make a deliberate choice to push back all the necessary fixations and passions of her recovery in order to allow a small space for the life that had been hers a year ago. Kate respected Lee's decision and tried hard not to push for every detail of a muscle gradually regained, a weight lifted, in the same way that she had respected Lee's choice of a caregiver, Lee's decision to come directly home from the hospital with full-time attendants rather than enter a rehabilitation clinic, and Lee's determination to keep some of the details of her care from her lover. Privacy is a precious commodity to anyone, but to a woman emerging from paraplegia, it was a gift of life.

So all Kate said was, mildly, "Well, don't overdo it."

"Of course not. What have you got?"

"Couple of articles by the expert on Fools. I was looking at one of them on the way here, and I swear it isn't written in English."

"Would you rather do my appendix to the grant application?"

"Tempting, but I think there's going to be a quiz on this."

Kate picked up the folder and Lee turned back to the terminal, and for the next hour the rusty gears of two minds independently ground and meshed. Kate looked over her two articles, decided to skip for the moment the one that used *exegetical* and *synthesis* in the first sentence, and began to read the other, a transcript of a talk given to some religious organization with an impressive name but an apparently generic audience.

HOLY FOOLISHNESS REBORN

The modern Fools movement began, as far as can be determined, in 1969 in southern England. Its earliest manifestation was on a clear, warm morning in early June, when three Fools appeared (with an appreciation for paradox that was at the movement's core from the very beginning) at the entrance to the Tower of London, that massive and anachronistic fortress which forms the symbolic heart of the British Empire. And, lest anyone miss the point, they arrived there from the morning service at St. Bartholemew-the-Great, a church founded by Rahere, Henry I's jester.

Had any of London's natives been watching, the behaviour of the taxi driver would have alerted him to the extraordinary nature of what was arriving, for the cabby, unflappable son of a phlegmatic people, stared at his departing passengers with open-mouthed befuddlement. Interviews with that driver and with the American tour which witnessed the appearance of Foolishness were more or less in agreement: One of the trio, the tallest, turned to pay the driver, adding as a tip a five-pound note and a red rosebud plucked from thin air. The three passengers walked a short distance away, dropped the small canvas bags they each carried, joined hands in a long moment of (apparently) prayer, and set about their performance. The cab driver shook himself like a setter emerging from a pond, put the taxi into gear, and drove off. The red rose he tucked into the side of his taximeter, where it gradually dried and blackened, remaining tightly furled but fragrant, until he plucked it off and threw it out the window over the Westminster Bridge nearly three weeks later.

He did not see his three passengers again, although as the summer passed he saw others like them. The original three, having bowed their heads and muttered in unison some chant barely audible even to the women who emerged from the toilets ten feet away, turned to face the Tower (and its tourists) full-face.

And an arresting trio of faces it was, too, glossy black on the right side, stark white on the left, hair sleeked back, and a row of earrings down the length of each left ear. Black trousers and shoes, white blouses and gloves, harlequin diamonds black and white on the waistcoats. The tall one alone had a spot of color: One of the diamonds on his waistcoat was purple.

What followed was a busking act such as even London rarely saw, street performance as one of the high arts. Part magic show, part political satire, part sermon, it seemed more of a dance done for their own pleasure, or a meditation, than a performance aimed at the audience—though audience there was, and quickly. The act of the three Fools was peculiarly compelling, faintly disturbing, wistful and wild in turns, austere and scatological, the exhortations of gentle fanatics, anarchists with a sense of humour;

three raucous saints who were immensely professional in their direct simplicity. The bobby who eventually moved them on had never seen anything quite like it. He had also never seen buskers who didn't pass the hat.

By the end of the summer, there were at least a dozen harlequin buskers in London, and others had appeared in Bath and Edinburgh. By Christmas, New York had its first pair, and the following summer they were to be found as far afield as Venice, Tokyo, and Sydney.

Then, around the second Christmas, the first tattooed harlequins appeared: the black half of their faces no longer greasepaint, but one solid and spectacularly painful tattoo from a sharp line down the center of the face, from the hairline to the chest. These half-and-halfs were the extremists, the most radical of a radical group, and although they never numbered more than a dozen, they were visible, confrontational, frenetically active, and disturbing: frightening, even. The other Foolish brothers and sisters contented themselves with the small tattoo of a diamond beneath the left eye, like a tear, but the handful of tattooed harlequins inevitably garnered the attention of the press, and the police. There had been arrests before, for such things as unlawful assembly and public nudity, but now the Fools (as they were known to the public through the various newspaper articles) began to collect more severe misdemeanors, and eventually felonies. One half-and-half in New York was so caught up in his performance that he picked up a small child and ran off with her; the little girl was greatly amused, the mother was not, and he was arrested for attempted kidnapping (a charge that was later dropped). Another assaulted a police officer who was trying to move him out of a crowded downtown intersection in Dallas. Four months later, the same man, out on bail but now in Los Angeles, reached the climax of his performance by pulling a revolver from his motley and shooting a young woman dead.

It was the death, too, of the Fools movement. The young man had a history of violence and severe mental disturbance, and the Fools were not to blame for providing him with an outlet, but they were all comprehensively tarred with the same brush of dangerous madness, and within a few months they had dispersed. Fools went back to the everyday life they had so often mocked: Fools bought clothes, bore children, voted in school board elections. And six teachers, two lawyers, a magistrate, two actors, four clergy of various denominations, and a junior congressional aide all wear the faint scar of a removed tattoo high on their left cheekbone.

The modern Fools movement of the early seventies sprang from a soil similar to that which nourished earlier Fools movements: The Russian Yurodivi, the classical Medieval Fool, the buffoonery of the Zen master—all came into being as a warning personified, a concrete and living statement that the status quo was in grave danger of smothering the life out of the spirit of the individual and the community. A church which no longer hears its parishioners, a government which is operating with its head in the clouds, a people which have moved too far from its source: The Fool's laughter serves to point out the shakiness of these foundations; the Fool seeks to save his community by appearing to threaten it. The essential ministry of a Fool is to undermine beliefs, to seed doubts, to shock people into seeing truth.

However, I shall not trespass on the lectures of my colleagues by going any further into the larger themes of the Fool movement, and in addition, I see that we have run short of time. Perhaps we might take just two or three questions from the audience.

The question-and-answer session that apparently followed was not recorded, and Kate turned to the next article with a sigh. This one was composed as a written, rather than oral, presentation, a reprint from a quarterly journal, and had so many footnotes that on some pages they took up more space than the text. Kate didn't think she really needed to know all about "Fedotov's analysis of this Russian manifestation of kenoticism," "Via's exploration of the kerygmatic nucleus of Gospel and the generative linguistic matrix of Greek comedy," or even "Harvey Cox's dated but valuable *Feast of Fools.*" The article was cluttered with names—Willeford and Welsford, Hyers and Eliade and Brown—and turgid with the concentrated essence of scholarship.

She contented herself with skimming, picking up interesting tidbits, mostly from the footnotes. "Holy Foolishness" was an accepted form of ascetic life in Russia, with thirty-six canonized saints who were Fools. Extreme Foolishness was used as a means of triggering Zen enlightenment. The Cistercian, the Ignatian, and the Franciscan orders of the Roman Catholic Church all had their roots firmly in Foolishness. (St. Ignatius Loyola regarded Holy Foolishness as the most perfect means of achieving humility, and St. Francis of Assisi was, as Lee had suggested, Foolishness personified.) There was an illiterate Irish laborer in the nineteenth century who lived the life of a Fool, and a tiny monastic order in the same country, founded about the time the tattooed harlequin in Los Angeles had murdered international Foolishness. The members of this Irish order, monks and nuns alike, wandered the roads like harmless lunatics, carrying on conversations with farm animals and then going home to pray.

So why not Erasmus, in twentieth-century San Francisco? Kate mused, turning to the third folder.

The loose papers it contained were a disparate lot, most of them handwritten, occasionally a mere scrap of paper, but mostly full sheets, though of a different size from standard American paper. The writing was in several hands, all ineffably foreign but for the most part legible. Some of the sheets were merely references, often with two or three shades of ink or pencil on the same page: titles and authors of books or, more often, articles. Kate glanced at these pages and left them in the file. Others had quotes and excerpts, with references, and yet others seemed to be Professor Whitlaw's own writing, perhaps thoughts for the book outlined on one page, much scratched out and emended.

A number of the pages were as unintelligible as the second article had been, one academic talking to others in a shared language. Others, however, were obviously meant for popular consumption, as the transcribed lecture had been. Kate picked up a few of these and read them:

There is no place [professor Whitlaw wrote] for the Fool in the modern world of science and industry. The Fool speaks a language of symbols and of Divinity. We forget, however, those of us who live our lives conversant with computer terminals and clayfooted politicians, with scientists who gaze into invisible stars or manipulate the genetic building blocks of living matter, that there is an entire population living, as it were, on the edge, who feel as powerless as children and cling, therefore, to any sign of alternate possibilities. They believe in the possibility of magic, the reality of Saints, and would not be surprised at the existence of miracles. The Fool is their representative, their mediator, their friend.

Judaism doesn't have fools; it has prophets. Mad—look at Ezekiel. Poor and uneducated—Jeremiah. Laughingstocks all—poor old Hosea couldn't even keep his wife from making a spectacle of them both. Jesus ben Joseph fit right in, preaching to the poor, the prostitutes, the scum, scratching his lice and calling himself the son of God—and the ultimate absurdity, God's only son strung up and executed with the other criminals: A royal diadem made from a branch of thorns, a king's cloak that went to the high throw, his only public mourners a few outcast women with nothing left to lose. Then, to cap it off, Christ the original Fool is decently clothed in purple, his crown traded for one of gold, he is restored to the head of his Church, and the transformation is complete.

But what consequences, when the jester assumes the throne? Someone must take his place in the hall, lest the people forget that the essence of Christianity is humility, not magnificence, that in weakness lies our strength.

(This page was marked: "Taken from personal communication, 12 October 1983, David Sawyer.")

The three thinkers of Deventes—Thomas à Kempis, Nicholas of Cusa, and Desiderius Erasmus—all based their thought on Foolishness.

The craving for security leads modern people to images of God that are powerful, demanding, and, above all, serious. We have lost the absolute certainty in God (God existing and God benevolent) which allows us to express religious ideas in freedom and good humour. In the twentieth century, God does not laugh.

Foolishness can be a hazardous business, and not only to one's mind and spirit. After all, one of the Fool's main activities is to make a fool out of others, to throw doubt on cherished wisdoms and accepted behaviours: in a word, to shock. If this is done too aggressively, without caution, the result is more likely to be rage than enlightenment. Foolishness does not usually coincide with caution. Even the less flamboyant Fools courted danger: The half-and-half extremists seemed almost to glory in it. I know of twenty-two cases of violence against Fools, all but one of them a direct result of some inflammatory word or action on the part of the Fool. One Fool spent three days unconscious in hospital, put there by a motorcycle gang member who became enraged when the Fool made fun of the motorcycle's role in the man's sexual identity. Another Fool had one foot amputated following a particularly aggressive mocking episode which began when a young man came out of a Liverpool pub with his girlfriend literally in tow, bullying and abusing her. The Fool stepped in and soon had a crowd gathered, all ridiculing the young man. A more experienced Fool would have then turned the barrage of criticism into a more long-term solution—some pointed suggestion perhaps, that real men do not slap women around—but this Fool was new to street work and lost control of his mob. The man stormed off, got into his car, came back to the pub, and ran the Fool down.

St. Francis wished his followers to become *joculatores*, clowns of God; his band of fools and beggars quickly became an order studded with intellectual giants.

How can a movement embodying the antithesis of organisation possibly deal with the modern world? When I wished to interview a certain Brother Stultus about the early days in England, he was not to be found. One of the brothers told me he had gone to Mexico (we were then in San Diego), but that was some weeks before. Stultus was not a young man, and I was concerned, but there was not much I could do. Some weeks passed, and a rumour reached me of a "crazy Anglo" who had taken up residence near the border patrol offices in Tijuana. I immediately drove down, and there found Stultus, living behind a garage, fed by the generous Mexican women, and waiting for rescue with sweet patience (in between periodic arrests for vagrancy by the frustrated police). Stultus, of course, carried no identification papers, and without them the U.S. Immigration Service would not allow him back in.

108

◆

ELEVEN

◆

He listens to those to whom God himself will not listen.

Kate closed the folder, unable to read any more. She felt as if she'd just finished Thanksgiving dinner: packed with more than she could possibly digest and experiencing the onset of severe mental dyspepsia. This wasn't cop business; this was tea-and-sherry-with-the-tutor business, Oxbridge-in-Berkeley business, Greek-verbs-and-the-nuances-of-meaning business, worse than memorizing the latest departmental regulations concerning the security of evidence and treatment of suspects. That at least was of personal interest, but this—she couldn't even convince herself it had anything to do with one charred corpse in Golden Gate Park. She thought it did, feared it might not, and all in all she had the urge to strap on her club and go rousting a few drunks, just to taste the grittier side of reality again. She scratched her scalp vigorously with the nails of both hands, knowing that there was no way she would be going back to continue her interview with Professor Whitlaw, certainly not tonight, and possibly not tomorrow.

She reached for the telephone.

"Al? Kate here. I had an interesting time with Professor Whitlaw." Hawkin listened without interrupting while she told him about the interview with the English professor and gave him a brief synopsis of the papers she had waded through, ending with, "Anyway, I thought I'd check and see if you still thought we needed to interview Beatrice Jankowski. I could do it tonight."

"We definitely have to see her again. She knows more about the victim than she was willing to tell us last week. However, if you want to go tonight you'll have to take someone else—Tom called in sick, I have to stand in for him on a stake-out."

"Hell. If this flu goes on we'll have to put out a white flag, ask the bad guys for a cease fire."

"We could make it another time, or I can ask around here for somebody to go with you. What's your preference?"

Kate thought for a moment. "Would you mind if I went by myself?"

"Martinelli, you're not asking my permission, are you?"

"No. I just wondered if you had any objections. It might be better anyway if I went alone; she might talk more easily."

"That's fine, whatever you like."

"Where's your stake-out?"

"The far end of China Basin."

"The scenic part of town. Dress warmly. We don't want you coming down with this flu, too."

110

"Yes, mother. Talk to you tomorrow."

Kate sat for a while staring at Lee's books until gradually she became aware that the voices she had been hearing for some time now were not electronic, but indicated a visitor. She wandered downstairs in hopes of distraction and found Rosalyn Hall, wearing not her dog collar but an ordinary T-shirt with jeans and looking to Kate's eyes eerily like a defrocked priest. She was standing in the hallway at the foot of the stairs, putting her jacket on, and Kate greeted her.

"Kate, good to see you again. As you can see, I took you at your word that Lee might be interested in the project, and wasted no time."

"I'm happy to do it, Rosalyn," said Lee.

"It's been tremendously helpful. I didn't know how I was going to pull that section together. I'm so grateful I ran into Kate the other day; I'd never have had the nerve to ask otherwise. So what did you think of Brother Erasmus?" she asked Kate, her eyes crinkling in humor.

"He's an experience," Kate agreed.

"I've never really talked with him, but I've heard a couple of conversations, if you can call them that. It's sort of like listening to a foreign language; you get a general sense of what people are talking about, but none of the details."

"It's a challenge for an interviewer all right."

"I can imagine. I saw him again the other day; he sure manages to get around."

"In Berkeley, you mean. Yes, I knew he was back there."

"Well, actually it was over here, down on Fishermen's Wharf last weekend. At least, I assumed it was him, though honestly I hardly recognized him, he looked so different."

"Why, what was he doing? Why did he look different?"

"He was performing, like that juggling act he does sometimes, but a lot more of it, and other things. Sort of clowning,

111

and some mime, but weird, a little bit creepy, and his face was painted—not heavily, like a clown's, just a really light layer of white on one side and a slight darkening of the other half—he looked like he was standing with a shadow across half of his face. And he wasn't wearing his cassock—he had on this strange outfit. Well, it wasn't strange, just sort of not right. He was wearing those sort of dressy khaki Levi's, but they were too short for him, and a striped T-shirt that had shrunk up and showed a little wedge of his stomach, and a pair of white athletic shoes so big, he kept tripping over them. Oh, and a watch. I've never seen him with a watch before."

"What day was this?"

"Saturday. I had a friend visiting, and you know how you only do the touristy things when friends and family come. I thought she'd like Ghirardelli Square."

"And that's where you saw him?"

"Across the street—you know that park where the vendors set up? Necklaces and sweatshirts? Lots of times street performers wander up and down there. Isn't that where Shields and Yarnell got their start?"

Kate had never heard of Shields or Yarnell, but she nodded her head in encouragement. However, it seemed that was about the sum of the report. After a bit more fussing and arrangements for the next phase of the grant application, Rosalyn hugged Lee and then left.

"Nice woman," Lee commented, her wheels purring after Kate on the wood of the hall. Kate turned and went into the kitchen to stand in front of the refrigerator.

"Did I have lunch?" she called to Lee. Nothing in the gleaming white box looked familiar.

"Once, but who's counting?" Lee answered. Kate fingered the increasingly snug waistband of her trousers and settled for an apple; Jon's cooking had its drawbacks.

"I'm going to have to be out tonight," she told Lee.

"I've been surprised you haven't had more calls at night," Lee said in resignation. "I expected it, with you back on duty."

"Yes, I've been lucky. It's been quiet—nobody feels like shooting anyone in the rain. But I need to talk to one of Brother Erasmus's flock, and Friday's one of the few times I can find her without a search."

◆

Sentient Beans was your typical Haight coffeehouse, self-conscious about its location and the sacred history of the district in the Beat movement and the Summer of Love. In this case, however, it was without the superiority of age, for its even paint and the cheerfulness of the furniture within gave it away as an imitation, set up by people who in 1967 would have considered an ice cream cone a mood-altering substance.

Still, it was a harmless enough place, and discreetly notified customers that the venerable Graffeo Company had deigned to supply it with French-roast coffee, the smell of which grabbed at Kate when she opened the door, a heady aroma, sharp and dark and rich as red wine. She ordered a latte and watched with approval as the man assembling it tipped the coffee over the steamed milk with a flip of the wrist rather than using the effete method of dribbling it cautiously over the back of the spoon to create multiple multicolored layers in the glass, a drink filled with aesthetic nuances but, to Kate's mind, lacking the pleasurable jolt of contrast between milk and coffee. Reverse snobbery, Lee had called it once, admiring on that distant occasion her own tall glass with at least nine distinct strata.

"Have you seen Beatrice tonight?" she asked as she paid.

"She'll be down in a bit," said the man, and slapped Kate's change down on the wooden bar. She picked up the dollars, tipped the rest of the change into the tips mug, and found a seat at a table with the surface area of a dinner plate. There was a guitarist at the far end of the L-shaped room, a woman all in black, with perhaps a dozen gold loops running up her ear and one through her nose. She was attempting classical music, with limited success: The notes kept burring and her fingers squeaked as they moved along the strings. However, the flavor was there, and Kate did not mind waiting.

Twenty minutes or so later, the guitarist took a break, and shortly after that, Beatrice came through the bar area and into the room, a ten-by-twelve artist's pad in one hand and a small tin box in the other. She sat down in the point of the L and without fuss opened the box, took out a black felt-tip pen, and began to sketch the person sitting in front of her, her pen flashing across the page in sure, quick gestures. In a couple of minutes, she put the cap on the pen, tore the page off the pad, and put it on the table, then stood up and moved to another vacant chair and another face. A mug marked FOR THE ARTIST had joined TIPS and FOR THE MUSICIAN on the wooden bar, and as people left, they tended to put some change and the occasional small bill in Beatrice's cup, even those who had not been sketched.

Eventually, when Kate had finished her second latte (this one decaffeinated) and was beginning to think she would have to approach the woman, Beatrice finished her dual portrait of a pair of nearly identical bristly-headed, metal-and-leather-clad punks, reached across her drawing on the table to pat the girl's black leather sleeve affectionately, and then took her pad and tin box over to Kate's table. She opened both and began to sketch.

"Hello, dear," she said. "I thought I might see you one of these nights."

"Hello, Ms. Jankowski."

"Beatrice, dear; call me Beatrice. I always feel that when

114

someone calls you by your last name, it's because they want something from you. Either that or they want you to know they are better than you. Funny, isn't it, something looks like respect but underneath it's a power trip. Do they still use that phrase, I wonder? My vocabulary is so dated, it's coming back into style. You need a haircut, dear. What's your name, by the way?"

"Martinelli. Kate," she corrected herself with a smile.

"Just Kate? Not Katherine?"

"Katarina," she admitted. Beatrice looked up from her drawing, both hands going still.

"Oh that's very nice. Katarina. It sounds like those beautiful little islands down south, near Santa Barbara, is it? Or San Diego? Kate is too abrupt. Do you have a middle name?"

"Cecilia," said Kate patiently.

"Katarina Cecilia Martinelli. Your mother was a poet. There's power in names, you know," she said, going back to her drawing. "Last names are safe, generic, but when you give someone your first name, you give them a part of yourself. What about your partner?"

"Al? You mean his name? It's Alonzo. Hawkin, and I don't know if he has a middle name."

Beatrice stopped again, to gaze in an unfocused way at the shelves over the bar. "Alonzo," she repeated softly. "Oh my. I am such a sucker for a pretty name. Other girls used to fall for eyes or a lock of hair, but I would just melt at a melodious name. My three husbands were named Manuel, Oberon, and Lucius. Of course, they were all bastards; you'd think I would learn. I don't think Alonzo would be a bastard though, do you?"

"No, but he's already spoken for." Kate exaggerated his marital status slightly for Al's own benefit.

"I figured he would be." She flipped the page of her sketchbook over to a fresh one. "But this chitchat is not why you're here, is it?"

115

"No."

"It's about that odious man."

"John? I'm afraid so."

"Oh, why can't you let him just . . . be dead?" she said crossly.

"Because if we let the 'odious' people be killed, where would it stop?"

"Oh, dear. You are right, I suppose. Very well," she said, turning to her pad again, "ask away."

"Do you know anything about John's history? Where he was from, what he used to do?"

"He never talked to me, not that way. I don't think he much liked women, certainly not to talk to. Not that he was gay, but a lot of men who sleep with women don't much like them."

"Did he sleep with many women?"

"Don't sound so surprised. Just because people don't have beds doesn't mean they lack sexual organs," Beatrice said, primly amused.

"Beatrice, I'm a cop, not a nun in a cloister," Kate reminded her. "I was surprised because the way you've described him made him sound unattractive. Were other women attracted to him?"

"He was presentable enough, and certainly kept himself cleaner than a lot of the men do. I found him repulsive, true, but he could have a very glib tongue when he wanted to bother, and many women fall for a clever line even more than they do a pair of shoulders or a handsome face. I'm sure he got his share of female companionship."

"Who in particular?" Kate asked, but Beatrice's lips went straight and she bent over the pad. "The homeless women in the park? Wilhemena?" Beatrice snorted. "Adelaide? Sue Ann?"

Kate tried to remember the names that had cropped up, but Beatrice shook her head. "Did he have lady friends in the area, then?" Kate asked, and thinking she saw a slight hesitation in the moving hand, she pressed further. "One of the women who has a house near the park? Or someone who works here?"

"Shopkeepers. He liked shopkeepers," Beatrice admitted.

"What kind? Bookstore, grocery store, restaurant, coffee shop—Beatrice, please tell me, I need to know."

Beatrice pursed up her mouth and rubbed her lips with the side of her thumbnail, a portrait of anxious thought. It wouldn't do for a woman living on the margins, dependent on the goodwill of her settled, more fortunate neighbors for what degree of comfort she managed to achieve, to offend them. Kate realized this and waited.

"Antiques," she finally muttered. "Junk really, but pretentious. I saw him inside the antique store on the corner of Masonic one morning before it opened. He kissed the owner; she let him out. He didn't see me."

"Is she the only one?" Beatrice shot her a look full of anger and closed her pad.

"I'm sorry," Kate said. "Thank you for that. I'll talk with her, and of course I won't tell her where the information came from. Is there anything else you know about him?"

Beatrice did not open her sketch pad again, but neither did she stand up and leave.

"Horses," she said suddenly. "He once said something about quarter horses, I think it was, one day when the mounted police went by. I suppose he was from a farming community of some kind, between the horses and the drawl."

"Drawl?" asked Kate sharply.

"Yes, he spoke with a drawl. Didn't you know that?"

"Nobody's mentioned it that I've heard."

117

"Oh yes. I mean, it wasn't strong, like Deep South, but it was there. Texas, maybe, or Arizona, though it sounded like he'd lived in cities for a while."

Kate thought for a minute. "You said you'd once seen him in a car with someone." Beatrice did not respond, but flipped open the sketch pad and thumbed the cap off her pen. "When you made your statement downtown," she elaborated. When the woman merely turned to a clean page and began to run her pen up and down, Kate's interest sharpened. So far this evening, Beatrice had shown little of the blithe, slightly disconnected stepping-stone quality of the earlier interview: Was it back, and if so, what had brought it? "Do you remember saying that?"

"It was a remarkably ugly car, considering how much money must have been spent on it."

"An expensive car. Foreign? A sports car? A big car? Cadillac? Rolls-Royce?"

"Just like a ten-gallon hat, all show and terribly impractical."

"Imagine the problems with parking it," Kate suggested, with success.

"Exactly."

"But at least he bought American," Kate offered tentatively, and held her breath. This system of interviewing a witness was inexcusable, leading questions compounded by guesses and utterly inadmissible as evidence, but there seemed no other way, and indeed, the responses kept coming.

"I never thought that a particularly good argument. The last car I owned was a Simca."

"The man driving the car looked the sort who would use that argument, though, would you say?"

"I suppose. The cost of gasoline certainly wouldn't trouble him," she added in a non sequitur.

"Was he actually wearing his ten-gallon hat when you saw him?"

"No." Ah well, it was a try, thought Kate. "He didn't have it on. A ridiculous notion, isn't it? A hat that literally held ten gallons would be big enough to sit in. It was on the backseat." By God. Bingo. Kate sat back in the flimsy chair.

"You remember what color the license plates were?" Might as well try for the big prize, if one's luck is in.

"Color? I don't remember any color. They weren't black and gold, though, I'm pretty sure." The old California plates had gone out of use about the time Kate had her first pair of nylon stockings, so that wasn't much help.

"I don't suppose you remember when this was that you saw the two men?"

"My dear Katarina, life on the street does not necessarily mean a person is brain-dead."

"I didn't—"

"Of course I remember. It was election day. The church served lunch outside that day because the hall was being used as a polling place and there was a mix-up over who was supposed to hold the soup kitchen instead, so they just worked inside and brought it out the back. Very apologetic, they were, but it was actually quite festive, I thought. Gave one a sense of participation in the democratic process. The last presidential candidate I voted for was George McGovern. He didn't win," she explained kindly.

"Er, no."

"I know that the man was in the city for a few days at least, because I remember seeing the two of them again on the Friday. They came in here. Didn't stay, just bought something to go, coffees probably, talked for a minute and looked around, then left. I was busy and didn't talk to them, but I think John saw me. I was a little nervous that he would come over, but he didn't, so that was all right, and he hasn't come in since, either. I did not like the idea of his taking over my Friday nights."

Beatrice took another thoughtful bite, then said suddenly in a muffled voice, "Texas!" Kate waited while she chewed and swallowed rapidly. "Pardon me. Texas, I'm sure, because of the star."

"Which star was that?"

"The license plate. The Lone Star State. That is Texas, isn't it? Or is it the yellow rose? No, I'm certain there was a star on it."

"The yellow—" Kate stopped, struck dumb, and slowly shook her head. The old bastard.

"What is it, Katarina? You look amused."

"Something Erasmus said—or rather, something he told me." He had told her by humming, over the breakfast table in Berkeley, a tune she had only half-recognized and ignored: "The Yellow Rose of Texas."

So, both Erasmus and Beatrice agreed that the mysterious womanizing John had probably been from Texas, and according to Beatrice, as recently as the first week of November he had retained a (wealthy?) possibly Texan connection.

"Did John smoke, do you know?"

"He did not."

"Did he wear false teeth?"

"My dear, I never looked in the man's mouth. Although, come to think of it, he occasionally hissed his s's, and once when he was eating a banana it sounded like strawberries, that click-crunch noise. Ask Salvatore," she said dismissively, starting to close up her pen, preparatory to moving on.

"Let me buy you a coffee," Kate suggested. "Something to eat?"

Beatrice stopped, suddenly wary, then resigned. "Very

well, dear. Krish there knows what I'll have."

Kate ordered herself yet another coffee, a decaffeinated cappuccino this time, and asked for whatever Beatrice liked, which turned out to be mulled apple cider with a toasted scone, a large dollop of cream cheese, and some plum jam. She arranged plates, cup, and cutlery onto the inadequate table, retaining her own cup for fear it would end up on her lap, and waited while Beatrice delicately cut her scone and scooped up cream cheese and jam in a practiced heap, then popped it into her mouth.

"I need to ask you a few questions about Brother Erasmus, now that I've had the chance to meet him." Kate's attempt to make the meeting sound like a social occasion fell flat beneath Beatrice's rather crumby words.

"You arrested him last week, I heard, and then let him go."

"No. There was no arrest; he was not even detained," she protested, stretching the truth slightly. "I gave him a ride back from Berkeley so we could take his statement, then we turned him loose. I admit it took us a while to get a statement, but that wasn't exactly our fault, if you know what I mean," she added pointedly. Beatrice got the point and laughed.

"I can imagine."

"Does he talk like that to everyone? Using quotes and sayings for everything he says?"

"Is that what he does? Good heavens. I knew he was using the Bible a great deal, but that would explain the sometimes . . . inappropriate things he says. Surely not *everything* he says comes from somewhere else?"

"That's what I was told."

"How extraordinary. How utterly sad."

"Why sad?"

"What I was talking about, the power of names, of words.

He must be very frightened of his own words if he never creates any. Terrified of his own thoughts, to push them aside for the thoughts of others."

Kate stared at Beatrice, who took a mournful bite of her scone. "You're an amazing person," she said without thinking.

"Oh no, not really. I just keep my eyes open and think about things. One thing about being on the street, there's lots of time for thinking."

"What are you doing here, anyway? I'm sorry if that's rude, but most of the street people I see are pretty hopeless. You're articulate, skilled—you could have a job."

"Oh indeed, I taught art history at UCLA," she said, and seeing Kate's astonishment, she added, "There's really quite an interesting intellectual community among the street people here. I've met an astrophysicist, a couple of other university and college teachers, three computer programmers, and a handful of published poets. To say nothing of the young men, and a few women, who make a deliberate choice to remove themselves from the race of the middle-class rat and as a form of practical philosophy choose this admittedly extreme form of freedom. Wasn't it Solzhenitsyn who said that a person is free only when there's nothing more you can take away from him? Dreary man, but unfortunately often right."

"And you?"

"Oh no, dear. You don't want to hear about me, it's not a very pretty story." Her voice remained light, but her eyes began to shoot around the room, looking for an escape from this topic. Kate relented and gave her one.

"Tell me about Erasmus, then. He won't, or can't, tell us anything except that he's a fool."

"I told you all I know about him. He comes to us on Sunday morning and leaves us on Tuesday. While he is here, he tells us stories from the Bible, sings hymns, leads us in prayer.

He listens; with all his being he listens, and does not judge. The disturbed are quieted; the drunks are calmed; the angry begin to see that there may be ways they can help themselves. He looks, and he sees; he listens, and he hears. This alone is an unusual experience for most homeless people: We are used to being either invisible or an annoyance. He brings dignity into the lives of those who have lost it. He is like . . . he is like a small fire that we warm our hands over. What else can I say?"

"But you don't have any idea who he is or where he came from?"

"He came here in the summer. It would have been two summers ago, I suppose. How time does fly. He gives us Sunday and Monday; he gives the people at this place with the holy hill Wednesday and Thursday."

"And the other days?"

"Travel, I suppose," Beatrice said dismissively, but her eyes began to roam and her fingers gave a twitch on the knife.

"Does it take two days to get back from Berkeley?" Kate asked mildly.

"I was never much for distance walking myself." Beatrice was retreating fast, but this time Kate would not let her go.

"Where does Erasmus go on Saturdays?"

"I have to get back to my drawing."

"Just tell me where he goes."

"The world is a big place."

"Where does he go?"

"It has many needs," Beatrice said wildly. "Even the world needs comfort."

"He is off comforting the world?"

"They don't deserve him. They don't understand him. All they see is the surface, shallow, silly, violent—no, not that, I didn't mean that!" she said quickly, looking frightened. "I meant crazy-*looking*; all they see is the act."

123

"Beatrice," Kate said evenly, "I know Erasmus performs for the tourists at Fishermen's Wharf. You haven't told me anything I don't know. I'm sorry if I've disturbed you, but I could see that you were trying to hide something about Erasmus and I wanted to know what it was." Kate did not make it a habit to apologize to witnesses she'd been pressing, but this woman, strong to look at, struck her as being too fragile to leave in an upset condition. Besides, she wanted her friendly and helpful in the future. "Trust me. I won't be misled by his act for the tourists. Okay? Good. There was just one other thing: Was there ever any direct animosity that you saw between Erasmus and John?"

This last question blew Kate's soothing words out of the water. Beatrice slapped the top down on her tin box, picked up box and pad, and rose to her feet.

"Don't I get my drawing?" Kate asked mildly. Beatrice tucked the box under her arm, flipped open the pad and tore off the page, and dropped it on the cluttered table. It was a caricature, a clever one, that emphasized the look of dry cynicism Kate sometimes felt looking out from her eye. She started to thank Beatrice, but the woman had already moved off to another table and was fumbling with unsteady hands at the clasp of her box. Kate put on her jacket, fished two five-dollar bills out of her purse to shove into the FOR THE ARTIST cup, and rolled the caricature gently into a tube.

It was raining lightly when she stepped out onto the street, raining heavily when she got home, and for the first time in her life she lay awake and wondered where the homeless were resting their heads this night.

♦

TWELVE

♦

The jester could be free when the knight was rigid.

Saturday morning was clear and clean and cold, and Kate stood drinking her coffee in a patch of sunlight that poured through a high side window onto the living room floor, wearing her flannel robe, talking to Al Hawkin on the telephone, and speculating with one part of her mind on how Beatrice and Erasmus fared this day.

"Fine. Good," she was saying. "No, I don't think there's any need for you to cancel. I'm only going because I'm curious, after Beatrice's reaction. He probably just talks dirty or something that embarrassed her; I don't think she was actually trying to hide anything from me. Right. Fine, yes I have Jani's number.

I'll call you if anything comes up; otherwise I'll talk to you tonight. Have a good time, Al. Say hi to Jani and Jules for me. Bye."

She pushed the off button and dropped the handset into her pocket, then closed her eyes and absorbed the pleasure of the winter sunlight in the silent house. Saturday mornings, Jon and Lee went to a pottery class, where they produced lopsided bowls and strange shapes from the unconscious. Three whole hours with a house that held only her was a treat she looked forward to every week; illicit, never mentioned, and resented when her job or an illness—Lee's, Jon's, or the pottery teacher's—took it from her. This morning she could have half of it before she went hunting Brother Erasmus in his Fishermen's Wharf manifestation.

Normally she kept this time for something unrelated to daily life: loud music, frozen waffles with maple syrup, a book in a two-hour bath. Not today, though. She pulled a pillow from the sofa and dropped it onto the patch of sunlight. A million dust motes flew up, and she settled herself with a fresh cup of coffee and the folders from Professor Whitlaw. Very soon this case would be pushed to a back burner, superseded by another, probably one considered more pressing than the odd death of a homeless man in a park. But Erasmus interested her—no, he bugged her. He was an unscratched itch, and she wanted him dealt with. So she read the impenetrable files for a second time, this time with a lined pad to write questions on, things she needed to know.

Did Erasmus have the scar of a removed tattoo on his left cheekbone? Might John have had one?

There must have been some organization behind the Fools movement. Where were the original Fools? Someone must have known Erasmus.

Who was the David Sawyer whose notes were marked as a

personal communication from 1983? A Fool?

Kate wanted more details on the crimes committed by Fools, both misdemeanors and felonies, primarily the names of those arrested for attempted kidnapping (later dropped) and the murder of the bystander in Los Angeles.

The sun had moved, and Kate scooted the pillow across the wooden floor so as to be fully in it again, then opened Professor Whitlaw's folder, the one with the loose scraps and notes. She picked up one page at random, and read:

> It used to be thought that only through the prayers of aescetic monks did the world maintain itself against the forces of evil, that monks were on the front lines of the battle against evil. Now, we are willing to grant monastic orders their place, for those of excessive sensitivity as well as a place of retreat and spiritual renewal for normal people. However, when a monk comes out of his monastery, we are baffled, and when confronted with a Saint Francis making mischief and behaving without a shred of decorum, we call him mad, not holy, and threaten him with iron bars and tranquillisers.
>
> Christianity is, by its core nature, more akin to folly than it is to the Pope's massive corporation. The central dictate of Christian doctrine is humility, in imitation of Christ's ultimate self-humbling. Christians are mocked, persecuted, small: The powerful so-called Christian empires are the real perversion of the Gospel, not the Holy Fool.
>
> One cannot be a Fool for Christ's sake and be truly insane. Holy Foolishness is a cultivated state, a deliberate choice. However, the movement's greatest

strength, its simplicity, is also its greatest weakness, for it cannot protect itself against the mad or the vicious. The innocent Fool is as helpless as a child before the folly of wilful evil. Hence the absolute catastrophe of the Los Angeles shooting.

The Fool is the mirror image of the shaman. The shaman's mythic voyage takes him from insanity into control of the basic stuff of the universe; the Fool goes in the other direction, from normality into apparent lunacy, where he then lives, forever at the mercy of universal chaos. Both remain burdened by their identities: the shaman paying for his control by personal sacrifice, and the Fool being in the grip of what Saward calls "the rare and terrible charism of holy folly."

Kate came to the end of the file without feeling much further along in her understanding. She set the folders on the table by the door, ate a breakfast of pear and a toasted bagel, and went to dress for her encounter with tourism.

♦

Given a sunny Saturday, even in February there will be a decent crowd in the Fishermen's Wharf area, meandering with children and cameras along the three-quarters of a mile between the glitzy Pier 39 and Ghirardelli Square, that grandfather of all factory-into-shopping-mall conversions. Kate parked in the garage beneath the former chocolate factory and made her way to the street that fronted Aquatic Park, but there was no sign of a six-foot-two elderly bearded clown. She went up the stairs back into Ghirardelli Square proper and found a puppet show in progress, but no Erasmus.

Back on the street, she crossed over to run the gauntlet of sidewalk vendors selling sweatshirts, tie-dyed infant's overalls, images of the Golden Gate Bridge painted onto rocks and bits of redwood, bead necklaces, toilet-roll holders in the shape of frogs and palm trees, crystal light-catchers, crystal earrings, crystal necklaces, and crystals to sew into the back seam of your trousers to center your energy. She was tempted to get one of those for Al, just to see his face, but moved on instead to the next stall, where a graying gypsy sold polished stones on thongs. Kate fingered a teardrop-shaped stone, dark blue with an interesting silvery line running through it.

"That's lapis lazuli, good for physical healing, psychic protection, and stimulating mental powers," the woman rattled off, adding, "The color would look good on you."

God knows, I could use some mental stimulation, thought Kate, although she told her, "I'm looking for a gift, for a blond woman."

The woman gave her a brief lecture on stone auras and personality enhancements, and Kate ended up buying a small necklace of intense lapis lazuli that was set in a delicate silver band. As the woman looked for a suitable box, Kate ran her eyes over the park again.

"Do you come here often?" she asked the woman.

"Seven years," was the laconic answer.

"There's a performer here I was hoping to see, an old guy, tall, does a clown act."

"You a cop?" Kate was surprised, as she had made an effort and dressed like half the women on the street.

"Yes. Why?"

"Just like to know who I'm talking to. That's eighteen bucks." Kate handed her a twenty; she gave her back two ones and the small white box. "I've got nothing against cops. My sister used to be married to one; he was okay. You're talkin' about Erasmus?"

"That's right. Have you seen him?"

"Not today. He usually comes down in the afternoon; mornings, he starts in front of the Cannery."

"I'll try down there, then. Thanks."

"Sure. It's the eyes," she said unexpectedly.

"What eyes?"

"Cops. Your eyes are never still, not if you've been on the streets. Flip-flip-flip, always looking into peoples' pockets, watchin' how they stand. Wear your sunglasses. And relax, sister. It's a beautiful day."

Kate laughed aloud, then sauntered off, feeling good. This was not a bad city, sometimes. She tended to forget that, what with one thing and another.

She made her way past the crowded cable-car turntable and turned downhill at the cart selling hot pretzels, strolling along the waterfront with her hands in her pockets and her eyes scanning the streets from behind the black lenses, humming a tune she did not recognize as coming from the silly musical video she had watched two nights ago. ("When constabulary duty's to be done, to be done, a policeman's lot is not an 'appy one, 'appy one.") She saw two drug scores and a cruising hooker, then a familiar face. She walked over and leaned against the wall next to the pickpocket and sometime informant.

"Hey, Bartles," she murmured. "How's doing?"

"Inspector Martinelli. Looking good. I'm clean."

"I'm sure you are, Bartles, and how about we stay that way? Such a pretty day, let's not spoil it for the folks from Nebraska, huh?"

"I'm not working, I told you. I'm just waiting for the wife."

" 'His capacity for innocent enjoyment is just as great as

any honest man's,'" she sang, out of tune, startling a passing young couple from Visalia.

"What're you going on about?"

"Just something I heard on the tube the other night. Bartles, I think when your wife's finished her shopping you should take her home. I'm in a good mood and if you spoil it, I might break one of your fingers getting the cuffs on you."

"I'm not working today," he insisted.

"Good. Neither am I. Have you seen a tall old man with a beard doing some kind of a clown act?"

"First she threatens me, then she asks me a favor."

"No threat, and it's not a favor. Just asking a civil question."

"You wouldn't know a—oh Christ, it's my wife. Get lost, will you?"

"Have you seen him?"

"Two blocks down, across the street. Now go!" he hissed.

Kate moved off, but not before she had seen the light of suspicion come on in the face of a thin woman in shorts and spike heels. She whistled softly to herself and turned into one of the nearby clothing shops, where she chose a hot pink nylon baseball cap that was embroidered with a truncated Golden Gate Bridge and the words SAN FRANCISCO, CALIFORNIA, buying it and a package of chewing gum. She paused at the tiny mirror beside a display of abalone earrings to put her hair up under the hat, then unpeeled the gum and took out a piece, which she never chewed by choice, but it rendered her infinitely more harmless than all the makeup in a theater. Chewing and humming and slouching behind her shades, she went to see the act of Brother Erasmus.

♦

THIRTEEN

♦

A certain precipitancy was the very poise of his soul.

It really was a stunningly beautiful morning, Kate thought with pleasure, the kind of day that tempts people from New York and Boise to move to California. It is easy to brave the earthquakes and the unemployment and the killing mortgages when a person can eat lunch outside wearing only a cotton shirt, knowing that much of the country is up to its backside in snow.

Strolling along in the carnival atmosphere, kites dipping out over the water, the air smelling of fish and aftershave, the waters of the Golden Gate sparkling, with the bridge, Mount Tamalpais, and the island fortress of Alcatraz looking on benevolently, Kate could forget for a few minutes that she was here on business. She paused to examine the odd wares of the shop that sold live oysters complete with pearls, stopped again to watch a young black kid standing on a box playing robot while his buddy made sure everyone had the hat held under their noses, and then she bought an ice cream cone—for camouflage, of course. By then she had spotted Erasmus. She went up casually, hiding behind hat and cone and the large crowd he had attracted.

He was dressed as Rosalyn Hall had described him, in khaki trousers, a too-small blue-and-white-striped T-shirt, and running shoes that were just a bit too long. He also had a Raiders cap perched on the back of his head and an exaggeratedly garish gold watch on his wrist. His face, as Rosalyn had said, was very lightly shaded. From the side where Kate stood, his face above the beard seemed slightly more dusky than usual, but when he turned around, she saw that the left side of his face was pale, almost chalky. Subtle, and disconcerting.

The most striking thing, however, was not Erasmus himself but his wooden staff: Propped upright against a newspaper vending machine, it wore on its carved head a miniature Raiders cap and a pair of child's sunglasses, and beneath its chin a scrap of the blue-and-white T-shirt fabric covered the worn piece of ribbon. Kate had not really noticed how like Erasmus the carving was, probably because the wood was so dark that the details faded, but it was all there: the beard, an identical beak of a nose, the high brow beneath the cap. The staff was Erasmus reduced to fist-sized essentials. Only its eyes were invisible behind the miniature black lenses.

Erasmus was talking to the staff. He seemed to be reciting a speech in a Shakespearean cadence (speaking with a clipped midwestern sort of accent), striding up and down in the small area of sidewalk that was his stage, seemingly unaware of any audience but the staff, which stood erect, gazing back enig-

133

matically at him from the orange metal newspaper box.

And then the staff spoke. For a moment, Kate felt the hairs on the back of her neck rise at the hoarse whisper, until she realized it was merely a very skillful ventriloquism she was hearing. Around her, the people in the crowd, particularly the newcomers on the outer fringes, stirred and glanced at one another with quick, embarrassed smiles. It was eerie, that voice, hypnotic and amazingly real. Across the shoulders, she caught a glimpse of two children on the other side of the circle, their mouths agape as they listened to the mannikin speak.

"A pestilent gall to me!" it said.

"Sir, I'll teach you a speech," offered Erasmus eagerly. He stood slightly bent, so as to look up at the face on the end of the wooden pole, and his stance, combined with the expression he wore of sly stupidity, changed him, made him both bereft of dignity yet somehow more powerful, as if he was under the control of some primal buffoon.

"Do," said the staff in its husky voice.

"Mark it, uncle: Have more than you show; speak less than you know—"

As the speech went on, Kate licked her ice cream absently, the wad of gum tucked up into her cheek, and tried to remember where she had heard this before. It must be Shakespeare, she thought. One of those things Lee had taken her to. What was it, though? One of the dramas. Not *Macbeth. The Tempest?* No, it was King Lear, talking to his fool. But here, the part of the king was being played by the inanimate staff, while the king's fool was the flesh-and-blood man.

"This is nothing, fool," hissed the staff.

"Then it's like the breath of an unpaid lawyer," said Erasmus gleefully. "You gave me nothing for it!"

This brought a laugh, from the adults at any rate. The

children did not giggle until the fool offered to give the staff two crowns in exchange for an egg.

"What two crowns will they be?" said the staff scornfully.

"Why, after I've cut the egg in the middle and eaten the meat, the two crowns of the egg." And so saying, Erasmus pulled two neat half eggshells out of thin air and placed them on the heads of two children. He turned back to the enigmatic wooden figure.

"I pray you, uncle, keep a schoolmaster, that can teach your fool to lie. I would like to learn to lie." He wagged his eyebrows up and down and the children laughed again.

"If you lie, sir, we'll have you whipped," growled the staff.

"I marvel what kin you and your daughters are!" Erasmus exclaimed. "They'll have me whipped for speaking the truth, you will have me whipped for lying, and sometimes I am whipped for holding my peace. I would rather be any kind of thing than a fool, and yet—I would not be you," he said, marching up to the staff and shaking his head at the wooden face. "You have pared your wit on both sides, and left nothing in the middle—and here comes one of the parings."

He raised his voice at this last sentence and looked pointedly over the heads of the people at a spot behind them. As one, they turned to see. Kate, with the whole mass in front of her, stepped away from the street to look down the sidewalk and saw—Oh no. Oh shit, Erasmus, you stupid old man, don't do this. Can't you see what you're messing with?

But of course he could. That was why he was standing there with his head down, grinning in wicked anticipation as he met the eyes of his target.

The young man was startled at the sudden spectacle of thirty or more people turning to stare at him. Wary, but constitutionally unable to back away from any confrontation, the

135

young man stopped dead, his eyes shooting from side to side as he tried to analyze the situation.

He was a small but powerfully built boy of perhaps nineteen or twenty wearing a tight tank top that showed off the muscles of a weight lifter. His chin and cheeks were dusted with a slight blond bristle and he swaggered in snug blue jeans and black Doc Marten boots that boosted his height almost to average. In his left hand he had a small brown paper bag with the glass neck of a green bottle protruding from it. His right arm was draped over the shoulder of an emaciated girl of seventeen or eighteen who had acne on her chin and chest, black roots in her blond hair, a fading bruise on her upper arm, a lip whose puffiness was not hidden by the lipstick she wore, and a pair of enormous black sunglasses that obscured a large part of her face. Kate had been on enough domestic calls to read the signs without thinking about it: Her careful walk and the arms crossed in front of her told Kate the girl's ribs hurt; her body language (leaning both into and away from the possessive arm) told Kate who had been responsible.

Erasmus, too, knew that something was wrong here. He held out a hand to the pair and called jovially, "Come my lad and drink some beer!"

"Uh, thanks, I got some," said the boy.

"Hasten to be drunk," Erasmus said smilingly. "The business of the day."

"I ain't drunk."

The staff now spoke up. "First the man takes a drink, then the drink takes a drink, then the drink takes the man."

The young man stood with his mouth open, his eyes going from the man to his curiously dressed stick and back again. He suspected mockery, but the number of spectators made it impossible either to shove the old man around or to back off.

"Wha' the fuck?" he asked.

"Where the drink goes in, there the wit goes out," commented the staff.

The boy squinted at the wooden object, then took his arm from the girl's shoulders to walk around and see it face-on.

"How's he do that?" The audience had begun to respond to this new act (all except for those with children, who had already faded away) and a murmur of chuckles greeted the drunk boy's confusion. He spun around belligerently to face them, and the onlookers glanced around for Erasmus to intervene, but he had moved, and they saw him now standing before the girl, her sunglasses in his hand.

Her left eye looked like something from a special-effects laboratory, swollen and black, the eyeball itself so bloodshot, it resembled an open wound. Silence fell immediately. With the others, Kate watched Erasmus bend slightly to look into the girl's good eye.

"A wounded spirit who can bear?" he said quietly, and reaching up with his right hand, he cupped it gently over her eye. The girl gazed up at him, as hypnotized as a rabbit, and did not even wince. After a moment, he stepped away and held out her sunglasses. She took them and her face once more disappeared behind them. No one watched her, though. Their eyes were on Erasmus, who turned back to the youth.

"A woman, a dog, and a walnut tree, the more you beat them the better they be."

The boy was confused by the old man's friendly smile and voice, and he nodded stupidly.

"Speak roughly to your little girl," Erasmus continued, "and beat her when she sneezes. She only does it to annoy because she knows it teases."

"Hey, wait a minute," objected the boy. "I never—"

"Hit hard, hit fast, hit often." Erasmus was still smiling, but

137

he did not look friendly now. He looked large, his eyes easily half a foot above those of the boy.

"I didn't hit her—"

"Jealousy is as cruel as the grave."

"What are you—"

"Cruelty has a human heart, and jealousy a human face; terror, the human form divine, and secrecy, the human dress."

"Jesus Christ. C'mon, Angela, this guy's nuts." The boy tried to move around Erasmus, but the older man moved to block his way to the girl.

The staff spoke up again. "It is human nature to hate those whom you have injured," it whined.

"Old man, you're asking for it."

Kate began to move through the back of the thinning crowd, cursing under her breath and looking for someplace to deposit the remnants of her cone. She knew what those young muscles would do to the old man, to say nothing of the boots. Erasmus bent to look into the young man's eyes, and for the first time he seemed to be trying to communicate, not just mock.

"I must be cruel," he said with a small shrug of apology, "only to be kind."

The boy hesitated, held not so much by the words as by the man's unexpected attitude, though even as Kate watched, it began to harden.

"What mean you," he said coldly, "that you beat my people to pieces and grind the faces of the poor?"

Silence held; then, said as a sneer: "The life of man: solitary, poor, nasty, brutish, and . . . short."

It was the deliberate stress given the last word that broke the boy, and his powerful right arm, with the paper-wrapped bottle now at the end of it, shot automatically out toward the old man's head. Kate threw herself against the arm before it made contact, but the impact swept all three of them into the girl Angela, against the wall behind her, and then tumbled them to the pavement in a heap. The raging boy flung his girlfriend off and was first to his feet, and if three men from the audience had not managed to drag him off, Kate would have had considerably more damage than three oval bruises on her shoulders and shins where his boots had hit home. She scrambled upright and shoved her police ID into his face, holding it there until it and her repeated shouts of "Police officer! I'm a police officer!" finally got through and she saw his muscles relax. The boy shook off the restraining hands but made no move to continue the assault.

The raucous gathering had finally attracted official attention, and several short coughs of a siren signaled the arrival of the local uniforms. The two men climbed out of the patrol car and moved their authoritative bulk into the center of activity, but Kate did not take her eyes from the young man until the uniformed officers had acknowledged her identity and were actually standing next to her. Only then did she turn and help Erasmus to his feet. He brushed himself off as if checking that he was in one piece, then, while Kate was making explanations that downplayed the entire episode, he went over to his staff, freed it from the newspaper box, and tucked it into his right shoulder. The effect was bizarre, like looking at a two-headed being, and Kate had to tear her eyes away.

The two uniformed officers were telling the crowd, what remained of it, to move on, and while the younger one dealt with the young man, the older one took Kate to one side.

"Inspector Martinelli, can you tell me what your interest is in the Brother there?"

"At this point, I don't know what my interest is," she admitted. "He's somehow involved in the cremation homicide in Golden Gate Park, but whether as a witness or something more, I just don't know."

"The reason I ask, he's a nice old guy, but he's like a magnet for trouble. Not always, or we'd move him on, but this is the third time, and once last fall we didn't get here fast enough. He got beat up pretty bad. I just thought if he was a friend or a relative, well . . . You know?"

"Would that have been in November?"

"Around then, yeah."

"I heard about that. I'll talk with him, see what I can do, but he has his own agenda, if you know what I mean, and self-preservation doesn't seem to be very high on it."

The crowd having dispersed, the two patrol officers turned their attentions to the young man and delivered a warning that even he seemed to find impressive (though, truth to tell, even before they began, he looked ill and without interest in beating up old men). When they had finished, he gathered Angela up and would have walked away, but Erasmus put out a gentle hand to stop him.

"Rejoice, O young man, in thy youth," he said quietly. The boy nodded and would not look at him, but Angela did, and to her, Erasmus said in a heartfelt exclamation, "Queen and huntress, chaste and fair," and then, with the emphasis of a judgment, told her, "None but the brave" (and here he pointedly ran his eyes over the boy) "deserve the fair."

The boy tugged at her and they moved off, but after half a dozen steps, Angela shrugged off the confining arm and the two of them continued side by side.

The two patrolmen suggested firmly that it was time Erasmus moved on. Kate reassured them that she would deal with it, and when another call came for them, they climbed back into the car and drove off. Kate waved her thanks. As soon as they had left, she turned on Erasmus.

"You could have been hurt, you stupid old man," she declared furiously. He did not seem to be listening as he watched the two young people go off down the street. He shook his head in sorrow.

"Such as sit in darkness and in the shadow of death."

"Talk about the shadow of death!" Kate stepped in front of him, though she practically had to jump up and down to interrupt his gaze. "That kid could have put you in the hospital. And you would have deserved it, for being such a damned . . . idiot."

He finally looked down at her, and his eyes crinkled up in a smile. "How forcible are right words."

"Damned straight they're right. Don't do that again, you hear me? I don't care what you think—it doesn't do anyone any good."

He looked again at the retreating backs and sighed. "We have scotched the snake, not killed it," he said, which Kate took as agreement.

"Just stick to juggling," she suggested. "I can't guarantee to stumble on you every time you get into trouble."

She knew in an instant that he did not believe she had just happened to show up here. He leaned on his staff, two identical heads sharing a good joke, and laughed at her. Even the wooden head seemed to be laughing at her, and she felt her face go red. There was absolutely nothing she could do, so she turned her back on him and walked away.

♦

FOURTEEN

♦

*With all his gentleness, there was originally
something of impatience in his impetuosity.*

Kate stalked off down the busy sidewalk, her face flushed, her
mind troubled, her shin and left shoulder sore, and her jaw aching. She stopped at the first trash bin she came to and spat out
the gum. How could people chew the stuff all day? They must
have jaws of iron. She pulled off the stupid pink hat, rolled it up
and stuffed it into the back pocket of her jeans, and ruffled her
short hair back into place with her fingers.

Could the man be schizophrenic? There was certainly
some kind of a split personality going on here, but whether it
was uncontrollable or an act, cynic that she was, she honestly
could not say. The performance had not been put on merely for

her benefit, of that she was reasonably sure. He could not have seen her until she had stepped back from the crowd, and the direction of the act had been already fully established.

What was that snippet in Professor Whitlaw's file? Something about Foolishness being a dangerous business. Kate could well believe that, if this was the pattern: One might as well tease a bull as the particular target he had chosen. Come to think of it, the bull would probably be safer.

And what was the point? Did Erasmus actually expect to change the way the boy treated his girlfriend? Or had he just been hoping to distract the young man, to take his attention away from the girl and—what? Allow her a chance to escape?

Oh, this was ridiculous. Erasmus wasn't all there, and looking for rational reasons for his behavior was pointless.

Still, he was clever, give him that. The more she thought about the scene she had just witnessed, the more impressed she was. Teasing a bull, indeed—and walking away intact, while the bull . . . what was the image she had in mind? Not a bull, some other powerful and savage animal. A wolverine or a cougar or something, seen long ago on a television nature program, being tormented and ultimately brought down by a pack of small, scruffy, cowardly coyotes or jackals.

At this point, Kate came to herself, finding that she was standing outside the elevator in the parking garage, feeling as bedeviled and set upon by her fanciful thoughts and images as the wolverine was by the coyotes (a lioness, perhaps it had been, and jackals). She was seized by the desire to lower her head and shake it in massive rage and befuddlement, but a family of honking New Yorkers came out of the garage and she controlled the urge. Don't frighten the children, Kate, she told herself, and grinned at them instead. The mother instantly herded her charges to one side and the father bristled in suspicion. Kate stood aside and allowed them to sidle past her, then went on into the garage. New Yorkers, she thought with a mental shake of the head. *They probably would have been less frightened if I had bellowed at them.*

Out on the street again, she pulled her car over into a loading zone and reached for her notebook and the car phone. The phone was answered after four rings by an English voice that by way of greeting merely stated the number she'd just punched out.

"Professor Whitlaw? This is Inspector Kate Martinelli."

"Yes, Inspector, what can I do for you?"

"I wondered if you might be free for an hour or so this afternoon?"

"Inspector, I'm terribly sorry, I have an informal tutorial that seems to be turning into a seminar, and I can't see that I'll be free much before tea."

"Er, right."

"I have six people here," the professor clarified, "and they look to be ensconced until hunger drives them out. Did you wish to review the material I set for you? Would tomorrow do as well?"

"No, it's not that exactly. I mean, yes, I'd like to go over it with you, but I found Brother Erasmus, and I wondered—"

"You found your Fool! Oh, grand. Where are you?"

"In my car, up near the Fishermen's Wharf area."

"Where can I meet you? I'll have one of the young people drive me. Surely one of them must have come in an automobile."

"Well, if you can get free, I'll come and pick you up."

"Even better. I'll dig out my Sherlock Holmes glass and my entomologist's bottle and meet you on the doorstep. Although come to think of it, etymology might be a more useful discipline for this exercise."

"Oh, certainly." *Whatever.*

"Inspector, I cannot tell you how grateful I am."

"For what? Messing up your day and dragging you across town to push your way through San Francisco's answer to the Tower of London?"

"I am ecstatic at the prospect, I assure you, Inspector."

"I'm glad to hear that. I'll be about ten minutes."

"I shall be ready."

When Kate turned the corner on the street where Professor Whitlaw was staying, she saw a group of young people on the steps of the house, forming a circle around an invisible center, which they all seemed to be addressing at once. When the car pulled up in front of them, Kate could see an extra pair of legs in the knot, and after a moment Professor Whitlaw peered out, her gray hair at shoulder level to the shortest of them. They gave way but followed her across the sidewalk to the street, still talking.

"Yes, dear," the professor soothed. "It'll keep until tomorrow. Just continue with your word studies." She climbed in beside Kate, pulled the door shut, and, as Kate pulled away from the protesting students, patted her hair. "My goodness," she said weakly, "Americans seem so very large, especially the young ones. What do their parents feed them?" She didn't seem to expect an answer, but sorted out the seat belt, lowered her black leather handbag onto the floor, put the black nylon tube of a fold-up umbrella on her lap and draped a tan raincoat over it, and folded her hands together. Sixty-eight degrees and not a cloud, not even a haze in the sky, but the well-dressed English-woman was ready for sleet.

"Where did you find him, this Erasmus?" she asked. "What is he doing?"

"He's in the very center of the tourist area, juggling, conjuring quarters out of the ears of children, and goading bulls."

"I beg your pardon?"

Kate laughed. "Sorry, not literally. It's an image that came to mind." She explained about the confrontation she had witnessed. Professor Whitlaw reached down for her handbag, snapped open the clasp and took out a small notebook, and wrote for a moment.

"How very interesting," she murmured.

"Why would he be doing this?" Kate asked. "I mean, I can see how a fool would want to help the homeless and I could sort of see the appeal that the seminary might have for him, but what is he doing here, dressed like a suburban refugee, risking arrest or worse—surely he must occasionally misjudge just how far he can push people before they explode? Dean Gardner said Erasmus had been hurt last November, and I assumed that he'd been beaten up in the street, but now I wouldn't be surprised if it had happened here."

"You are quite right. Fools have never been content unless they were putting themselves at risk—from violence, from cold and starvation, whatever edge they were near, they would go closer. A medieval court fool would insult the king; the early Christians embraced martyrdom: It's all a means of courting madness."

"It is a kind of mental illness, then?"

"Oh no. Well, I couldn't say in this case, not having studied your friend Erasmus, but for a true Fool, a Holy Fool, the madness is always simulated. It is a tool, not a permanent state. I should perhaps qualify that by saying that there were some Holy Fools who had, in an earlier period of their lives, undergone a period of true insanity, but they came out of it, through conversion or enlightenment, and then later, if they returned to it, would only do so deliberately. You might say that they would choose to lose rational control."

"I don't understand why. A tool for what?" Other than a

means of establishing an insanity plea for murder, she did not say aloud.

"For teaching. A fool who has relinquished control, who has submitted to chaos, is in a sense no longer a person, not an individual with a will and a mind of his own. You saw how Erasmus deferred to the staff he carries. Typically, even an inanimate object has more will than a fool. And because he is not his own person, he can be all people; he can be a reflection of whatever individual he is facing. That is why a fool is so troubling; he's a mirror, and mirrors can be frightening."

Kate waited until she had negotiated Geary Street before she spoke. "I'm sorry, it's a pretty theory, but I can't see what it has to do with the man Erasmus."

"I am putting it in theoretical terms, perhaps. I should apologize for my airy-fairy academic language, which makes the process sound theoretical, but I assure you it's quite real. Why do you think your fool so angered that young man? Not just because he was irritating him. Erasmus was reflecting the boy's own ugly face back to him, showing him that he, a strong, a powerful young man, what you would call 'macho,' would stoop so low as to hit, not only a frail young woman but even an old, feeble man. Judging by the behavior I have witnessed in the past by experienced fools, I would speculate that Erasmus, left alone, would probably have defused the lad's anger by carrying it to exaggeration, by actually lying on the ground and inviting the young man to savage him. And then, having shocked the fellow into immobility, he would have brought the lesson to a close by identifying himself, Erasmus, the near victim, with the girl, the man's perpetual victim. Now, *that* is teaching, and I suspect that even in its interrupted form the lesson will not cease to niggle at the man for some time. Every time he looks at the young woman, for a while."

147

"If you're right, it'd be a clever thing to teach in our domestic violence program—lie down and let the husband boot you before arresting him."

"Of course, it isn't quite that simple, is it? It's not a technique at all; it's a response from the fool's inner being. And, seeing the effect this fool has had on one far-from-gullible police officer, I must say I am quite looking forward to meeting him."

♦

At first it looked as if the professor would not get her wish, because when Kate drove past the place where Erasmus had been performing, he had obeyed the patrolman's order and was no longer there. Nor did they spot him anywhere along the strip of shops and shows, all the way up to the Maritime Museum. Along the drive, however, there had been various tantalizing smells, french fries and onions and grilling hamburgers, topped off by a waft of chilis and onions that lay over Ghirardelli Square.

"I haven't had any lunch," Kate declared. "Do you mind if I stop off and get something, then we can do another drive-by?"

"That's quite all right with me."

Kate drove around into Fort Mason and stopped as close to Greens Restaurant as she could get, ran in and bought a juicy sandwich of eggplant and red peppers and cheese, a bag of fruity cookies for the professor, who had said that she'd already eaten lunch, and ran back out. She pulled the car back out into the Marina and parked, and they ate while watching the joggers and Frisbee players and people lying with their faces turned to the winter sun. Professor Whitlaw ate one cookie and then opened the door and got out to stand and gaze over the grass to the waters of the Bay and the tracery of the Golden

Gate Bridge. Kate gathered up sandwich and car keys and went to stand with her.

"You have a very lovely city here," said the professor. "A jewel in a golden setting. Do you know, London is built on one of the most active rivers in the world, and yet in most of the city you'd never know the river was there. I've often thought that would be the definition of a modern city: One has absolutely no idea of the natural setting."

"It would be hard to ignore the Bay and the hills here."

"Yes, I fear San Francisco is doomed never to achieve modernity. What a blessing. Do you suppose that is a kite that young man is wrestling with, or a tent?"

"God only knows. We'll have to wait and see if he gets it in the air."

The results were inconclusive. The winged dome with the dragon stitched on one side was briefly airborne but hardly aerodynamic. Kate crumpled her sandwich wrapper and tossed it into a nearby can.

"Ready?" she asked.

"Yes," Professor Whitlaw said, and turned back to the car. "I really must do this more often. It's ridiculous, to come to a magnificent place like this and see only the insides of walls. I believe I've seen more of the city in the last hour than I have the entire three weeks I've been here." She turned to Kate and humorously half-inclined her head. "Thank you for the tour."

"Any time."

In the car, they rolled down the windows. Kate turned back toward Fishermen's Wharf.

"Are you from London, then?" she asked.

"Oh no, dear. Rural Yorkshire originally, then Cambridge, followed by several years teaching in London. I hated it there. So insular and gray. Chicago seemed wide open, bracing after

London. That is where I first came in this country, to a teaching job. Although I admit California seems like a different country entirely. I first got to really know the Fools movement in Chicago and on the East Coast, Boston and New York."

"Even though they started in England."

"Yes, ironic, wasn't it? I knew of them in England, of course, but they were of peripheral interest to me then—a friend who later became a colleague had a passion for them. Eventually the passion proved contagious. My actual field is the history of cults, but there's so much that is depressing in cult behavior, I found Fools a refreshing change. They are one of the few groups who understand that religion can be not only joyous but fun. He doesn't seem to be here, does he?" She sounded disappointed as Kate drove slowly past the place where Erasmus had been two hours earlier.

"No, but we'll try farther up. One of the vendors said he's usually there in the afternoon."

There was one crowd, at the beginning of Aquatic Park, but that was only the line waiting for the cable car to be rotated. They rounded the park, dodging a flock of Japanese tourists and a laden station wagon from Michigan, and then, on the path sloping down from the road to the waterfront, there was another crowd: From its center rose the back of a familiar graying head.

Kate pulled into a no-parking area, propped her police identification on the dashboard, and trotted around the car to help Professor Whitlaw out.

"He's down there. See where that child with the ball just ran?"

The professor set off determinedly in her sensible shoes, with Kate at her side. Halfway down the slope, the din from the street musicians across the road faded, and the wind stilled. Kate could hear him now, not what he was saying but the

150

rhythm of his voice as he chanted some other man's words. A few more steps, and Professor Whitlaw faltered. Kate's hand shot out to grasp the woman's elbow, but she had not stumbled, and now she picked up her pace as if anxious to reach her goal.

The voice of Brother Erasmus rose and faded as his head turned toward them and then away. They were still in back of him.

". . . a rich man to go through the eye of a needle than . . ." he said before his words faded again. The brief phrase had an extraordinary effect on the professor, however. She gave a brief sound, like a cough, and raised her hand as if to pull away the shoulders that were blocking her view of the speaker, but then, realizing the futility of it, she began to work her way around to the right, craning her neck and going up on her toes, to no avail. This close, even Kate couldn't see him.

They were directly in front of him now, separated by four or five layers of people, and although his words were clear, Kate did not hear them. All her attention was on Eve Whitlaw, that dignified English professor who was now practically whimpering—she *was* whimpering, with the frustration of being unable to move the bodies ahead of her, those shoulders clad in knit cotton, shining heads of hair a foot above her own. Finally she just put her head down and began to push her way in, Kate close on her heels.

He saw Kate first. His eyes rested on her calmly, sardonically, as if to say, Are you here again, my child? And then they dropped to look at the tiny woman emerging from the circle of onlookers before him. Kate saw the shock run through him, saw him rear up, his two-toned face draining of color, his head turning away even though his eyes were riveted on Eve Whitlaw. His mouth, his entire body were twisting away from her, and the expression on his face could only be one of sudden and complete terror.

"David?" the professor cried. "David, my God, I thought you were dead!"

And with her words, he turned and bolted through the crowd.

♦

FIFTEEN

♦

*The man who went into the cave was not the man
who came out again.*

Kate would never have thought that a seventy-year-old man
burdened by a wooden staff and overly large shoes could have
evaded her, but this one did. His early advantage through the
thinnest edge of the crowd while Kate was wading out from the
very center got him to the road first. He shot across, to a
screeching of tires and the blare of angry horns, and by the
time Kate had threaded her way between the camper van and a
taxi, he had vanished. He had to have entered Ghirardelli
Square somehow, but the shopkeepers all looked at her dumbly
and none of the other closed doors would open. Red-faced and

cursing her lack of condition, she went to her car to radio for help but then stopped to think.

What difference did his running make? That had not been the flight of a guilty man upon seeing a police officer; indeed, he hadn't been the least bit disturbed at seeing her. She could hardly have him arrested for fleeing an old acquaintance—because that's what he had been doing. He knew Eve Whitlaw, and she knew—David? Kate put down the handset and got out of the car. She could always put out a call for him later, if she needed to.

Professor Whitlaw was sitting on a bench, looking pale, hugging her large black handbag to her chest. Kate sat down beside her.

"Are you all right?"

"Oh yes, dear. Upset. It was a shock. For him, too, obviously. Oh my, how very stupid I was, bursting in on him like that."

"You know him," Kate said, not as a question. "I mean personally."

"Oh my yes, I know him. Knew him. We worked together for ten years, what seems like a long, long time ago."

"David . . . Sawyer?"

"You know of him, then?"

"There was a note in your file, a personal communication from David Sawyer, dated October 1983."

"Lord, yes. I had forgotten that. Just three months before he disappeared. We all thought he was dead."

"Why? What happened?"

She closed her eyes and put a shaky hand across her mouth. Kate looked up and noticed the last of the crowd, lingering to have the excitement explained. She shook her head at them and they began to drift away.

"I don't think I can go into it just here and now," said the professor. "I feel very unsettled. I should like to pull my thoughts together first, if you don't mind."

Truth to tell, she was looking old and badly shaken.

"That's fine. Let me take you back to your house; we can have a cup of tea. Isn't that what I'm supposed to offer you?" The professor smiled at her gratefully.

"The English panacea, yes. Tea for upsets, tea when you've been working, tea for hot and cold, thirst and hunger, tea to ease an awkward conversation. Yes, we shall drink tea."

♦

While the kettle was heating in the cheerful pine kitchen, Kate borrowed the telephone in the study, closing the door behind her. She reached Al Hawkin on the third try, neither in his car nor in his office, but at home. She could hear the television in the background.

"Al, this is Kate. I'm glad I reached you; I thought you might be in Palo Alto."

"Jani's got a conference this weekend, so I'm catching up on paperwork and watching the moss grow on my carpet. What's up?"

"Professor Whitlaw knows who Erasmus is. I took her to see him, down on the lawn of Aquatic Park, and when he spotted her, he ran—literally. He was frightened of her, Al."

"You were there? And he got away from you?"

"I know," she said, embarrassed. "Only as far as the shops, but one of them was either hiding him or had let him out through a back door. I didn't think I should make a big thing of it, though. I mean, he's hardly your average Joe, if we want to pick him up again."

"Where are you now?"

155

"At Professor Whitlaw's house down in Noe Valley. She's going to tell me what she knows about Erasmus, or I should say David Sawyer. Do you want to hear it?"

"Give me the address," he said, and when she had described how to find the place, he growled, "Fifteen minutes. I need to shave first."

"Oh, give her a thrill, Al. She'll think you're doing undercover work."

He grunted and dropped the phone, and Kate replaced her own receiver, then stood looking at the walls of books that rose up on all sides. Two sides, she saw, were filled with an unlikely combination of medical texts (with an emphasis on childhood diseases and allergies) and best-seller hardbacks with brightly colored dust jackets (novels and the sort of non-fiction books everyone talks about but no one reads). One wall and the narrow shelves beside the door had been cleared for use by the temporary resident; these books were mostly old and lacking dust jackets, with library stickers on their spines. Ignoring the whistle of the teakettle and the sounds of cups and spoons, Kate ran her eye slowly over the assembled volumes until she found what she had thought would be there: *The Fool: Order Through Chaos, Clarity from Confusion* by David M. Sawyer, M. Div., Ph.D. She pulled it out, then saw another with the name Sawyer on the spine, a slim volume called *The Reformation of the Catholic Church.* She carried them both with her out to the kitchen and laid them on the oak table, which was looking slightly less polished than it had two days before.

"You've found David's books," noted Professor Whitlaw. She put down the plate she was carrying and reached out for the book on top, the *Church* title. She held it in her right hand and, pinching the hollow of the binding between her left thumb and forefinger, she ran her fingers up and down the

156

spine a couple of times before putting the book down again with an affectionate pat.

"These are the only ones he wrote?"

"There are two more, which I've loaned out, and he was halfway through a fifth one when he disappeared."

"If you don't mind I'd like my partner to hear about Sawyer's disappearance, too. His name is Al Hawkin; he'll be here in about ten minutes."

"Of course not, I don't mind waiting."

Kate looked again at the two books, which gave her a topic of peripheral conversation. "Isn't that a broad sort of reach, from Catholicism to Fools? I thought scholarly types tended to specialize more than that."

"The Reformation book was his Ph.D. thesis, an investigation into how early Protestantism changed the Roman Catholic Church. And yes, you'd think the two topics unrelated, but David was interested in the ways an existing organization, when confronted by rebellion, moves not away from but toward its opposition. After Luther, the Roman Catholic authorities—" She was off, in full-fledged scholarly flight, and Kate did not even try to follow her. She just nodded at the pauses and waited for the doorbell to ring.

When Hawkin arrived (shaven and dressed in tan shirt, tie, and tweedy sport jacket), the pot of tea had to be emptied and made anew, the plate of what the professor called "digestive biscuits" refilled, and tea begun again. Eventually they were settled, refreshed, and ready. Kate took out her notebook.

"You want to know about David Sawyer," Professor Eve Whitlaw began. "I first met David in London in 1971. It was July, the beginning of the long vac, and I was in the reading room of the British Library when he came up to my table and demanded to know why for the third time he had requested a book, only to be told that I had it. He was over from America, looking into the Fools movement, which was barely two years old and had caught his fancy. Our interests overlapped, so for the rest of his stay, which was, I think, a couple of weeks, we joined forces. Academically," she added sternly, although the vision of even the most platonic relationship was inevitably amusing, given nearly two feet in height difference. Seeing neither suspicion nor humor in either bland detective face, she went on. "He was married and had a son. The family stayed in Chicago that summer, although the next year they came over with him. His wife was younger than he was, and the child was eight or nine."

"Where are they now?" Kate asked.

"I think you'd best let me tell the story as it comes, if you don't mind. As I said, we joined forces. I drove him around southern England to the various Fool centers, and he helped me with my work. He had a remarkable understanding of cult psychology, and he knew everyone in the field, it seemed. After he'd left, we corresponded. That first spring we wrote a joint article for a journal. The next summer when he came over with his family, they hired a house near Oxford, and for two months I practically lived with them. His wife was the loveliest person, had just finished her Ph.D. in early-childhood education, and their son was sweet, too. He had a mild speech defect and was at that sort of unformed age, but he had occasional sparkles of joy and intelligence. Ay, what a grand summer that was.

"At the end of it, I went back to gray old London and they flew back to Chicago, and two months later I had a telephone call from David asking if I'd be interested in applying for a job. Teaching undergraduates, to start with, with some research time. I jumped at it, and I got it, and we worked together for the next ten years. They were the best ten years of my life," she said, pursing her lips as if to keep from having to speak further.

"Now comes the hard part. Perhaps I should point out that David was considerably higher up the ladder than I was. He worked almost exclusively with graduate students and on his own research. In a way, that was a pity, because he was one of the most stimulating lecturers I've ever heard. I used to pull him into my classes regularly, just for the pleasure of seeing their faces light up, and to see him respond to them. When he talked about church history, his voice would make poetry out of the councils and the heresies. Brilliant.

"But for the most part, he had graduate students. Some of them were very good; a few were mediocre—he found it difficult to refuse anyone outright; he thought it better to let them discover their own limitations. There were a few disappointments, a couple of kids who were angry when they finally realized they weren't world-movers, but mostly it went smoothly. Until Kyle.

"I never liked Kyle Roberts, and I don't think it's only hindsight talking. I didn't trust him, and I told David so, but he said it would be fine, that it was only Kyle's rough edges. Kyle came from a very poor family, made it through on some minority scholarship, although he looked straight Caucasian to me, and basically he assumed the world owed him a living. What he wanted was to be a full professor at Yale, no less. David thought . . . Oh God. David thought it was funny. He thought that when Kyle really knew what he was getting into, he would settle for teaching in some lesser university, or a college. He should have taken his master's degree and gone away, because he had a wife and two children to support, but his work was just good enough to keep him in the program. David and a couple of the others used to give him part-time jobs, research assistant and teaching aide, but I wouldn't have anything to do with it. I thought, frankly, that it was cruel to encourage a man who had working-class manners, a family to feed, and no brilliance to think of himself as top academic material.

"Well. By the autumn of 1983, he had been in the program for five years. The first of the men and women he had entered with began to finish their programs, but he hadn't even had the topic for his dissertation approved, much less written it. Now, that's not all that unusual—a Ph.D. varies tremendously in how long it takes—but for him it was becoming a real problem, because in his own eyes he was brilliant.

"Then in early December, one of the assistant professors announced that he was leaving, and Kyle went to David and said that he wanted the job. It was utterly impossible, of course. He might just have qualified as a candidate if he'd had the thesis in its final stages, but when he had not even begun to write it? There were at least forty others who would be completely qualified, so why lower the standards in order to get Kyle Roberts?

"It all happened so quickly. Looking back, that's the most baffling thing, that there was no time for clouds to form on the horizon, no warning. Kyle confronted David, and David finally told him the truth about his academic future. Politely at first and then, when Kyle just refused to understand, David became harder, until he finally lost his temper and said that Kyle was deluding himself if he thought he'd ever reach higher than assistant professor, and that he, David, would be hard put to write a letter of recommendation even for that.

"Kyle had never had anyone he respected tell him that, and it simply shattered him. I saw him when he left David's office—the whole building heard the argument—and he was just white. Stunned. I will never forget how he looked. And I know, I knew then, that any one of us could have rescued him, just by putting a hand out. . . . But we didn't. He'd become too much of a leech to risk making contact. I let him walk past me.

160

"He went home. But on his way, he stopped at a sporting goods store and bought a shotgun, and when he walked through his back door, he loaded it and shot his wife, his eight-year-old son, and his three-year-old daughter. The police later decided that he must have sat there for nearly an hour, and during that time he must have found his anger again, because instead of killing himself, he went to find David. It was dark. He went to David's home. David was not back yet, but his wife and son were there, and so Kyle shot them both and then finally turned the gun on himself. Jonny died. He was nineteen. Charlotte, David's wife, had a collapsed lung, but they saved her. She got out of the hospital just in time for Christmas.

"David was utterly devastated, empty—an automaton. He wouldn't go out, except to buy food for Charlotte and pick up her prescriptions. He wouldn't talk to me; when I went to his house, he would not even look at me. The administration arranged for a leave of absence, of course, but he didn't even sign the papers they sent him until the chair of the department went and stood over him.

"Finally at the end of January, Charlotte was well enough to travel, and she went home to her parents' house on Long Island. He drove her to New York and then went back to their house, just long enough to type out his letter of resignation, arrange a power of attorney for his lawyer so that all his personal assets could be transferred immediately to Charlotte, and make three phone calls to friends. I was one of them. All he said . . ." She swallowed, blinking furiously. "This is very difficult. All he said was that his vanity had . . . had killed five people and that he— Oh God," she whispered as the tears broke free. "He said he loved me and wished me all good things, and would very probably not see me again. And he asked me to take care of Charlotte. . . . Thank you." She seized the box of tissues Hawkin had put in front of her and buried her face in a handful of pink paper. "Ten years ago last month," she said, and blew her nose a final time, "and it seems like yesterday."

She got up and walked into the kitchen, where she stood on the stool to splash water onto her face, then dried it with a kitchen towel and came back to the table.

"We all assumed that he had gone somewhere and killed himself. He was very nearly dead already. And then today I see David Sawyer looking like an old derelict and acting the Fool for tourists, and he runs at the sight of my face. And," she added a minute later, "he is somehow involved in a murder. Yet another murder. Oh, poor, poor David."

Holding her threadbare dignity around her, she stumbled down from the tall chair and walked away down the hallway. A door opened and closed. Kate blew a stream of air through her pursed lips and looked at Hawkin.

"I could understand if someone had bashed *him*—Erasmus, or Sawyer. I've seen two good solid motives for killing him in the last few hours. But as for him killing someone else, I haven't seen anything."

"John was a blackmailer," said Hawkin quietly.

"And he found out about Kyle and threatened to tell the other street people, so Erasmus bashed him to keep him quiet? I can't see it, Al. Sorry."

"He ran."

"From her, not from me."

"She knows who he is. She'd give you the motive and ID him. Maybe if you hadn't been there he would have lured her off to a quiet corner and whacked her one, too."

She leaned over the table to study his face, but it told her nothing.

"Are you serious, Al? Or are you just playing with this?"

"I'm mostly trying it out for size, but I will say that I'm not too happy he made a run for it. I don't like the idea of him skipping town."

"Okay, you're the boss. Do you want to put a call out for him tonight or wait and see if he shows up in the park tomorrow?"

"We can wait. Meanwhile, see what you can find out about this Kyle Roberts thing. Where's Sawyer's wife now; was it really an open-and-shut murder/suicide; did Roberts have family that might want to even things up a bit?"

"Such as a five-foot-eleven white male with a Texas accent who called himself John?"

"Such as. You know anyone in Chicago?"

" 'Anyone' meaning anyone on the police department? No."

"I don't, either. Well, I met someone at a conference once, but he and I had differing views on such things as search-and-seizure and putting down riots. He wouldn't give you the time of day. What about Kenning down in Vice? He had a brother, didn't he?"

How, wondered Kate, could I have forgotten either Hawkin's phenomenal memory or his personal-touch method of getting information? When they had worked together before, she had tended to turn to the computer; Al depended on someone's cousin Marty who had been mentioned at the last departmental ball game.

"I'll ask," she said. Computers didn't have it all.

"Well," he said, "I don't know that we can do anything else here. You want to start the background search on him? I'd do it, but I'm testifying in that Brancusi case Monday and I need to go over it carefully. It's going to be a bitch."

"No problem, I'll get it going. Except—how about you call Kenning and ask for his brother's name? He's probably home watching the game, and you're more likely to know when it's over than I am." She grinned at him and he, unembarrassed, grinned back.

"Paperwork, you know?" he said. "I only turn on the tube for the noise."

"Sure, Al. Have a beer for me, okay?"

"Talk to you later. Thank the professor for the tea." He let himself out, and a minute later Kate heard a car door slam and an engine start up. She picked up Sawyer's book on fools and began to leaf through it, waiting for Professor Whitlaw to emerge, but she had barely started the introduction before the door opened and the professor came down the hall.

"I apologize," she said. "As I said, it was a shock. Now, please tell me what I may do to help my old friend."

"Er, I don't really know."

"I must see him again."

"I'll let you know when we find him." They owed her at least that much, Kate figured, but something in her voice alerted the professor.

"You sound as if you have some doubts about it."

"He may go to ground for a few days," she said evasively.

"You don't think it'll be more than that, do you? He won't run away completely, surely."

Kate always hated this sort of thing. With a suspect, you knew where you stood: Never answer questions; don't even act as if you heard them. With a witness, just evade politely. But with an important, intelligent, and potentially very helpful witness, evasion created a barrier, and she couldn't afford that.

"Professor Whitlaw, we don't know what to expect, and I doubt you could help us any in figuring it out. I'd say offhand that the David Sawyer you knew is gone. He's Brother Erasmus now, and Brother Erasmus could do anything."

"Not murder, in case you are thinking of him as a suspect. Not as David Sawyer, and not as a fool."

"I hope you're right. He's an appealing character."

"That hasn't changed, at any rate. Perhaps there's more of David there than you think."

"We shall see. Thank you very much for your help with his identity. And I take it that you would be available for assisting in an interview with him?"

"That's right; you said he was difficult to communicate with. I had forgotten, in all the uproar. Yes, certainly, I shall be glad to help. Perhaps I'd best brush up on my Shakespeare."

"That reminds me—the name of his son. You said it was Jonny, I think?"

"Short for Jonathan, yes. Why?"

"The first time I met him, he seemed to be trying to explain himself to me and Dean Gardner, and he said something about vanity, and Absalom, and he also said that David loved Jonathan."

"Odd. Isn't it Jonathan who loved David?"

"That's what the dean said. He seemed to think it was very unusual for Erasmus to change a text." Although, come to think of it, he had done so again that day. Surely the Lewis Carroll poem told us, Speak roughly to your little *boy*?

"I'm sorry, but I find it difficult to imagine a fool who is so structured in his utterances."

"Imagine it. But if as you say his son was named Jonathan, then perhaps he was trying to tell us that he believes his 'vanity' led to the death of his son. That's very close to what you've just told me, which proves that he can communicate; he can even change his quotations if he wants to badly enough."

"Oh dear. I'm afraid I'm getting too old for this kind of

mental gymnastics. I shall have to think about what you've told me."

"That's fine; there's nothing more you can do now, anyway. You have my number, if you think of anything. Thanks again for your help. I'll let myself out."

♦

SIXTEEN

♦

He suffered fools gladly.

It was dark outside but still clear. Kate got into her car and drove to the Hall of Justice. By the time she arrived, her bladder was nearly bursting from the cups of tea she'd drunk, and she sprinted for the nearest toilet before making her way more slowly to her office, the coffeepot, and the telephone. It was Saturday night, although early yet; business would pick up soon. Her first phone call was to her own number.

"Jon? Kate. I'm going to be stuck at the office for a while. I hope not too long, but don't hold dinner. Oh, you didn't, good. Are you going out? Well, if you decide to, give me a ring and let me know who's there instead, okay? Thanks. Oh, I hope not more than a couple of hours, maybe less. Fine. Right. Bye."

Then the computer terminal and the other telephone calls, and when Al called with Kenning's brother-in-law's (not brother; Al, unusually, had gotten it wrong) name and home number, she called through to the Chicago police, found that the man was on duty the next morning, and decided that little would be gained by bothering him at home on a Saturday night. There was no trace of David Sawyer on the records—hardly surprising, since David Sawyer had virtually ceased to exist a decade before.

There was not much more she could do tonight, so she gathered her coat and made her way to the elevators, deaf to the ringing telephones and shouts and the scurry of activity. She stepped aside when the doors of the elevator opened and two detectives came out, each holding one elbow of a small Oriental man in handcuffs, with dried blood on his shirt and a monotonous string of tired curses coming from his bruised mouth.

"Another Saturday night," she said as she slipped through the closing doors.

"And I ain't got nobody," sang the detective on the man's left arm. The doors closed on the rest of the song.

Outside, in the parking lot, Kate was seized by a feeling of restlessness. She should go directly home, five minutes away, let Jon have his evening out, but she'd told him two hours, and it had been barely forty minutes. Time for a brief drive, out to the park.

Erasmus—Sawyer—no, Erasmus—habitually spent Saturday with tourists and then Sunday in the park, roughly four miles away. Did he walk? Was he already in the park now, bedded down beneath some tree? Where did he keep his stash, his bedroll and clothing, the small gym bag Dean Gardner had fetched from the CDSP rooms and which had been returned (with its contents of blue jeans, flannel shirt, bar of soap, threadbare towel, and three books) when Erasmus had been turned loose after making what could only loosely be called his statement?

Kate got into her car and turned, not north to home but west into the city. She drove past the high-rise hotels and department stores and the pulsing neon bars and busy theaters into the more residential areas with their Chinese and Italian restaurants and movie theaters, the pet stores and furniture showrooms closed or closing, until she came to the dark oasis that was Golden Gate Park.

The park held over a thousand acres of trees, flowers, lawn, and lakes, coaxed out of bare sand in painful stages over patient decades, wrenched from the gold-rush squatters in the 1850s and now returning to their spiritual descendants a century and a half later, for despite the combined efforts of police and social services and parks department bulldozers, a large number of men and women regarded the park as home.

Kate drove slowly down Stanyan Street and along Lincoln Way, cruising for street people who were not yet in their beds. At Ninth Avenue, a trio of lumpy men carrying bedrolls leaned into one another and drifted toward the park. She turned in, got out of her car, and waited for them under a streetlight.

"Good evening, gentlemen," she said. Astonished, and suspicious, they stumbled to a halt, eyeing her. "I'm looking for Brother Erasmus. Have you see him?"

"She's a cop," one of them said. "I seen her before."

Kate reached into her pocket and drew out a five-dollar bill that she'd put there a minute before. She folded it in half lengthwise and ran it crisply through her fingers. "I just hoped to talk with him tonight. I know he's usually here in the morning, but it would save me some time, you understand."

" 'S tomorrow Sunday?" asked the second man, with the

slurred precision of the very drunk. The others ignored him.

"He don't come on Sa'day," stated the third man. "You have to wait."

"Do you know where he is tonight?"

"He's not here."

"How do you know?"

"Never is."

Kate had to be content with that. They hadn't told her anything, but she gave them the five dollars anyway and left them arguing over what to do with it, spend it now or save it until tomorrow. All three had looked to be in their sixties but were probably barely fifty. She turned to look at them over the top of her car, three drunk men haggling in slow motion over a scrap of paper that represented an evening's supply of cheap wine.

"Where did you serve?" she called on impulse. They looked up at her, blinking. The third man drew himself up and made an attempt at squaring his shoulders.

"Quang Tri Province mostly. Tony was in Saigon for a while."

"Well, good luck to you, boys. Keep warm."

"Thank you, ma'am." The other two men automatically echoed his thanks, and she got into her car and turned around and reentered the traffic on Lincoln Way.

In the next twenty minutes, she gave away another fifteen dollars and got more or less the same answer from a woman with darting eyes who pulled continuously at her raw lips with the fingers of her left hand; from a sardonic, sober elderly gentleman who would not approach close enough to take the contribution from her hand but who picked it up from the park bench with a small bow once she had retreated; and from the monosyllabic Doc, whom she recognized from the initial interviews.

Satisfied, she left the park, intending to go home but then finding herself detouring, taking a route slightly north of the direct one, and finally finding herself in front of the brick bulk of Ghirardelli Square, still lighted up and busy with Saturday night shoppers. Oh well, she was nearly home; she would only be a little late.

There were four shops that Erasmus might have slipped into that afternoon, plus two blank and locked doors and a stairway up to the main level of shops. Two of the shopkeepers had at the time seemed merely harassed and innocent on a busy afternoon, one of them had been with a woman who was contemplating an expensive purchase and had not seemed the sort to shelter an escaped fool, but the fourth— Kate thought that she would have another word with the fourth shopkeeper, smiling behind his display of magic tricks and stuffed animals.

She parked beneath the NO PARKING sign in front of the shop and strolled in, her hands in her pockets. The man recognized her instantly; this time his amusement seemed a bit forced, and he was flustered as he made change for the woman who was buying a stuffed pig complete with six snap-on piglets. Kate stood perusing the display of magic tricks until the customer left and he was finally forced to come over to her.

"Can I help you with something?" he asked.

"I'm interested in disappearing tricks," she said. She picked up a trick plastic ice cube that had a fly embedded in it, studying it carefully. "I had something large disappear, right in front of me. I'd like to know how it was done. I know that magicians don't like to tell their secrets, but"—she put down the joke ice cube and leaned forward—"I would really like to know."

As she'd thought, he folded immediately. "I—I'm really sorry about that; I didn't know—I mean, I could tell you were a cop, but I thought you were just hassling him. They do it, to the street artists and stuff, and he's such a harmless old guy, I

171

just thought it was a joke when he came shooting in here and held his finger in front of his mouth and then ducked behind the curtain."

So he'd been standing there less than ten feet away. Hell. She went and looked at the small, crowded storage space. He sure wasn't there now.

"How did he know this was here?"

"He comes here every week. Oh yeah, I sell him things sometimes, magic stuff—you know, scarves and folding bouquets, that sort of thing. He changes clothes here and leaves his stuff in the back while he's working. I don't mind. I mean, he's not that great a customer, never spends much money, but he's such a sweet old guy, I never minded. What did you want him for?"

"Did he go out through the back?"

"Yes, that door connects with a service entrance. I let him out after you'd gone."

"Did he leave anything here?"

"He usually does; he changes out of his costume and leaves it here, but this time he was in a hurry. He just wiped the makeup off his face, took his coat out of the bag and changed his shoes, and took the bag with him."

"Well, all I can say is, don't complain about crime in the streets if a cop asks for your help and you just laugh in her face."

"What did he do?" the man wailed, but Kate walked out of the shop and drove off.

When she got home to Russian Hill, Lee had gone to bed, Jon was sulking over a movie, and her dinner was crisp where it should have been soft, and limp where it had started crisp. However, she consoled herself with the idea that at least she knew how Brother Erasmus avoided carrying his gear all over the city with him.

172

♦

SEVENTEEN

♦

There was never a man who looked into those brown burning eyes without being certain that Francis Bernardone was really interested in him.

For the first time since he had come to San Francisco, Brother Erasmus did not appear on Sunday morning to preach to his flock of society's offscourings, to lead them in prayer and song and listen to their problems and bring them a degree of cheer and faith in themselves. The men and women waited for some time for him in the meeting place near the Nineteenth Avenue park entrance, but he did not show up, and they drifted off, singly and in pairs, giving wide berth to two newcomers, healthy-looking young men wearing suitably bedraggled clothes but smelling of soap and shaving cream.

At two in the afternoon, Kate called Al Hawkin. "I think

he's gone, Al," she told him. "Raul just called; he and Rodriguez hung around until noon and there was no sign of him. All the park people expected him to show; nobody knows where he might be. Do you want to put out an APB on him?"

"And if they bring him in, what do we do with him? We couldn't even charge him with littering at this point. Unless you want to put him on a fifty-one-fifty."

"No," she said without hesitation. Putting Sawyer on a seventy-two-hour psychiatric hold would keep him in hand, but it would also open the door wide for an insanity plea, if they did decide to charge him. Beyond that, though, was a personal revulsion: Kate did not wish to see Brother Erasmus slapped into a psychiatric ward without a very good reason. Damn it, why did he have to disappear?

"It may come to that, but let's give it another twenty-four hours."

"Okay. And, Al? I talked to the guy in Chicago; he's going to fax us some records when he can dig them out. And before that, on my way in, I stopped by and talked with that antique-store owner Beatrice told me about." She reviewed that conversation for him, the trim woman in her fifties who had seemed mildly disturbed by her occasional lover's death, but mostly embarrassed, both by the affair's becoming public knowledge and by how little she actually knew about the man: He was not one for pillow talk, it seemed. She did say that he had a fondness for boastful stories about an unlikely and affluent past, which she dismissed, and a habit of denigrating the persons and personalities of others, often to their faces.

"Which is pretty much what we've heard already."

"I know. Well, I'll let you know if the Chicago information comes in. Talk to you later."

"Look, Martinelli? Don't get too hooked on this. You don't have anything to prove." There was silence on the line for a long time. "It's Sunday," he said. "Go home. Work in the garden. Take Lee for a drive. Don't let it get to you, or you'll never make it. Understand?"

"Yes, sir."

"Don't give me that 'sir' bullshit," he snapped. "I don't want to work with someone who obsesses about their cases."

"Al!" Kate started laughing; she couldn't help it. "You're a fine one to talk about being obsessive. What are you doing right now? What did I interrupt?"

His silence was not as long as hers had been, but it was eloquent.

"Look, Martinelli," he said firmly, "that Brancusi case doesn't look good, and there's a lot hanging on my testimony tomorrow. I don't think you can call that obsessive. I'm just doing my job. I only meant—"

"Go work in your garden, Al. Go for a walk on the beach, why don't you? Go to a movie, Al, there's a—"

He hung up on her. She put the receiver down, still grinning, and went home to pry some weeds out of the patio bricks.

♦

Monday morning, Al was in court and Kate was in Golden Gate Park. While Al was being dragged back and forth over the rougher parts of his testimony, Kate walked up and down and talked with people. She ignored the women with shiny strollers and designer toddlers, the couples soaking up winter sun on spread blankets, the skaters and bikers, and anyone with a picnic. The homeless are identified by the mistrust in their eyes, and Kate rarely chose wrong.

She talked with Molly, a seventy-one-year-old ex-secretary who lived off a minute pension and spent her nights behind an apartment house in the shelter that covered the residents' garbage cans. Some of them left her packets of food, she'd received a blue wool coat and a nice blanket for Christmas, and yes, she knew Brother Erasmus quite well, such a nice man, and what a disappointment he wasn't at the service yesterday. A couple of the others had tried to lead hymns, but it just wasn't the same, so in the end she'd just marched down the road and gone to a Catholic church, although she hadn't been to a church in twenty years, and it was quite a pleasant experience. Everyone had been so nice to her, welcomed her to have coffee and cookies afterward, and what do you know, as she got to talking to one of the girls who was serving the coffee, it turned out that they needed some help in the office, just three or four hours a week, but wasn't that a happy coincidence. It'd mean she could buy a real dinner sometimes, such a blessing, dear.

Then Kate talked with Star, a frail young woman with the freckles of childhood across her nose and a curly-haired four-year-old son who leaned on his mother's knee as she sat on the bench, his thumb in his mouth and his eyes darting between Kate and the hillside behind them, where three small children in Osh-Kosh overalls and European shoes giggled madly as they lowered themselves to the ground and rolled, over and over, down the lawn. Star's hair was lank and greasy and she had a cold sore on her mouth, but her son's hair shone in the wintery sun and he wore a bright jacket. Star had lived on the streets since her parents in Wichita had thrown her out when she was four months pregnant. Her son Jesse had been born in California. Her AFDC was screwed up; the checks didn't come. So they'd been in shelters the last few weeks. Yeah, she knew Erasmus. Funny old guy. At first she stayed away from him, thought he was weird. After all, an old guy who wants to give a kid a toy, a person has to be careful. But after a while he seemed okay. And he was really good with Jesse. He gave him a party for his birthday back in November, a cake for God's sake, with his name on it, big enough for everyone in the shelter. And last month when Jesse had a really bad cough, it was just after the AFDC screwup, Brother Erasmus had just handed her some money and told her to take Jesse to the doctor's. Well no, he hadn't said it like that; he talks funny, kind of old-fashioned like. But he had said something about doctors, and it was a good thing they went, because it was pneumonia. Jesse could have died. And she was sorry Erasmus wasn't here yesterday, because she had wanted to talk to him. It was sort of an anniversary—a whole year she'd been clean now. Yeah, she didn't want Jesse growing up with a junkie for a mom. And what if she went to jail—what'd happen to him? And there was a training program she thought she might start, wanted to talk to Erasmus about it. Well no, he didn't really give advice, just sometimes in a roundabout way, but talking to him made things clearer. Yeah, maybe she'd sign up anyway, tell him about it next week.

Star was seventeen years old.

Kate saw her three army buddies from the other night, two of them lying back on their elbows in the grass with their shirts off, the third one curled up nearby, asleep. Yes, they had missed Erasmus yesterday, especially Tony. He got really wild when the Brother didn't show, started shouting that the old guy'd been taken prisoner, that they had to send a patrol out to get him back. "Stupid bastard," commented the veteran with the collar-to-wrist tattoos, not without affection. The other one shrugged. Nightmares last night, too, and now there he was, sleeping like a baby. Maybe it was time to head south. Not so cold in the south, get some work in the orange groves. If she saw the old Brother, tell him the infantry said hi.

She looked down at the sleeping Tony as she turned to go. His coat collar had slipped down. Behind his right ear, a patch of scalp the size of Kate's palm gleamed, scar tissue beneath the sparse black hair.

Mark was next, a beautiful surfer boy, lean tan body with

long blond curls. Kate wondered what the hell he was doing still loose, but there he was, looking lost beneath the bare pollarded trees in front of the music concourse. Sure, he knew Brother Erasmus. Brother Erasmus was one of the twelve holy men whose presence on earth kept the waves of destruction from sweeping over the land. Every so often one of them would die, and then a war would break out until he was reborn. Or a plague. Maybe an earthquake.

Then there were Tomás and Esmerelda, standing and watching the lawn bowling. They were holding hands surreptitiously. Esmerelda's belly rose up firm and round beneath her coat, and she did not look well. *Sí*, they knew who Padre Erasmus was. No, they hadn't seen him. *Sí*, they had an enormous respect for the padre. He wasn't like other padres. He had married them. *Sí, verdad*, an actual ceremony. Yes with papers. Did she want to see them? Here they were. No, of course they had not filed them. They could not do that. Tomás had been married before, and there was no divorce in the Catholic Church. *Sí*, the padre knew this. But this was the real marriage. This one was true. And to prove it, Tomás had a job—working nights. And they had a house to move into on Wednesday. Small, an apartment, but with a roof to keep out the rain and a door to lock out the crazy people and the addicts and thieves, and there was a stove to cook on and a bed for Esmerelda. Tomás would work hard. If it was a boy, they would name it Erasmo.

Three of the men she talked with would not give her their names, but they all knew Erasmus. The first one, shirtless on a bench, his huge muscles identifying him as recently released from prison even if his demeanor hadn't, knew her instantly as a cop and wouldn't look at her. However, his hard face softened for an instant when she mentioned the name Erasmus. The second man, hearing the name, immediately launched into a description of how he'd seen Erasmus one night standing on

Strawberry Hill, glowing with a light that grew stronger and stronger until it hurt the eyes, and then he'd disappeared, a little at a time. Kate excused herself and walked briskly away, muttering, "Beam me up, Scotty" under her breath. The third man knew Erasmus, didn't like her asking questions about him, and was working himself up into belligerence. Kate, unhampered by bedrolls and bulging bags, slipped away, deciding to stick to women for a while.

♦

"They love him." Kate threw her notebook down on the desk and dropped into the nearest chair. Her feet hurt; her throat ached: Maybe she was coming down with the flu.

Al Hawkin pulled off his glasses and looked at her. "Who loves whom?"

"The people in the park. I feel like I'm about to book Mother Teresa. He listens to them. He changes their lives. They're going to name their kids after him. Saint Erasmus. God!" She ran her fingers through her hair, kicked off her shoes, walked over to the coffee machine, came back with a cup, and sat down again. "Hi, Al. How'd it go in court?"

"The jury wasn't happy with it. I think they'll acquit. The bastard's going to walk." Domenico Brancusi ran a string of very young prostitutes, a specialty service that circled the Bay Area and had made him very rich. He was also very careful, and when one of his girls died—an eleven-year-old whose ribs were more prominent than her breasts—he had proven to be about as vulnerable as an armadillo.

"I'm sorry, Al."

"American justice, don't you just love it. I was looking at the stuff your friend in Chicago sent."

"Did it come? Was there anything?"

"Two blots on Saint Erasmus's past. A DUI when he was

twenty-five—forty seven years ago—and then ten years later he plead guilty to assault, got a year of parole and a hundred hours of community service."

"Any details?"

"Not many. It looks like what he did was pick up a chair in a classroom and try to brain somebody with it. They were having an argument—a debate in front of a class—and it got out of hand. The gentle life of the mind," he commented sardonically.

"Damn the man, anyway," she growled. "Why the hell did he have to run off like that?"

"Exactly."

"What?"

"Why did he run?"

"Oh Christ, Al, you're not going to go all Sherlock Holmes on me, are you? 'The dog did nothing in the night,' she protests. 'Precisely,' says he mysteriously."

"You are in a good mood, aren't you?" observed Hawkin. "Have you eaten anything today?"

"Now you sound like my mother. Yes, I had a couple of hot dogs from the stand in the park."

"There's the problem. You've got nitrates eating your brain cells."

"Since when do you care about nitrates? You live off the things."

"No more." He placed one hand on his chest. "I am pure."

"First cigarettes and now junk food? That Jani's a powerful woman."

Al Hawkin stood up and lifted his jacket from the back of his chair. "Come on, Martinelli," he said. "I'll buy you a sandwich and you can tell me about the Brother Erasmus fan club."

◆

EIGHTEEN

◆

Some might call him a madman, but he was the very reverse of a dreamer.

It was now two weeks since John had been killed, thirteen days since his funeral pyre had been lighted, and Kate woke that Tuesday morning knowing that her case consisted of a number of details concerning a fine lot of characters, but the only link any of it had was a person she would much prefer to see out of it entirely.

Kate had been a cop long enough to know that likable people can be villains, that personality and charisma are, if anything, more likely to be found attached to the perpetrator than the victim. She liked people; she sent them to jail: no problem.

But damn it, Erasmus was different. She could not shake

the image of him as a priest, but it wasn't even as simple as that. She had, in fact, once arrested a Roman Catholic priest, with only the mildest hesitation and no regrets afterward. No, there was something about Erasmus—what it was, she could not grasp, could not even begin to articulate, but it was there, a deep distaste of the idea of putting him behind bars. She would do her job, and if necessary she would pursue his arrest to the full extent of her abilities, but lying in bed that Tuesday morning she was aware of the conviction that she would never fully believe the man's guilt.

Well, Kate, she said to herself, you'll just have to dig deeper until you find somebody else to hang it on. And with that decision, she threw back the covers and went to face the day.

Her hopeful determination, however, did not last the morning. When she arrived at the Hall of Justice she found two notes under the message clip on her desk. The first was in Al Hawkin's scrawl, and read:

Martinelli, you're on your own again today, I'm taking Tom's appointment with the DA. Back at noon, with any luck.

—Al

The other had been left by the night Field Ops officer:

Insp. Martinelli—3:09 A.M., Tuesday. See the woman 982 29th Ave., after 11:00 A.M. today. Info. re the cremation.

At five minutes after eleven, Kate was on Twenty-ninth Avenue, looking at a row of pale two-story stucco houses with never-used balconies and perfunctory lawns. Number 982, unlike most of its neighbors, did not have a metal security gate in front of the entrance. It did have a healthy-looking tree in a

Chinese glazed pot sitting on the edge of the tiled portico. When she pressed the doorbell, a small dog barked inside, twice. She heard movement—a door opening and a vague scuffle of footsteps above the noise of traffic. The sound stopped, and Kate felt a gaze from the peephole in the door. Bolts worked and the door opened, to reveal a slim woman slightly taller than Kate, her graying blond hair standing on end, her athletic-looking body wrapped in a maroon terrycloth bathrobe many sizes too large for her. Kate held out her identification in front of the woman's bleary eyes, which were set in rounds of startlingly pale skin surrounded by a ruddy windroughened forehead and cheeks. Ski goggles, Kate diagnosed.

"Inspector Kate Martinelli, SFPD. I received a message that you have information pertaining to the cremation that occurred in Golden Gate Park two weeks ago. I hope this isn't a bad time."

"Oh no, no. I was up. The friend who was watching my dog just brought her back. Come on in. Would you like some coffee? It's fresh." She turned and scuffled away down the hallway, leaving Kate to shut the door.

"No thank you, Ms. . . . ?"

"Didn't I leave my name? No, maybe I didn't. I'm Sam Rutlidge. This is Dobie," she added as they entered the kitchen. "Short for Doberman."

Doberman was a dachshund. She sniffed Kate's shoes and ankles enthusiastically and wagged her whip of a tail into a blur, but she neither jumped up and down nor yapped. When Kate reached a hand down, Dobie pushed against it like a cat with her firm, supple body, gave Kate a brief lick with her tongue, and then went to lie in a basket on the lowest shelf of a built-in bookshelf, surrounded by cookbooks. Her dark eyes glittered as she watched them.

"That's the calmest dachshund I've ever seen," said Kate.

"Just well trained. Sure you won't have some?" She held out the pot from the coffeemaker. It smelled very good.

"I will change my mind, thanks."

"Black okay? There isn't any milk in the house, none that you'd want to drink, anyway."

"Black is fine. Do I understand that you've been away, Ms. Rutlidge?"

"Skiing. I've been in Tahoe for the last couple of weeks, I got back after midnight last night. It was stupid to call at that hour, I guess, but somehow you don't think of the police department as working nine to five."

"The department works twenty-four hours. Some of us are allowed to sleep occasionally. How did you hear about the cremation?"

"I was reading the papers. I'm always so wired when I get in after a long drive, especially at night, there's no point in going to bed, since I just stare at the ceiling. I make myself some hot milk, soak in the bath, read for a while, just give myself a chance to stop vibrating, you know? So anyway, I went through my mail and then started leafing through the newspapers—the neighbor brings them in for me—and I saw that article about the body being burned, the day I left."

"You left for Lake Tahoe on the Wednesday?"

"Early Wednesday. I like to get out of the Bay Area before the traffic gets too thick."

"You didn't see any news while you were at Tahoe?"

"I was too busy."

"So you read about it at—what, one or two this morning?"

"About then. Maybe closer to three."

"What made you think to call us?"

"Well, the first papers were really general, and aside from the fact that it was so close to here, I didn't really think about it. I mean, I don't know any homeless people."

184

Kate made some encouraging noise.

"Then for a couple of days, there wasn't anything, or if there was, I didn't see it—I wasn't reading very carefully. Then on Monday, there was another article, with a picture, and as soon as I saw the man, it all came back to me."

"Which man was this?"

In answer, the woman stood up and went out of the room. The dog raised her sleek head from her paws and stared at the door, attentive but not concerned, until Sam Rutlidge came back with a section of the paper, folded back to a photograph. She laid it on the table in front of Kate and tapped her finger on the bearded man who was standing on a lawn in front of about twenty other men and women, reading from a book.

"Him. I saw him coming out of the park, not far from the place where they . . . burned the body the following morning. I saw him Tuesday morning. And he seemed really upset."

"What time was this?"

"About quarter to ten. I had an ten o'clock appointment and I was running late because of a phone call, so I was in a hurry. I usually go up a block to the signal or down to Twenty-fifth to get onto Fulton, but I was in such a rush and it would've meant turning the car around and there was a truck down the block, so I just went straight down to Fulton and turned left as soon as I could." She glanced uncomfortably at Kate the defender of law and order. "I'm a careful driver; I've never had a ticket. Looking back, I know how stupid it was, to shove my way in when the traffic was thick and the pavement was wet from the fog, but as I said, I was in a hurry and not thinking straight. I cut it kind of close, and one of the cars slammed on its brakes and honked at me as I moved through his lane to the outside lane."

"Don't worry about it," Kate said. "I'm not with the traffic division."

"Yes, well. It was stupid. I wouldn't have hit the car, but I did scare him, and he went past, shaking his fist out the window at me. And then I saw that man." She pointed toward the newspaper. "I noticed him because he seemed to be shaking his fist at me, too, but as I went by, I could tell he wasn't even looking at me. He'd have had to turn his head to see my car, and he hadn't; he was looking straight ahead."

"What was he looking at?"

"Nothing, as far as I could tell. He was coming out of the park on one of the paths, not quite to the pavement, and he was holding that big stick of his, shaking it, sort of punching it into the air as he walked along."

"You'd seen him before?"

"Oh yes, he's a regular in the park. We call him 'the Preacher.' "

" 'We' being . . ."

"There's a group of us who run three times a week and then go for coffee. We tend to see the same people."

"Did you ever talk with him?"

"The Preacher? Not really. He'd nod and wave and one of us would call hi, but nothing more. He struck me as kind of shy. Always neat and clean, and polite. Which is why it was so odd to see him behaving that way. I mean, some of the street people are really out of it; they really should be on medication, if not hospitalized. Of course, thanks to Reagan, we don't have any hospitals for the marginally insane, only for the totally berserk. But I don't need to tell *you* that."

"Would you mind showing me just where you saw him?"

"Sure, I need to take Dobie for a walk, anyway. Just let me get some clothes on. Help yourself to more coffee. I'll just be a few minutes."

It was with some irritation that Kate heard a shower start, but Sam Rutlidge was as good as her word, and in barely seven minutes she came back into the kitchen, dressed in jeans and a UCSF sweatshirt, her wet hair slicked back and a pair of worn running shoes in her hand.

"Sorry to be so long," she said, dropping onto a chair to put on her shoes. "I hate getting dressed without having a shower first. Makes me feel too grungy for words."

"No problem. Dobie's a good conversationalist."

Dobie had, in fact, only eyed her closely. Now, however, she emerged from her basket and went to stand at her owner's feet, tail whipping with enthusiasm. When the woman rose, the dog turned and galloped like a clumsy weasel down the hallway to the front door. Rutlidge put on a jacket and took down a thin lead to clip to Dobie's collar, and down the steps they went.

They walked down to Fulton, where Rutlidge paused and pointed.

"I turned onto the road here," she said. "Moved over into the right lane, the other driver accelerated to pass me, and then I saw the Preacher. Just about where that crooked 'No Parking' sign is. See it? He was walking toward the road at an angle, as if he was headed to Park Presidio."

"Was he carrying anything other than his staff?"

"Not that I saw, but then I couldn't see his right hand, just his left, and that was holding his stick."

"What was he wearing?"

Sam Rutlidge wrinkled up her forehead in thought while Dobie whined restlessly. "A coat, brownish, I think. It came almost to his knees. Some dark pants, not jeans, I don't think. Dark brown or black, maybe. And he had a knit hat, one of those ones that fit close against the skull. That was dark, too. I only saw him for about two or three seconds. I don't think I'd have given him a second glance if it hadn't been that his anger was so obvious—and uncharacteristic."

"Okay. Thank you, Ms. Rutlidge, you've been very helpful," said Kate, polite but careful not to appear overly enthusiastic or grateful. "I'll need you to sign your statement when I get it drawn up. Could you come by and sign it?"

"Tomorrow's not very good. I'll have a long day at work."

"What do you do?"

"I'm a technical writer. Boring, but the pay is good. Do you want my number there? You can call me and arrange a time to meet?" They exchanged telephone numbers and then Rutlidge and her small sleek dog turned right toward the signal where Thirtieth crossed into the park, while Kate walked to the left until she was across the street from the point where the dirt path met the paved sidewalk, marked by a post with a crooked NO PARKING sign. There was no need to cross the road and follow the path through the trees; no need to look for scraps of yellow on the trees. She knew where she was. She stood looking at the park, at the path along which an angry Brother Erasmus had stormed on a Tuesday morning two weeks ago, leaving behind him the area that, twenty hours later, would be surrounded by great lengths of police tapes. Behind those bushes, sometime that morning, John the nameless had lain, bleeding into the soil until the life was gone from him.

She walked back to her car and set into motion the process of obtaining a warrant for the arrest of one David Matthew Sawyer, aka Brother Erasmus, for the murder of John Doe.

♦

NINETEEN

♦

. . . The valley of humiliation, which seemed to him
very rocky and desolate, but in which he was
afterwards to find many flowers.

They picked him up near Barstow.

Two sheriff's deputies spotted him less than a hundred
miles from the Arizona border, walking due east along the
snow-sprinkled side of Highway 58, barely twenty-four hours
after the APB went out on him. They recognized him by the
walking stick he used, as tall as himself and with a head carved
on the top. He did not seem surprised when they got out of
their car and demanded that he spread-eagle on the ground. He
did not resist arrest. Besides his staff, he was carrying only a
threadbare knapsack that held some warm clothes, a blanket,
bread and cheese and a plastic bottle of water, and two books.

He seemed to the sheriff deputies, and to everyone who came in contact with him, a polite, untroubled, intelligent, and silent old man. In fact, so smiling and silent was he that the sheriff himself, on the phone to arrange transportation for the prisoner, asked Kate if the description had neglected to say that Erasmus was a mute.

The Sheriff's Department already had a scheduled pickup to make in San Francisco, and in light of the state budget and in the spirit of fiscal responsibility, they agreed to take Erasmus north with them. Kate was there to receive him when he was brought in Thursday night, even through it was nearly midnight. He spotted her across the room, nodded and smiled as at an old friend one hasn't seen in a day or two, and then turned back to the actions of his attendants, watching curiously as they processed his paperwork and transferred the custody of his person and his possessions to the hands of the San Francisco Police Department. Brother Erasmus was now in the maw of Justice, and there was not much any of them could do about it.

When the preliminaries were over and he was parked on a bench awaiting the next stage, Kate went over and pulled a chair up in front of him. He was wearing the clothes he had been picked up in, minus the walking stick, and she studied him for a minute.

She had seen this man in various guises. When she first met him, he had appeared as a priest, wearing an impressive black cassock and a light English accent. Among the tourists, he had dressed almost like one of them, a troubling jester who did not quite fit into his middle-class clothing or his midwestern voice. When ministering (there was no other word for it) to the homeless, he had looked destitute, his knee-length duffel coat lumpy with the possessions stashed in its pockets, watch cap pulled down over his grizzled head, sentences short, voice gruff.

Tonight she was seeing a fourth David Sawyer. This one was an ordinary-looking older man in jeans and worn hiking boots, fraying blue shirt collar visible at the neck of his new-looking thick hand-knit sweater of heathery red wool, lines of exhaustion pulling at his face and turning his thin cheeks gaunt. (He did not, she noted absently, have a scar below his left eye from the removal of a tattoo.) He sat on the hard bench, his head back against the wall, and looked back at her out of the bottom half of his eyes, waiting. After a moment, he shifted his arms to ease the drag of the metal cuffs biting into his bony wrists, and she was suddenly taken by a memory of their first confrontation. He had held out his wrists to be cuffed, and now she had cuffed him, just sixteen days after the murder had been committed.

There was no pleasure in the sight.

"Your name is David Sawyer," she said to him. There was no reaction in his face or in his body, just a resigned endurance—and, perhaps, just the faintest spark of humor behind it. "Eve Whitlaw told us who you are, and we've been in touch with the police in Chicago. They told us what happened back there, Professor Sawyer. We know all about what Kyle Roberts did."

This last brought a response, but not an expected one. The flicker of humor in the back of his eyes blossomed into a play of amusement over his worn features and one eyebrow raised slightly. Had he said it in words, he could not have expressed any more clearly the dry admiration that she could fully comprehend all the complexities of that long-ago incident. Within two seconds, the eloquent expression had gone, and all traces of humor with it. He looked tired and rather ill.

"Look not mournfully into the past," he said softly. Hell, she thought, disappointed. She'd been hoping, since seeing him, that this current, rather ordinary manifestation of Sawyer/

Erasmus might have regained the power of ordinary speech, but it didn't seem to work that way.

"I have to look into the past, David," she said, using his first name in a deliberate bid for familiarity. "I can't do that without asking questions about the past."

"Not every question deserves an answer."

"I think tomorrow, when Inspector Hawkin and I talk with you, we will ask some questions that not only deserve an answer but demand it. We are talking about a human life, David. Even if he wasn't a very pleasant person, which I have heard he wasn't, the questions deserve an answer."

"Murder, though it have no tongue, will speak with most miraculous organ."

"You knew it was murder from the first time I laid eyes on you, didn't you, David? How was that? No, no, don't answer that, not tonight," she said quickly, although there was no sign that he was about to respond, not even a flash of fear at being trapped into an admission. She wasn't about to lay the groundwork for his defense lawyer to claim she had badgered him into giving inadmissible evidence.

That reminded her: "Are you going to want a lawyer present while you are being questioned, David? We will provide you with one if you want."

He had to search his memory for a moment, but eventually he came up with an answer, spoken with a small conspiratorial smile that was nearly a wink of the eye. "There are no lawyers among them, for they consider them a sort of people whose profession it is to disguise matters."

"I guess that's a no. Okay. Let us know if you change your mind." She stood up, and his eyes followed her, though his head had not moved from the wall during their conversation. "I will see you tomorrow, then. I hope you get some sleep tonight." This last was intended merely as a wry comment and unspoken apology for the racket of the place, but it served only to draw the man's attention to his surroundings, and for the first time he looked about him. His gaze traveled over the tired walls, the loud, bored policeman, the drunk and belligerent and bloody prisoners, and he shuddered; the whole length of him gave way to a deep shiver of revulsion, and then he shut his eyes and seemed to withdraw. Kate stood up and caught the eye of the guard to nod her thanks and signal that she had finished with this prisoner, but before she could move away, she heard Sawyer's voice, speaking quietly, as if to himself, but very firmly.

"Go and sit in thy cell," he said, "and thy cell shall teach thee all things."

Kate gaped at him, but his eyes remained shut, so in the end she threw up her hands and took herself home to her own unquiet bed.

◆

TWENTY

◆

*Men like Francis are not common in any age, nor
are they to be fully understood merely by the
exercise of common sense.*

The interrogation, if it could be called that, began the next
morning, the last Friday in February. Of the three of them gathered in the stuffy room, Al Hawkin was the only one who
looked as if he had slept, and even he came shambling down
the corridor like an irritable bear. He did not like having his
hand forced, he did not like arresting someone with less than
an airtight case, and most of all he did not like jousting on the
way in with reporters who treated the whole thing as something of a joke.

"Christ, Martinelli, were you in such a hurry to see him
that you couldn't have arranged for the sheriffs to have car

trouble or something? We've only found two of his hidey-holes, don't even have the warrants for them yet, and I'm supposed to conduct an interrogation on the strength of his being in the neighborhood at the time the victim was bashed? And to put the frosting on the whole absurd thing, the victim's still a John Doe! Give me strength," he prayed to the room in general, and walked over to fight with the coffee machine.

"What was I to do?" she demanded. "He would have been in Florida by next week, or Mexico City."

"Of course we had to have him brought in. Just maybe not quite so fast."

Stung by the unreasonableness of Hawkin's demands, Kate stalked off to call for the transport of Erasmus from cell to interrogation room.

So the three of them came together for the second time, Kate sulky and sleepless, Sawyer looking every one of his seventy-two years, and Hawkin so perversely cheerful, he seemed to be baring his teeth.

This was to be an interrogation, unlike the earlier non-committal interview. An interview might be considered the polite turning of memory's pages. Today the purpose was to rifle the pages down to the spine, to shake the book sharply and see what might drift to the floor. Politely, of course, and well within the legal limits—the tape recorder on the table ensured that—but their sleeves were metaphorically rolled back for the job. The only problem was, the process assumes that the suspect being interrogated is to some degree willing to cooperate.

Kate, as had been agreed, opened the session with the standard words into the tape recorder, giving the time and the people present. Then, because Hawkin wanted it on record, she readvised Sawyer of his rights. The first snag came, as Hawkin had anticipated, when Sawyer sat in silence when asked if he understood his rights. Hawkin was prepared for this, and he sat forward to speak clearly into the microphone.

"It should be noted that Mr. Sawyer has thus far refused to communicate in a direct form of speech. He has the apparently unbreakable habit of speaking in quotations, which often have an unfortunately limited application to the topic being discussed. During the course of this interview, it may occasionally be necessary for the police officers conducting the interview to suggest interpretations for Mr. Sawyer's words and to note aloud any nonverbal communications he might express."

Hawkin sat back in his chair and looked at the older man, who nodded his head in appreciation and sat back in his own chair, his long fingers finding one another and intertwining across the front of his ill-fitting jail clothes. Somehow, for some reason, life was slowly leaking back into his mobile face, and as animation returned, the years faded.

"Tell me about Berkeley," Hawkin began. There was no apparent surprise on the fool's part at this unexpected question, just the customary moment for thought.

"We shall establish a school of the Lord's service," he said, "in which we hope to bring no harsh or burdensome thing."

"I don't understand what you mean," said Hawkin flatly. Sawyer merely twitched a skeptical eyebrow and said nothing. Hawkin's practiced glare was no match for the older man's implacable serenity, either, and it was Hawkin who broke the long silence.

"Are you saying you find it restful there?"

"Oh Lord, support us all the day long, until the shadows lengthen and the evening comes, and the busy world is hushed, and the fever of life is over, and our work is done. Then in Thy mercy grant us a safe lodging, and a holy rest, and peace at the last."

This heartfelt prayer, simply recited by a man who so obviously knew what it was to be tired, gathered up the ugly little room and gave pause to the proceedings. Kate thought, This is why he is so curiously impressive, this man: When he says a thing, he means it down to his bones. Hawkin thought, This man is going to be hell before a jury: They'll be eating out of his hand. He cleared his throat and pushed down the craving for a cigarette.

"So, you go to Berkeley for a rest. Do you go there regularly?"

There was no answer to this, only patient silence, as if Sawyer had heard nothing and was waiting for Hawkin to ask him the next question.

"Do you have a regular schedule?"

Silence.

"You spend time in San Francisco, too, don't you? In Golden Gate Park? With the homeless? Why won't you answer me?"

"Not every question deserves an answer," he replied repressively. It was one of the few times Kate had heard him repeat himself.

"So you think you can choose what questions you answer and which you won't. Mr. Sawyer, you have been arrested for the murder of a man in Golden Gate Park. At the moment, the charge is murder in the first degree. That means we believe it was premeditated, that you planned to kill him and did so. If you are convicted of that crime, you will go to prison for a long time. You will grow old in prison, and you will very probably die there, in a room considerably smaller and less comfortable than this one. Do you understand that?" He did not wait for an answer other than the one in Sawyer's eyes.

"One of the purposes of this interview is to determine whether a lesser charge may be justified. Second-degree murder, even manslaughter, and you might sleep under the trees again before you die. Do you understand what I am saying, Mr. Sawyer? I think you do.

"Now, I don't know if you planned on killing the man known as John or not. I can't know that until you tell me what happened. And you can't tell me until you drop this little game of yours, because the answers aren't in William Shakespeare or the Bible; they're in your head. Let's get rid of these word games—now, before they get you in real trouble. Just talk in simple English, and tell me what happened."

There was no doubt that Hawkin's speech had made an impression on the man, though whether it was the threat or the appeal was not clear. He had sat up straight, his hands grasping his knees; now his eyes closed, he raised his face to the overhead light, and his right hand came up to curl into the hollow of his neck, as if grasping his nonexistent staff. For three or four long, silent minutes he stayed like that, struggling with some unknowable dilemma. When he moved, his hand came up to rub across his eyes and down to pinch his lower lip, then dropped back onto his lap. He opened his eyes first on Kate, then on Hawkin. His expression was apologetic, but without the faintest degree of fear or uncertainty.

"Truth," he began, "is the cry of all, but the game of the few. There is nothing to prevent you from telling the truth, if you do it with a smile." He gave them the smile and sat forward on the edge of his chair to gather their attention to him, as if his next words would not have done solely themselves. "Dread death. Dry death. Immortal death. Death on his pale horse." He paused and held out the long, thin fingers of his right hand. "Will all great Neptune's ocean wash this blood clean from my hand? No. Your brother's blood is crying to me from the ground. And the Lord set a mark upon Cain. A fugitive and a vagabond shall you be on the earth." He paused to let them think about this, his eyes going from one face to the other. He drew back his hand and commented in a quiet voice that made the thought parenthetical but intensely personal: "Death is not the worst. Rather, to wish for death in vain, and not to gain it." After a moment, he sat forward again and held out his left hand, cupped slightly as if to guide in another strand of thought. Putting a definite stress on the misplaced names, he said, "Then David made a covenant with Jonathan, because he loved him as he loved his own soul. And David stripped himself of the robe that was upon him, and gave it to Jonathan. And then he shall go out to the altar which is before the Lord and make atonement for it. He shall go no more to his house. He shall bear all their iniquities with him into a solitary land. I have been a stranger in a strange land. And the ravens brought him bread and flesh in the morning, and bread and flesh in the evening, and he drank of the brook. I met a fool in the forest, a motley fool. A learned fool is more foolish than an ignorant one. Let a fool be made serviceable according to his folly." He stopped, saw that he had lost them, and pursed his lips in thought. Then, with an air of returning to kindergarten basics, he began again. "The wisdom of this world is folly with God. If anyone among you thinks that he is wise now, let him become a fool so he may become wise. To the present hour we hunger and thirst, we are poorly clothed and buffeted and homeless. We have become, and are now, as the refuse of the world, the offscouring of all things. We are fools for Christ's sake."

"So you're saying you do this as some kind of religious exercise?" Hawkin asked bluntly. Kate couldn't decide if he was acting stupid to draw Sawyer out or because he was irritated.

"I count religion but a childish toy, and hold there is no sin but ignorance."

"Then I guess I must be burning in sin," snapped Hawkin, "because I don't know what the hell you're talking about."

Sawyer sat back again with his fingers across his stomach and eyed Hawkin for some time, his head to one side, before making the stern pronouncement, "A living dog is better than a dead lion." Kate glanced at him sharply and saw a sparkle of mischief in the back of his eyes. He looked sideways at her and lowered one eyelid a fraction. Hawkin did not see the gesture, but he was staring at the man with suspicion.

"What does that mean?" he demanded.

"He who blesses his neighbor in a loud voice, rising early in the morning, will be counted as cursing."

"Look, Mr. Sawyer—"

"Do not speak in the hearing of a fool, for he will despise the wisdom of your words."

"Mr. Sawyer—"

"He who walks with wise men becomes wise, but the companion of fools will come to harm."

Hawkin stood up abruptly, his face dark. "All right, take him back to the cells—" he began, but he was drowned out by Sawyer's sudden loud stream of words.

"A whip for the horse, a bridle for the donkey, and a rod for the back of fools," he asserted. "Like a thorn that goes into the hand of a drunkard, is a proverb in the mouth of fools. Like snow in summer or rain at the harvest, honor is not fit for a fool. A man without—"

The door closed behind Al Hawkin, and Sawyer, on his feet now, stood tensely for a moment, then relaxed and smiled at Kate as if the two of them had just shared a clever joke. "A man without self-control," he said slyly, "is like a city broken into and left with no walls." He sat down again.

Kate did not smile back at him. "Why do you antagonize people? Al Hawkin's a good man. Why make an enemy of him?"

Sawyer shrugged. "The way of a fool is right in his own eyes. A fool speaks his whole mind."

"That's exactly what we're trying to get you to do, David. Your whole mind, not just the games."

"It is a happy talent to know how to play."

She leaned forward, her arms flat on the table. "Do you really take death so lightly?"

"Remember, we all must die."

"And you honestly think that justifies murder? You?" she said pointedly. "Think that?"

The ghostly presence of Kyle Roberts visited the room, and on the other side stood his innocent victims: Kate saw in the worn face across the table that Sawyer felt them there. He finally broke her gaze, and his throat worked before he answered.

"What greater pain could mortals have than this: to see their children dead before their eyes?"

"You know, I'd have thought that would make you more willing to help us, not less." He did not answer. "All we want is for you to talk to us. No games, just talk." Still nothing; but she had not expected a response. Time to end it. "You're tired, David. Think about it for a while, see if you don't change your mind. We'll continue this discussion later."

Kate stood up, went to the door, and looked on as the guard prepared to take Sawyer back to his cell. The prisoner paused in the doorway, with the guard's hand on his elbow, and looked down at Kate.

"I well believe thou wilt not utter what thou dost not know. And so far will I trust thee, gentle Kate." He turned and allowed himself to be led away. She went back into the interrogation room and turned off the tape recorder, then took out the tape and carried it downstairs, where she slid it into the other machine that stood on Hawkin's desk and waited while he ran the tape back a short way and listened. Erasmus ranted; the door slammed; Kate's voice reproved their suspect; he answered her. When the tape clicked, Hawkin switched the machine off.

"Well done. That's just what I had in mind. We'll let him stew today. I'll lead another session tomorrow morning, and then you can take over. Stop by and hold his hand for a few minutes before you go home today, okay?"

"If you say so."

"I want him softened up. The DA'll have him sent off for psychiatric evaluation the first part of the week. If we keep him longer than that and then they decide he really is nuts, we're risking a harassment charge."

"Is it really necessary, the evaluation?"

"For Christ sake, Martinelli, the DA couldn't possibly take it to trial without. You heard him in there. He was raving. It may be an act, but after forty-eight hours in custody, it isn't likely to be drugs or booze."

"I don't know, Al. He makes a weird kind of sense."

"*Weird's* the word for it."

"I mean it. I think I'll make a copy of that tape, if you don't mind."

"Studying it for secret meanings?"

"I thought I might have it translated."

TWENTY-ONE

But after all, this man was a man.

On Sunday afternoon, Kate assembled her team of translators. They met at the house on Russian Hill to avoid the problem of transporting Lee's wheelchair up and down stairs. At two o'clock, Kate left the house and drove across a rain-lashed San Francisco to fetch Professor Whitlaw, and when they returned, they found Dean Gardner already ensconced in front of the fire in the living room.

On her trip out, Kate had stopped to photocopy the transcripts of the first two interviews, both the abortive one from Friday morning and the longer but even less productive Saturday session. The one from Sunday morning had not yet been transcribed, but she had the tapes from all three.

Coffee and tea and the preliminary rituals were dispensed and then Kate handed out Friday's interview. The rain on the windows sounded loud as Lee, the dean, and the professor all dove into the pages with the quick concentration of people who live by the written word, all three with pencil in hand. Kate followed more slowly behind them. She had two pages yet to go when the two academics and then Lee began to discuss what they had read, but since she knew how the story ended, she allowed her stapled sheaf to fall shut.

"I should make a couple of comments about what you've read. First, Inspector Hawkin's abrasiveness was more or less deliberate, and certainly he played it up when Sawyer responded to it. In the first two sessions, the idea was to make me look like a paragon of understanding; for some reason Erasmus—Sawyer—had already responded to me, and there was a degree of rapport before his arrest."

"Good heavens," said the professor. "Do you mean to tell me that isn't just an invention of the television police dramas? There is even a name for the technique, isn't there?"

"Good cop, bad cop," suggested the dean.

"That's right."

"We use it a lot," answered Kate, "though it's not as simple as it sounds. Perpetrators—the accused—are human beings, and most of them want to be told that they're not really all that bad. Sympathy is a much more effective tool, whether you're in an interrogation or in a street confrontation, than swagger and threat. All we did was exaggerate an existing situation to emphasize the contrast and make me appear, frankly, on his side."

"And was David taken in by this little play, Inspector?"

"Professor Whitlaw, your friend David is a tired, confused seventy-two-year-old man who has been living in a carefully constructed dream for the last ten years. I think he is partially

204

aware that he is being gently manipulated, and I think he is allowing it.

"I want to be up front about this. What I'm looking for is a way of making David Sawyer talk. I could tell you it's for his own good; I could even tell you I want to help acquit him of the charges because I don't think he's guilty, but I'm not going to bullshit you. I don't know if he did it or not. I think he would be capable of hitting out in a moment of great anger; I think most people are. I do not believe it was premeditated, and, in fact, I think the charge will be reduced next week.

"So. What I'm saying is this: Yes, I'm a cop, and yes, it is my job to compile evidence against your friend. There may be things you don't want to tell me, and there are sure to be things I'm not going to tell you. Are those ground rules acceptable?"

Professor Whitlaw looked determined and nodded, Dean Gardner looked devious and reached for the Saturday transcript, and Lee—Lee was looking at Kate as if she'd never seen her before.

"Hey," said Kate with a shrug. "It's what I do."

Lee let out a surprised cough of laughter and shook her head. Kate handed her the transcript.

Kate did not bother to read along, as the session was clear enough in her memory. Instead, she went into the kitchen to make another pot of coffee and put on the kettle for Professor Whitlaw's tea, and as she stood and waited, her eyes went out of focus and she thought about what she had just told them.

A great deal of any police officer's time is spent on the thin line that divides right from wrong. Representatives of Good, cops spend most of their life in the company of Bad, if not Evil, and often find more to talk about with the people they arrest than with their own neighbors. In a fair world, ends do not justify means; to a cop, they have to.

She had gone to see Erasmus on Friday before she left, as

Hawkin had asked. She found him sitting on the bunk in his cell, his eyes closed and his lips moving in a murmur of prayer or recitation. His head came around at the sound of her approach and he watched her come in, his eyes neither welcoming nor antagonistic, simply waiting. She sat down on the bunk next to him.

"Hello, Erasmus. David. Are you comfortable?" She laughed at the sweep of his eyes. "Yeah, I know, stupid question. What I meant was, can I bring you anything?"

"O, thou fairest among women!" he said in wan humor.

"I don't know about that. Something to eat tomorrow? Jail food isn't the greatest."

"The bread of adversity and the water of affliction."

"I hope it's not quite that bad."

"The abundance of the rich will not suffer him to sleep," he said in a gentle refusal of her offer.

"I wasn't offering rich abundance, but I might stretch to a cheese sandwich and some fruit."

His eyes lighted up at the last word, though he did not say anything.

"Nothing else?"

He hesitated, then said, "I had rather than forty shillings I had my Book of Songs and Sonnets here."

"Your books? From your backpack. Yes, I'll have them brought to you. Writing materials? Another blanket?"

He smiled a refusal, then his right hand came up and nestled into his neck, his index finger stroking his beard. He cocked his eyebrow at her. "Thy rod and thy staff, they comfort me," he suggested.

"Um, your staff? I'm sorry, I don't think I could get that approved." Even if I could get the laboratory to hurry up with it, she thought.

He shrugged a bit wistfully. "Naked came I into the world,

and naked shall I return. The Lord gives, and the Lord takes away. Blessed be the name of the Lord."

She hesitated and then risked a joke. "I don't think even Inspector Hawkin himself thinks he's God."

His smile was warmly appreciative, but somehow she got the uncomfortable feeling that she'd given something away. She stood up, and he rose with her.

"I'll see if I can get your books released tonight, and I'll see you in the morning. Good night."

He surprised her by putting up a finger to stop her, then bent down to look into her face. "Be strong, and of good courage," he told her. "Be not afraid." And when she could find no answer to that, he merely touched her shoulder and, sitting back down on the too-short bunk, said, "I will lay me down to sleep, and take my rest."

That last little episode was what she had had in mind when she said that David Sawyer was cooperating with his seduction. He knew what she was doing, and moreover he knew what it was doing to her.

No, she did not like cozying up to that old man in order to pry him loose from his secure rest; she was honest enough with herself to admit that she felt dirty using his affection against him. Feeling dirty was, of course, an occupational hazard, and so far it had never kept her from doing her job.

But all in all, she would much rather play bad cop.

♦

The readers in the living room were coming back to life and the coffee had finished dripping, so she moved back out to be hostess for a few minutes. When the cups were full and hot, she paused, the tape of the Sunday session in her hand.

"Al Hawkin was not there this morning. This was partly technique but mostly because he had other commitments." (As if Al would allow previous commitments to stand in the way of an important interrogation session unless it was toward a greater goal, Kate thought to herself.) "I conducted the interview" (stick with that less-loaded term) "and another sat in—and only sat in. I don't think she said a word the whole time, except for saying Hello when I introduced her to Erasmus. Sorry—Sawyer."

"His *nom de folie* does seem to fit him better than the workaday David Sawyer," agreed Dean Gardner.

Kate slipped the cassette into the player and sat down with a cup of coffee. Her own voice came on, sounding stifled and foreign as it always did, with the formalities, then explaining to the prisoner Hawkin's absence and Officer Macauley's presence. After that the interview began.

The recording, on more than one cassette, ran for nearly three hours, and there was even more silence on it than Kate remembered. Long stretches of silence. Many questions were unanswered, or perhaps unanswerable; at other times, remarks were offered that seemed to have nothing to do with Kate's questions—even at the time, Kate had thought that the pronouncements seemed plucked out of thin air. Hawkin, on the telephone afterward, had been greatly encouraged: There had been no antagonism, and he had interpreted Sawyer's mute periods as the first signs of stress, the lapse of confidence that would open him up. Kate was not sure of that. She had been in the room with Sawyer and she had witnessed no lack of confidence. If anything, he seemed to be reconciling himself to his surroundings. When he came into the room, he stood easily in himself, he submitted to the handcuff rituals without noticing them, and he was beginning to look with interest at his jailers and fellow prisoners. Last night, the guards had told Kate, he had sung to the other inmates and read from his book of poetry. It had been, she was informed, the calmest Saturday night in a long time.

No, Kate did not think Erasmus was building up to a revelation; she was afraid he might be settling down to a new home.

Had the tape recorder been voice-activated, the tape they were listening to might have run under two hours. As it was, by the time it ended, Kate was laying out plates and forks and the cold salads Jon had left for them. They helped themselves and carried their plates and glasses back to the sofas and the fireplace. Kate shoveled a few bites down and then opened her notebook.

"Now," she began, "there are two reasons I've asked you to help me with this. The first, as I mentioned, is that one of you might have an idea about how we can get David Sawyer to talk to me about the murdered man. The other is to help me decipher what he's already told us. It would take me years to track down the references and meanings you probably know instantly."

"I don't know about Professor Whitlaw," began the dean.

"Eve, please," murmured the professor.

"Eve, then. But it would take me hours to figure out sources for most of the quotes Erasmus uses."

"I don't think we need all of them. How about if we concentrate on the ones that don't seem to have much bearing on the question that we're asking at the time."

"What do you hope to gain?" the professor asked doubtfully.

"I won't know unless I find it. You see, in an investigation like this we may ask a hundred useless questions for every one that turns out to be of importance. The hope is that a thread end may appear in the process."

"The method is not precisely scientific," said Professor Whitlaw, sounding disapproving.

"That side of it is not. It's an art rather than a science," Kate stated, hoping she sounded confident rather than apologetic. The dean and the professor seemed satisfied, though the therapist lowered her gaze to her plate and did not respond.

"For example. Dean Gardner, when—"

"Philip."

"Philip. When I first met you, Erasmus said something about—where is it? Here . . . Jerusalem killing the prophets, and you interpreted that as a reference to hens, and therefore eggs, and so decided he wanted omelets for breakfast." Lee was frowning and Eve Whitlaw smiling at the convoluted reasoning. "Now, I'm assuming there are other places in the Bible or Shakespeare or wherever where hens are mentioned. Why did he choose this one?"

Philip Gardner scowled at the first page of the thick sheaf of papers. "Yes, I see what you mean. The Beatitude he quoted before that was definitely from Luke, not Matthew, so it wasn't a tie-in from that. And before, let's see. It was Corinthians."

The professor had put her plate aside and picked up her own papers. "Perhaps the link in his mind was thematic rather than—what, bibliographic? I see he was citing Paul's criticisms of the Corinth church for not accepting the negative side of being prophets—that is, being perceived as silly or mad. It is a reasonably close parallel to 'Jerusalem killing the prophets,' don't you think?"

"Was Sawyer saying that he is a prophet, would you say?" Kate asked.

"I don't think we should read too much into his choice of passages," the professor objected. "It strikes me that he uses whatever is to hand, then cobbles the phrases together as best he can. A bit like a collage, where the overall effect is more the point than the parts that go to make it up."

"Would you agree with that, Lee?"

210

"A Freudian would say that each phrase has to be analyzed in regards to its setting, but I am no Freudian. However, I think you do have to be aware of the sources—where they come from and what's going on in the place he lifts them from—and to be sensitive to any themes and patterns that may appear. It's like a collage I saw once, Eva, to use your analogy. It was a giant picture of an empty chair with a book on the floor next to it, but when you got up close you saw that the whole thing was made up of snippets of naked female bodies, cutouts of portions of breast and navels and throats. Knowing that changed the meaning of the final collage considerably. Which was the whole point."

"Philip?"

"I agree, the overall picture is more important than the component parts. For one thing, I don't think Erasmus regards himself as a prophet. A prophet is chosen, often despite his wishes, and spends his time exhorting, preaching, driving people toward right behavior. In my experience, Erasmus seems to spend a great deal of his time listening, and when he does preach, it's often far from clear what he thinks you should do. No, he's no prophet. Although he may well be a saint."

Kate looked at him, startled, but he did not appear to be joking.

"Are you serious?"

"About his potential sainthood? Oh yes. You have to remember that even Francis of Assisi was a man before he was a saint. Why not Erasmus?"

She could think of no way to answer that, so Kate turned back to her notes. "Why not indeed? Tell me about his choice of passages that first day, out on the lawn at CDSP. What is Corinthians? Why would he use it so much?"

♦

It was very late when the meeting broke up, and Kate felt more battered than enlightened. It had been a slow and laborious process, and humiliating, an ongoing admission of her own profound ignorance. She had persisted, however, and in the car, driving back from delivering Professor Whitlaw to the Noe Valley house, she came to certain conclusions.

First of all, she abandoned any hope of finding a hidden meaning in Sawyer's utterances by looking at their original context. Occasionally he used a phrase to refer to a story or episode, but those were generally characterized by the marked inappropriateness of the phrase, such as when he referred to the dead man as "He was not the Light" to give the man a name. For the most part, Sawyer used a quotation as raw material, hacked from its setting regardless.

Beyond that, Kate was not sure what she had expected. However, she did not feel it had been a wasted day. Without knowing why, she felt she had been told the layout of a dark room: She still couldn't see where she was going, but she could begin to sense the shapes and obstacles it contained.

And as she turned up Russian Hill, she began to play with the idea of meeting Erasmus on his own ground. Could her team of translators assemble enough quotes of their own to enable her, as their mouthpiece, to put David Sawyer on the spot?

Could it be that he was waiting for someone to do just that?

TWENTY-TWO

Never was any man so little afraid of his own
promises. His life was one riot of rash vows; of
rash vows that turned out right.

When the phone rang at 2:20 on Wednesday morning, Kate's first thought was how she'd forgotten this jolly side of working homicide. Her second thought was that David Sawyer had attempted suicide.

"Martinelli."

"Inspector, this is Eve Whitlaw."

"Professor Whitlaw?" Kate dashed her free hand across her eyes and squinted at the bedside clock. Yes, it was indeed the middle of the night. "What is it?"

"It's about David. I know why he does it."

Does it, not *did* it, Kate noted dimly. "And that couldn't wait?"

"I thought, before you sent him to that mental institution—"

"He's already gone." Actually, it was just to the psychiatric ward at San Francisco General.

"Is he? Oh dear. Well, perhaps it's for the best."

"It's also required. I doubt he'll be gone long. Was there anything else, professor?"

"Did you not want to hear my thoughts? There is a distinct internal logic to his actions, once one understands the starting point."

"Professor, could it wait until morning?"

"Is it that late? Why, what time—oh good Lord, I had no idea. I was sitting here thinking and—oh how appalling of me, you poor thing. Yes, by all means, ring me in the morning. Go back to sleep, dear."

Kate hung up with a chuckle and, savoring the delicious feeling of reprieve, curled up against Lee and did indeed go back to sleep.

In the morning, Professor Whitlaw was bristling with apologies. Kate drank half her coffee just waiting for a chance to get a word into the telephone receiver, and she then arranged to meet the professor at a café downtown at eleven o'-clock. The professor was quite willing to break her other appointments for the morning, but Kate decided that she did not need to break her own.

She did have to cut it short, though, and even then she came into the café late, shaking the rain from her coat. She spotted the professor's gray head at a corner table, bent toward a book, a cup frozen halfway between saucer and lip, forgotten. Kate sat down. Eve Whitlaw looked up, startled, sipped from the cup, made a face, and let it clatter onto the saucer.

"Inspector, how lovely to see you. You're looking remarkably fresh, considering your disturbed night."

Before she could launch into more apologies, Kate greeted her, offered her more tea, or a meal, and when both were refused went over to the counter and ordered herself a double cappuccino and a cheese sandwich. Thus fortified, she went back to the table, where she found the professor hunched forward, ready to pounce.

"I will not bore you with further apologies for my deplorable manners, Inspector, but I must apologize for the slowness of my intellect. It has taken me since Sunday evening to see the obvious. The problem is," she said, as if laying out the basic premise for a lecture—which indeed she was—"I am an historian, and as such I am accustomed to approach theological questions as historical questions. That is, they are tidy, complete, finished. It is very difficult to visualize a modern phenomenon in the same way: it keeps moving about, and one can not foresee its consequences. Rather the same, I suppose, as an early-fourth-century theologian would be unable to visualize the real importance of the Council of Nicaea, or a bishop of the time to imagine the immensity of what Luther was doing. I'm sorry, I'm dithering.

"What I am trying to explain is why I couldn't see what is happening to David when we first looked at it on Sunday afternoon. You, of course, were approaching it from a legal point of view, your friend saw it from a psychological one, Philip Gardner can see David only as the colorful Erasmus, and I was stuck at seeing Erasmus as a perversion of David Sawyer. This morning at that ungodly hour, I finally turned it around, placed him in an historical setting, and looked at his actions as if they indeed held an internal logic, rather than simply reflecting the irrational reactions of a severely traumatized man." She leaned forward to drive her point home. "The key idea here is, 'covenant.'"

Kate swallowed her bite and tried to look intelligent.

"A covenant is some kind of agreement, isn't it?"

"A biblical covenant could be anything from an international treaty to a business arrangement. It was regarded as a sacred commitment, legally and morally binding, absolutely unbreakable. The relationship between the Divinity and the people of Israel was covenantal, for example. I should have known immediately that was what David was doing—he used the idea twice in explaining himself, the first time when he was talking to you and Philip Gardner in Berkeley, the second in the interview on Friday. The passages were on both lists, but I was seeing it as one of his loosely metaphorical quotations, or expressing a psychological truth, not a literal one."

"What difference would that make, precisely?"

"A great deal. You see—well, let me take a step back here." Take several, thought Kate. "What you see in David is a conjunction of two very different religious traditions that have been brought together by his personal disaster and welded together by his need. The idea of covenant is one of them—we'll come back to that. The other is the tradition of the Holy Fool, a figure David spent much of his adult life studying. Ten years ago, David took a long-delayed but decisive action and told Kyle Roberts that there was no future, no real future, in the academic world for him. David now attributes his harsh words to his own vanity, which I assume means that he was too proud of his own status to recommend an inferior scholar for a post that he, Kyle, was not suited for. I agreed with him at the time, and still do: One cannot allow oneself to be known as a person who recommends duds; the academic world is too small and too unforgiving for that. At any rate, David's criticism was the spark that set off a badly unbalanced and volatile personality, and David's family, his beloved son, as well as three other innocents, were destroyed in the explosion.

"Now, one of the most basic characteristics of the fool, either a secular or a religious one, is that he is without a will. Even inanimate objects are more self-willed than a fool. Think of some of Charlie Chaplin's brilliant bits where he wrestles with chairs and clothing and lengths of wallpaper and such and then is beaten by them. Look at the way your Erasmus depends on his scepter—a classic piece of foolishness, by the way. He has no will; he makes no choices; he is wafted to and fro by powers he cannot control. Even when he appears forceful and aggressive, he is acting only as a mirror. David, in fact, took this to an extreme, though I admit a logical one: He does not even have words of his own."

She waited until she saw that Kate had followed her this far, saw Kate begin to nod, and continued.

"Only a brilliant man like David could have managed it. And, more than brilliance. I am not so ready as Dean Gardner to attribute sainthood to David, but he did have a point, and David's charisma was always considerable.

"What I think happened, then, is that at the point in David's life where he had to choose between death—remember what he said, that the only thing worse than death was wanting death and being denied it?—and some tolerable form of life, he chose a life of absolute surrender, of complete will-lessness. Complete and daily sacrifice, without any risk of doing harm to another by taking positive action, a form of service to humanity that was properly demanding and might go some way to make up for what he was responsible for—and here's where the idea of covenant comes in. Guilt is a feeling with a limited life span, and David could not take the chance that someday—in a year, or three years, or five—the initial impulse that drove him to

217

live the life of a Fool would fade and he would find some excuse to resume his normal life. So he ensured that it would be permanent by declaring a covenant, an unbreakable oath said, I venture to say, over the dead body of his son.

"A covenant is either whole or it is broken—nothing in between, no amendments or retractions. In the most archaic forms, the symbolic recognition of a covenant is a split carcass, down the halves of which a flame is passed or the people walk. In fact, in the Hebrew language a covenant is 'cut,' not just made, which serves as a reminder that if one party goes back on his part of the agreement, he may be split down the middle as the carcass was.

"I can see I'm losing you, and I freely admit that it's a very cerebral explanation. In fact, I doubt very much that David thought of it in anything like this manner. His was, I imagine, a 'gut' response to the option of suicide. The fool's way of thinking came naturally to hand—it fit—and he clamped on the oath, sworn on his son's body, like a suit of armor. No—more than armor; like an exoskeleton, a rigid carapace that held him together and allowed him to justify living. The inflexibility of the vow, the safety of speaking in other men's words, the freedom that comes with letting go—that has become his life. A life of service to the homeless, of ministering in different ways to the spiritually impoverished middle classes and to the dangerously isolated seminarians."

"And now, jail," said Kate slowly. "And probably prison."

"What do you mean?" Professor Whitlaw said sharply.

"I have had the strong feeling the last few days that Sawyer is reconciling himself to being incarcerated, that he doesn't really care whether he's in or out. At any rate, he certainly isn't afraid of it anymore, like he was at first."

"God. Oh God. Yes, I can see that. His ministry in prison. Oh Lord, what can we do?"

"We must make him talk. We have to find out what he knows about John's death. Professor Whitlaw, I am being horribly unprofessional by saying this, but frankly I have serious doubts that David Sawyer killed the man. However, I think he knows who did. He must tell us."

The café lunch tide that had risen around the two women was now starting to ebb, and Kate only now became briefly aware of her surroundings. After a long time, Professor Whitlaw looked up at her, and to Kate's astonishment the woman did not seem far from tears.

"I want David back, you do understand that. He was my best friend in all the world, and I have missed him terribly, every day, for all these years. However, much as I would rejoice in having him return to himself, I have to admit that what you want could finally destroy what remains of his life. If you make David break this strange vow of personal speechlessness, you will force him to break faith with his murdered son, and I suspect that for David that would be intolerable. It would negate the whole last ten years of his life. I do not wish to be overly dramatic, but I very much fear that if you break his oath, you will break him. You could kill him."

"What would you recommend we do?"

"You might find the real murderer."

Kate suppressed a surge of irritation. "Yes," she said dryly.

"Other than that, frankly, I do not know what you can do. Self-preservation is too low a priority for him to respond to that particular appeal, and you have already tried to convince him that he has the responsibility to help bring the man's killer to justice, with no result whatsoever. Unless you can convince him that his silence positively harms others, I can't see that you'll budge him."

Kate began to pile her dishes together. She did not say anything, could not say anything without it being inexcusably

219

rude. Even a "Thank you very much" would inevitably sound like sarcasm, and this woman was only doing her best. Still, even with all the pretty words she'd dressed it in, she had told Kate no more than she knew already: Erasmus would not talk; Sawyer would not save himself. So she said nothing. Professor Whitlaw, however, had one more observation to throw in.

"Martyrdom has always been the act of fools. It's the ultimate absurdity, giving up one's life for an idea."

"Martyrs stand for something," Kate said, suddenly fed up with words. "There's nothing to stand for here. He's just being stupid, and a real pain in the neck."

With that judgment, she tipped her plate into the tub marked DISHES and walked out into the rain.

♦

TWENTY-THREE

♦

. . . The abrupt simplicity with which Francis won the attention and favour of Rome.

A few days later, David Sawyer was returned to the jail, along with a lengthy psychiatric evaluation that said, in effect, that the man was eccentric but quite sane enough to stand trial. That evening, on her way home, Kate stopped by his cell to see him. She stopped in the next night as well, to take him a book of poetry that Lee had sent, and the next. It soon became a part of her day, and twice when she was out in the city and might normally have gone directly home, she found herself making excuses to drop by her office first and then go up to the sixth floor for a few brief words.

Kate was not the only one to fall beneath the spell of

Brother Erasmus. One evening he held out a flowered paper plate and offered her a home-baked chocolate chip cookie. A child's drawing mysteriously appeared, Scotch-taped to the wall of his cell. Once, late, following a long and depressing day, Kate entered the jail area and heard the sound of Sawyer's voice ringing out clear and loud among the astonishingly silent cells. When she came nearer, she saw him stretched out on his narrow bed, reading aloud from a book called *The Martian Chronicles*. The other inmates were sitting, lying down, or hanging on their bars, listening to him. Kate turned and left. Another night, even later, Kate passed by on business and heard a voice singing: a repetitive tune, almost a chant, with every second line exhorting the listener: Praise Him and glorify Him forever.

He had visitors, too, over the next couple of weeks. Those of the homeless who could work up the courage to enter the daunting Hall of Justice came for brief visits: Salvatore once, the three Vietnam vets once each, Doc and Mouse and Wilhemena twice each. Beatrice came four times in the first six days after he had returned to the jail. From Sawyer's other worlds came Dean Gardner, who visited regularly, and Joel, the grad student who had given Erasmus rides to Berkeley. There was a steady stream of others from the seminary, professors, staff, and students, and from Fishermen's Wharf, the owner of the store that sold magic supplies and the crystal woman.

Brother Erasmus even had his own newspaper reporter, who had adopted him and argued with his editor about the newsworthiness of a jailed homeless man. Ten days after Sawyer had been brought back to San Francisco, the reporter's efforts paid off with a full-page human-interest story in the Sunday edition on homeless individuals, one of whom was Erasmus. Photographs and interviews of the homeless men and women connected to him, and of their more settled neighbors, succeeded in drawing a picture of the homeless population as a community of wise eccentrics. The feature spread resulted in a great deal of cynical laughter among those responsible for enforcing the law, a flurry of letters to the editor in praise and condemnation, a brief increase in the takings of the panhandlers across town, and even more visitors for David Sawyer.

It was a popular article, and two days later the reporter submitted another, smaller story, this one looking at the murder case itself in greater detail. His editor cut out half the words and changed it from an investigative piece to one with a greater emphasis on the people involved, but still, there it was in Wednesday's paper, with interviews of five of the homeless, a review of the facts, and photographs of Erasmus, Beatrice, and the colorful Mouse.

The guards grumbled at the number of visitors they had to handle for this one prisoner. However, they did not stop bringing him plates of food their wives had made and snapshots of their dogs.

The only person Erasmus flatly refused to see was Professor Eve Whitlaw. Everyone else he listened to, smiled at, prayed with, and presented with a pithy saying to take away with them, but the English professor from his past, he would have nothing to do with. She tried twice but not again.

During the weeks after David Sawyer's arrest, Kate had been immensely busy, not only with the case against Sawyer but with another investigation that she and Hawkin had drawn, the lye poisoning of an alcoholic woman (who had looked to be in her sixties but was in fact thirty-two), which could have been either accident or suicide but was looking more and more like murder. It involved long hours of interviewing the woman's large and predominantly drunken extended family, and it left Kate with little time to spare for Erasmus, safe in his cell.

It was over a month since the murder, and Kate felt the

Sawyer case slipping from her. She had neither the time nor the concentration to pursue it further, and she was uncomfortably aware that she might let it go entirely but for the continued entreaties of Dean Gardner and Professor Whitlaw. She came home late on a Monday night, aching with exhaustion, cold through, and hungry, and found a series of five pink "While You Were Out" slips lined up for her on the kitchen table: Philip Gardner, Eve Whitlaw, Rosalyn Hall, Philip Gardner, Eve Whitlaw.

Fortunately, it was too late to return the calls. However, she no longer had much of an appetite. She poured herself a tumbler glass of raw red wine, drank it up as she stood in the kitchen, filled up the glass again, and took it to bed.

♦

Things looked rosier in the morning, as she lay with Lee's arm around her shoulder while they drank their morning coffee.

"You see," Kate was saying, "what I had hoped to do was assemble enough quotes of my own to meet him on his own ground. I even got a book of quotations and started it off—'The vow that binds too strictly snaps itself' and 'I hate quotations. Tell me what you know,' that kind of thing. But I can't do it. I just don't have time to memorize the whole damn book."

"You saw the notes, that Eve and Philip Gardner called?"

"I did. I'll call them later."

"She's only here for another month, did you know that?"

"So she told me. About six times. I don't know what I can do, Sawyer won't see her."

The phone rang.

"Oh hell, it's not even eight o'clock."

"Let the machine get it," Lee said, but Kate was already stretched across to the telephone.

"Yes?" she demanded. "Oh, Al. Hi. Yeah, I was expecting someone else. What's—Who?" Kate became quiet and listened for a long time, unconsciously disentangling herself from Lee's embrace until she was sitting upright on the edge of the bed. "What do they think about her chances?" she said finally, listening again. "Okay. Sure. Do you have someone at the hospital? Good. See you there, twenty minutes." She hung up and went to the closet.

"That wasn't about David Sawyer, was it?" Lee asked.

"David . . . Oh. No, it's another case—fifty suspects and now one of the family decided he knows which of his cousins did it and so he took a shot at her early this morning. Several shots, through the wall of her bedroom, and one of them hit her. They're all nuts, the whole family. No, I won't bother with breakfast."

The shower went on and, after two minutes, off again. Kate emerged, her hair wet but her clothes on, kissed Lee absently, and left. Lee listened to her lover's feet on the stairs, the familiar pause in front of the closet while the wicked gun was strapped on, then the front door opened and closed. A car started up on the street outside, where Kate had left it instead of rattling the garage door late last night, and she was gone. Lee sighed and set about the laborious business of the day.

♦

Not that night, nor the next morning, but the following day over dinner the conversation was resumed.

"You know what you were saying the other day about trying to put together a bunch of quotations to throw back at David Sawyer?" Lee began.

"Fat chance of that now. There're two more members of that woman's family in jail now; they were going at each other with chains in the dead woman's front yard. There used to be a rose bed. Do they give prizes for the most dysfunctional families? This crew would take the gold."

"I was wondering if there would be any reason you couldn't have Philip Gardner and Eve do it for you? Come up with zinging quotes, that is."

"He's still in jail."

"I know he's still in jail; is there any reason why you can't have a conference of half a dozen people? Using the two of them as translators, like you thought of before, only in two-way translation, into and out of Erasmusese?"

"There are problems in allowing civilians—friends—in on an interview," Kate said slowly.

"Insurmountable problems?"

"I'd have to talk to Al," Kate finally said.

"Do. Because if you have to argue with him using his own language, you'd better have someone who speaks it as well as Philip and Eve do."

"You're right. In fact—no, maybe not."

"What?"

"I was just thinking that he and Beatrice seem very close. If she'd be willing to help us, it might make it less adversarial. I don't know if that would help or not."

"I think it would be a good idea."

"I'll have to talk to Al about it. I could probably find Beatrice before Friday night, although I suppose we'd have to do the interview on Saturday anyway to work around Dean Gardner's schedule. I'll talk to Al," she said again finally.

Al agreed, with strong reservations but a willingness to try anything that might loosen David Sawyer's guard. Philip Gardner agreed; Eve Whitlaw agreed. The conference was set for ten o'clock on Saturday morning, regardless of whether Beatrice had prior commitments.

But when Kate went to Sentient Beans on Friday evening to talk to the homeless woman, Beatrice was not there. Beatrice had not been there the week before, either.

Kate stood listening to the angry young owner, feeling the cold begin to gather along her spine.

◆

TWENTY-FOUR

◆

Praised be God for our Sister, the death of the body.

"You scared her off." The young man behind the wooden bar was gripping the latte glass as if he were about to throw it at her. His name was Krishna, but he had obviously been named after one of the god's more violent manifestations.

"Could you explain that please, sir?" Kate asked politely, keeping an eye on the glass.

"You probably did it on purpose. That's harassment. You could tell her nerves were bad."

"Are you telling me you haven't seen Beatrice Jankowski since the night I was here? That was nearly a month ago. I've seen her since then."

"She was in once," the man said grudgingly.

"Twice," said a woman's voice from behind him. The woman herself appeared, carrying a tray of clean cups, which she slid into place beneath the bar. She was very small, with hard, slicked-back unnaturally black hair, at least a dozen loops and studs in her ears and one through her nose, and kind, intelligent brown eyes. Kate recognized the guitarist from the night she had come here. "We didn't see her last week, and we haven't seen her since then, but she was in a couple of times after you were here."

"How do you remember when I was in? One face on a busy night."

"I noticed you. Beatrice talked about you. But we were a little concerned last week when she didn't show, and we've been keeping an eye out for her in the neighborhood. She's not around."

"You haven't filed a missing-persons report?"

"For a homeless woman? Who'd listen to us?" snorted the man.

The woman answered Kate as if he—her husband?—hadn't spoken. "I decided that if she didn't come in tonight, I would report her missing. I called the hospitals, but she's not there. My name is Leila, by the way."

The man turned to her, his grip on the glass so tight now that white spots showed on his knuckles. "You called the—I thought we agreed—"

"Oh, Krish, of course I called. What if she was sick or something?"

"But she was here two weeks ago?" Kate asked loudly, to interrupt the burgeoning argument.

"Just like always," Leila said.

"And she said nothing to indicate that she would not be here?"

"No. In fact, she said, 'See you next week, dear,' just like she always does. Did." Leila was worried now, taking police interest as evidence that something was very wrong.

"I wouldn't be too concerned, not yet. I just wanted to pass on a message from a friend of hers who's in custody."

"Brother Erasmus?"

"Yes. You know him?"

"Not personally. Though I feel like I do, since she talked about him all the time. She went to see him in the jail."

"I know. But not for a while, apparently, because he was asking about her," she embroidered.

"How long? Since he's seen her?"

It was in the small beat before Kate answered that she acknowledged her own apprehension.

"I don't know," she said slowly. "I'll have to check."

The stark possibilities lay there, and nothing Krishna or Leila could add changed them any. Finally, she asked for the use of their telephone and began to cast out her lines of inquiry.

The logs at the jail revealed that Beatrice Jankowski had last visited David Sawyer on Wednesday the ninth of March, two days before she had not appeared at Sentient Beans to wash her clothes and sketch the customers.

A call to the morgue confirmed that there were no unclaimed bodies in San Francisco that remotely matched Beatrice's description.

Al Hawkin was not at home and had not yet arrived at Jani's apartment in Palo Alto. Rather than beep him, she left brief messages at both numbers, on his machine and with Jani's daughter Jules, and then went back out into the coffeehouse, where she found Leila cleaning the tables.

"Did Beatrice leave anything here?" she asked.

"Probably. There's a little cabinet in the back we let her use."

"Does it lock?"

"There's a padlock. We kept one key, gave her the other."

"Just the two keys?"

"That's all."

"May I have the key, please?"

Leila let a cup and saucer crash down onto the tray. "Oh God. What did you find out?"

"Not a thing. I'm not going to open the cabinet, and I'll give the key back to you if Beatrice turns up. I'd just be more comfortable keeping it in the meantime."

Leila dug into the deep pocket of her baggy black silk pants and drew out a fist-sized bundle of keys. She flipped through it, unhooked a cheap-looking key, and handed it to Kate. "There's nothing much in there. Her sketch pad and box, a few clothes, odds and ends."

"It's good of you to let her use it."

Leila actually blushed. "Yes, well, I've been there myself, and she's getting too old to live out of plastic bags."

Kate opened her mouth to ask if Beatrice slept here occasionally, then closed it again. Time enough for questions that might compromise the insurance and zoning. She merely wrote out a receipt, pocketed the key, thanked Leila, and went back out to her car.

◆

In the Homicide room, at her desk, on that Friday night, Kate sat for a long time and stared at the telephone. She did not want to pick it up. She wanted to go home and rub Lee's back or watch some inane musical video or listen to Lee's voice reading from a novel. She did not want to make these telephone calls because she was afraid of what she was going to learn, and when she learned it, she knew whom she would blame.

Kitagawa and O'Hara came in then, speaking in loud

voices, and in order to avoid having to talk to them she picked up the receiver and tucked it under her ear. She began to look up the telephone numbers and then made her calls.

After the fifth call, a faint hope began to stir: Maybe she had been wrong. Alarmist. But the optimism was premature: At the seventh morgue, this one in Santa Cruz, they had a Jane Doe, Beatrice's size, Beatrice's age, with Beatrice's hair and eye color. She'd been found four days ago up in the hills, by hikers. Dead at least three days before that. Not pretty. Sure, there'd be someone there all night.

Kate sat and rubbed her eyes, hot and gritty and wanting nothing but to close for a long time. Too late to phone Lee, let her know she wouldn't be in? Yes, it really was. Lee used to sleep very little—four, five hours a night. Now she needed eight hours, or she ached. Sometimes took a nap. Why are you thinking about that? Kate asked herself. Christ, this is a shitty job.

Phones had been ringing on and off. Now Kate heard her name called, and she automatically picked up the receiver.

"Martinelli. Oh, Al, thanks for calling. Sorry to wreck your weekend. Yeah, she disappeared, but I think I found her. The Santa Cruz morgue. Yeah, I know. I'm going down to see her. Want me to call you from there? You don't have to come. You're sure? You promise Jani won't hate me? Well, leave her a note; maybe you'll be back before she wakes up. I'll leave now. Right. Bye."

♦

It was like old times, driving a sleeping Al through the rain into the Santa Cruz Mountains. This time, however, their goal was not the forest site of three murdered children, their first case together a year earlier, but the sterile, temporary repository of one elderly woman.

232

When Kate rolled to a stop and pulled on the parking brake, Al woke up, ran his hands over his face, and bent forward to look at the windshield. "It's déjà vu all over again," he commented.

"How about next year, come March, we arrange a case that takes us to Palm Springs or something?"

"I'll put in a voucher for it tomorrow. Do you know where—"

"Through there."

Into the cold, inhuman space that smelled of death, up to the body, leaning over the gray face: Yes. Oh yes: Beatrice Jankowski.

"I hadn't realized how old she was," Kate said bleakly.

"She had false teeth," commented the morgue attendant. "Taking them out makes anyone look shriveled up. Is her family going to want her shipped, do you know?"

"I don't know if she had a family."

"We'll hang on to her for a while, then."

"Do you have a copy of the autopsy report?" Al asked.

"I don't think so. You'd have to check with the investigating officer. I think that was Kent Makepeace. I can tell you it was homicide." He reached down and turned Beatrice's head to one side, revealing the damage beneath the clotted gray hair on the right side of her skull, between the ear and the spine. "Somebody hit her, hard."

◆

TWENTY-FIVE

◆

Many of his acts will seem grotesque and puzzling to a rationalistic taste.

The mere fact that an identity had been given to a body in the morgue hardly justified rousting the investigating detective out of his bed at four o'clock on a Saturday morning. Even Al Hawkin had to admit that. So he and Kate found an all-night restaurant and ate bacon and eggs in an attempt to fool their bodies into thinking it was a new morning rather than a too-long night, and at six they made their way to the county offices. At 6:30, Hawkin succeeded in bullying an underling into phoning Makepeace. At seven o'clock, they were in his office being shown the case file.

"That's right," he was saying, fighting yawns. "Completely nude, no false teeth, not even a hairpin."

"She wore several rings," Kate commented.

"That's in the path report. Couple of nicks on her fingers, scratches that showed where the rings'd been cut off her postmortem. Her hands were so arthritic, I'd guess he tried to pull them off and couldn't get them over her knuckles, so he had to cut them. She was also moved around after death, a couple of rug fibers and marks on her legs, probably transported in a car's trunk. Nothing under her fingernails but normal dirt—she didn't scratch her attacker, no defense marks on her hands, nothing. About the rings, though." He sounded as if he was beginning to wake up, and he took a large swallow of coffee from his paper cup to increase the rate of coherency. "We did a ground search, especially up and down the road. Among the crap they picked up was a ring. There should be a photograph here somewhere." He dug back into the file, flipped through the glossy photographs of the nude woman sprawled in the leaves, gray hair snarled across her face, and pulled out the picture of a large fancy ring with a cracked stone. He laid it on the desk between them.

Kate peered at it. "It looks like one of hers. I'd have to ask her friends to be sure. Where was it?"

"Whoever dumped her pulled off the main road down this dirt road." His finger tapped a long-range photo that showed Beatrice as a mere shape in the corner. "He couldn't go any farther because of the gate, but you can't see the place from the road. The ring was on the left side of the road going in, where it might have fallen when he opened the driver-side door. If it was in his pocket, say, and fell out. Of course, it could've been there for a week or two." He sipped at his coffee, then added, as if in afterthought, "There was a partial on the ring, halfway de-

235

cent. So let us know when you have prints on a suspect. Other than that, we didn't find a thing. Wasn't raped or assaulted, no signs that she was tied up, just a sixty-odd-year-old woman in fairly good condition until she ran into a blunt instrument."

"The pathologist doesn't seem to have much to say about the weapon," Hawkin commented. He had put his glasses on to look through the file.

"There wasn't much to say. No splinters, no rust or grease stains, no glass splinters. A smooth, hard object about two inches in diameter. Three blows, though the first one probably killed her. Could've been almost anything. What's your interest in her, anyway, to drag you down here in the middle of the night?"

"It's related somehow to the body that was cremated in Golden Gate Park," Hawkin replied.

"No kidding? I read about that. And I used to think we had all the loose ones rolling around here."

"We have our share. Can I have a copy of all this?"

"Sure. Here, you take any duplicates of the pictures. If you want copies of the others, let me know and I'll have them printed. Let me go turn the Xerox machine on."

♦

Kate turned the car toward the mountainous Highway 17 and began climbing away from the sea. The morning traffic was light, the rain had stopped at some time during the night, and Kate drove with both eyes but only half a mind on the road.

"It was the newspaper story," she said abruptly.

"What was?"

"Her picture was in the Wednesday paper. The article quoted her as saying she'd seen John talking with a stranger from Texas; she seemed to think we should let Sawyer go because of that. Two days later, she was missing."

For a long time, Al did not answer. Kate took her eyes off the road for a moment to see if he had fallen asleep, but he was staring ahead through the windshield.

"You don't agree?"

"We don't know anything about the woman. It's a little early for jumping to conclusions."

Silence descended on the car. Kate had been tired earlier but now, boosted by two cups of stale coffee from the doughnut shop Hawkin had spotted just before the freeway entrance, she felt merely stupid. She followed the road up and out of the hills and into San Jose, where the freeways were always busy.

Nearing Palo Alto, she spoke again. "I'll drop you at Jani's, then?"

"No, go on to the City. I changed my mind; I want to be in on your group meeting this morning with Sawyer."

"I was thinking we'd probably cancel it," said Kate, surprised.

"This is all the more reason not to."

◆

TWENTY-SIX

◆

. . . Something happened to him that must remain
greatly dark to most of us, who are ordinary and
selfish men whom God has not broken to
make anew.

The interrogation had been scheduled to begin at ten o'clock.
Kate and Hawkin were back in the city by then, but they did
not join David Sawyer in the interview room at ten. At eleven
o'clock, he was still by himself in the room, his hands in his lap,
his lips moving continuously in a low recitation. Twice he had
glanced at the door, and on the third time he caught himself
and made a visible effort to relax. Since then he had appeared
to be in meditation, his long body at ease and his eyes open but
not focused on any object.

At 11:20, the door opened. Hawkin came in first, followed

by Kate. Both of them looked clean and damp, though their bodies and eyes betrayed a sleepless night.

There were three vacant chairs in the room, but neither detective sat. The man in the jail garb blinked gently at them and waited, and then the third figure came through the door and he instantly got to his feet, his face shut-down and hard, and made as if to sidle past his old friend to the door, looking accusingly not at her but at Kate.

Hawkin put out a hand to stop him. "Please, Dr. Sawyer," he said quietly. "Sit down."

Sawyer's head came around and the two men gazed at each other while the old man, alerted by some nuance of tone, tried to gauge what lay behind the words. He studied Hawkins' stance and eyes and looked down warily at the manila envelope Hawkin held in his hand before he accepted the detective's unspoken message: Before, we were acting out a game. Before, we had time to play with animosity. The game is over now.

The message that said: Bad news coming, David.

"Please," Hawkin repeated quietly.

After a long minute, without breaking their locked gaze, Sawyer moved back to the table and lowered himself into his chair. Only then did he look at Kate, sitting poised to take notes, and then at Eve Whitlaw, and when he took his eyes from her and turned back to Al Hawkin, on the other side of the table from him now, he drew breath and opened his mouth.

"No," interrupted Hawkin, one hand raised to stop Sawyer from speaking. "Don't say anything yet. Listen to me before you commit yourself to speech. I've been told you're very good at listening." Hawkin waited until the older man had slowly subsided into the plastic chair. He then leaned forward and, choosing his words carefully, began to speak.

"Five and a half weeks ago, a man was killed in Golden

Gate Park. A number of your friends decided to cremate the body, in imitation of a similar cremation you had supervised three weeks earlier, that of a small dog. The attempted cremation confused matters a great deal, but eventually it proved to have no direct connection with the man's death.

"You, however, attracted our suspicions from the very beginning. You would not answer our questions, you had no alibi for the time of death, and you seemed to have something you were hiding. On the nineteenth of February, you fled from Inspector Martinelli and a woman who could identify you. And then when a person who lives near the park told us that you were in the vicinity at the general time the man was killed, and in a state of agitation, the case against you seemed fairly tight. It appeared that you had been blackmailed by the man John and finally hit him in the head in anger. No, much as I would like to hear what you could come up with by way of a response, I'd really prefer if you would just listen."

Hawkin slouched down in the chair, playing with the clasp on the envelope that lay on the table between them.

"However, I don't think you killed him. I know you could have. I know you have a short temper, for all your years of saintly behavior, and you could easily have lost it and swung at him with that stick of yours. But I don't think you would have been capable of standing by and waiting for him to die. And I don't believe you could have broken the skull of his dog three weeks before that. And I know damn well that you were in custody eight days ago and that therefore you could not have committed the murder of your friend Beatrice Jankowski."

It took a moment for the information to lodge in his mind, but when it did, the effect was all Hawkin had aimed for: Shock, profound and complete, froze David Sawyer's hands on the edge of the table, kept him from moving, stopped the breath in his body.

240

"Yes. I'm very sorry," said Hawkin, sounding it. "Beatrice died last week. Inspector Martinelli and I just identified her body a few hours ago." He pushed back the flap on the envelope and slid the photograph out onto the table, pushed it across in front of Sawyer, and withdrew his hand. The old man stared uncomprehending at the black-and-white photograph of Beatrice Jankowski's face that had been taken on the autopsy table just before she was cut open. She lay there calmly, her eyes closed, but was very obviously dead.

Sawyer closed his own eyes and his hands came up to his face, pressing hard against his mouth and cheeks as if to hold in his reaction—vomit, perhaps, or words—but he could not hold back the tears that squeezed from beneath his closed eyelids, tears utterly unlike the simple, generous, childlike stream he had cried so freely on the first occasion Kate had seen him. These were a man's tears, begrudged and painful, and he clawed at them with his long fingers as if they scalded his skin.

They all waited a long time for him to take possession of himself again. Even Professor Whitlaw waited, as she had been instructed, though she palpably yearned to go and comfort him. They waited, and eventually he raised a bleary red-eyed face from his hands and accepted the tissue that Al Hawkin held out to him.

Hawkin then sat forward until his arms were on the table and his face was only inches from the stricken features of the prisoner.

"Dr. Sawyer, you had nothing to do with the deaths of your son and the wife and children of that madman Kyle Roberts. You believe you did, because grief has to go somewhere, but the truth of the matter is, you were in no way responsible.

"Beatrice Jankowski's death is a different matter. You know who the dead man was, and you know who killed him. You may even know why. You wouldn't tell us because of this vow of

241

yours. You figured the man was such a miserable shit-filled excuse for a human being, his death was hardly a reason to break your vow. You played God, David, and because you wouldn't answer our questions a month ago, because you distracted us and slowed down the investigation, he came back. He heard a rumor that Beatrice had seen him; he probably read the interview in the newspaper where she hinted that she could identify him, so he came back for her. He killed her, David. He broke her skull and he cut those distinctive rings from her fingers and then he stripped her naked and dumped her body down in the mountains, because you had made up your mind to be noble in prison rather than answer our questions."

Although she had been briefed on what to expect, Professor Whitlaw started to protest. Kate stopped her with a hand on her arm, but it was doubtful that either Sawyer or Hawkin noticed.

"Tell me, David," Hawkin pleaded, nearly whispering. "You know who did it; you know why; you even know where he is—you were headed for Texas when they picked you up in Barstow, weren't you? You know everything and I don't even know what the dead man's name is. David, you have to suspend this vow of yours. Just long enough to give me the information I need. Please, David, for God's sake. For Beatrice's sake, if nothing else."

Kate saw David Sawyer's surrender. With a jolt made of triumph and sorrow and revulsion at Al Hawkin's superb skills, she could see the old man succumb, saw the moment when he buckled off the only thing that had held him together through ten hard years. His mouth opened as he searched for words, his own words, a foreign language spoken long ago.

"I . . ." he said, then stopped. "My name . . . is David Sawyer."

Eve Whitlaw stood up and went to him, taking up a position behind his chair, her hands resting on his shoulders. He raised his right hand across his chest to take her left hand and, fingers intertwined, he appeared to gather a degree of strength, then continued.

"You know . . . who . . . I am. You know . . . about Kyle Roberts. I . . . do not need to say anything about . . . that. You need to know about the man who died. The man . . . you know as John . . . was sick. Mentally. His mind and his . . . spirit had become twisted. He . . . enjoyed . . . power over others. He was rich." Sawyer stopped and with a visible effort pulled himself together. His tongue, so easy and fluent with the complex thoughts of others, seemed unable to produce a sentence more complicated than a four-year-old's. When he resumed, his words were more sophisticated, but each phrase, occasionally each word, was set apart by a brief pause.

"John was actually a very wealthy man, and he . . . left his home and his business to . . . wander. There are others like him on the streets. Not many, but always a few who choose the nomadic way of life for . . . various reasons, rather than falling into it. He did not change, though. He was—he had been a cutthroat businessman, in land speculation and development. He was proud of his . . . shady dealings. When he came onto the streets, he remained . . . sly and manipulative. In many ways, I believe he derived more pleasure from controlling the . . . destitute and the downtrodden than he had from breaking his business rivals.

"When I came to San Francisco in August, a year and a . . . half ago, I . . ." He seemed suddenly to run dry of words. It took a moment with his eyes closed, while he searched for the source, before they began to flow again. "I met John. He had only been here a few months himself. I knew immediately that there was something . . . wrong with him, and as I watched him move among his friends—and they were friends, real friends—I

243

. . . felt he was like a jackal, watching for weakness in the herd. I . . . avoided him as best I could, and we went our separate ways. Until November, All Saint's Day, when one of his victims tried to commit suicide.

"The man recovered, but something had to be done. So, I offered myself to John. I allowed him to think I possessed a great and awful secret that would . . . devastate me were it to become known. There was such a secret, of course, but I greatly exaggerated the effects of public knowledge to make it more . . . appealing to John. I . . . dropped hints to encourage him to concentrate on me. I did not stop his . . . activities entirely, but I . . . became his main focus."

"How much did he find out?" Hawkin asked quietly.

"I do not think he knew the entire story. He would make guesses, and I would react, you see? He knew there had been deaths, in an academic setting. He knew I felt responsible for those deaths. I believe he hired an investigator; a man was asking questions about me, about eight months ago. But no, I think he would have let me know in . . . clear ways had he known the full truth.

"It succeeded, in distracting him from others. The most . . . unpleasant part of the affair was his increasing sense of intimacy with me. Not physically, of course, but emotionally. He took to confiding in me, as I said, recounting the details of his past business coups. He thought it amusing to take something from another, even if he did not actually desire it. He told me a long story once, how he had stolen away the wife of a rival, saw them divorced, and then refused to marry her. He preferred to destroy a thing rather than see it in the hands of another. A very twisted man."

He stopped again, allowing his head to fall back against Eve Whitlaw's shoulder.

"Can I get you anything?" Kate asked. "Coffee? A glass of

244

water?" He smiled at her with his eyes and shook his head minutely before looking back at Hawkin.

"I hope you are recording this," he said. "I'm not going to tell it twice."

"We're recording it."

"Good. So. That was John. You needed to know."

"What was his real name?"

"John was his middle name. Alexander John Darcy, of Fort Worth, Texas. I thought of him as John Chrysostom, who was called 'Golden-Mouthed.' Now I will tell you what I know about his death.

"John had a brother who lived near Fort Worth. The two men had been business partners until John left. His leaving created many difficulties for the brother, whose name is Thomas Darcy. John was greatly amused at the problems. Deals were suspended and money was lost because his signature was unavailable."

As the fluency returned to David Sawyer's tongue, Kate was aware of other changes, as well. His posture in the chair had become an awkward slump. His right hand remained intertwined with the professor's, but his left hand wandered up and down, feeling his shirt front, plucking at his trouser legs. And his face—she was briefly reminded of the Dorian Grey story, for as Sawyer's features relaxed from the attentive and thoughtful pose she had always known there, they aged, becoming almost grim with the sense of burden borne. With a shock, Kate realized that the man in the chair across from her was no longer Brother Erasmus.

"A few months ago, John found out two things. First, a piece of land that had been left him and his brother jointly— 'worthless scrub,' he called it—was now surrounded by town and a freeway and had become very valuable. Then he discovered that sometime before, Thomas had begun the legal process of declaring his missing brother dead. John was almost dancing with pleasure at the thought of confounding his brother's plan."

"He told you these things?"

"Everything. I was safe, you see. I had to listen, and he knew I would not tell the others that, for example, he had money and an apartment he used sometimes. He knew I disapproved of everything he did. Perhaps you could even say I detested it. He felt my reaction, and it gave him wicked pleasure. Yes, *wicked* is, I think, the word for the man. Not evil, simply wicked."

"What did he do about his brother?"

"He played games with the telephone at first. He called Thomas, hinting at who he was. Finally he came out in the open. They hadn't been in touch for five years or more. Thomas was at first shocked, and then he became angry and said he thought it was a hoax. John told him where he was. Thomas flew out here in—I don't know. September? October? He also drove out once, a month or so later. John kept him dangling for weeks, offering to sign the deed papers, then withdrawing."

"Did you meet him?"

"Once. I saw him several times."

"Could you describe him, please?"

"Your sort of build, Inspector Hawkin, only shorter. He wore heeled boots, glasses. Brown hair going gray, tan skin, stubby little hands."

"Did he wear a hat?"

"The first time I saw him, no. He was dressed as a normal businessman. The time he drove out, he looked like a cowboy, with snakeskin boots and a hat with a turned-up brim—a cowboy hat."

"Do you remember the make of car?"

"I didn't see it."

"How did you know he had one, then?"

"John described it. He said it was big and ostentatious because his brother had a small . . . sexual organ."

"Did he smoke?"

"Thomas or John?"

"Either."

Sawyer thought for a moment. He looked now like an tired old ex-professor on the skids, and it would have taken a considerable leap of the imagination to place him in a black cassock.

"John smoked cigars, expensive ones, from time to time. I never saw him with a cigarette, although he carried one of those disposable lighters. I don't remember about Thomas, but I was only with him about ten or fifteen minutes."

"Think about it and let me know if you come up with anything."

"He may have been a smoker, come to think of it," Sawyer said, sounding surprised. "His hands—they were tidy. Small, fussy hands. But the nails were discolored, yellow. Like a smoker's." The pauses between his words were becoming brief, more sporadic. His speech was almost normal, but he looked so tired.

"Is there anything else you know about Thomas Darcy?"

"He was here in San Francisco on the day his brother died."

"Was he, now?" Hawkin almost purred with satisfaction.

"Yes. I normally saw John before I would go to Berkeley. I would meet him somewhere in the park, often in Marx Meadow before I walked up to Park Presidio, where Joel picked me up. That is where we met that day."

"What time did you meet him?"

"In the morning. Perhaps nine. We walked through the

meadow and up into the trees, and he told me that his brother was coming to see him again. And he told me that he had decided what to do about the piece of land his brother was so desperate to sell. He told me . . . he said he had made up his mind to disappear again, but before he went, he was going to sign over his half interest in it. Sign it over not to his brother, but to me."

"What?"

"Yes. Can you imagine? It wasn't enough to confound and rob his brother; he had to do it in a way that would take over my life, as well. The property was worth four or five million dollars, he told me. It is not possible to own that much money; he wanted it to own me."

"What was your response?"

"I was angry . . . very angry. I thought . . . I had hoped that after more than a year of working with him, he would begin to grow, to let go of his wickedness. Instead, it had grown within him. I was so incensed, I shouted some words at him and then walked away from him. In fact, it took me so long to calm myself that I forgot about Joel. He had waited and then left. I had to walk and thumb rides across the Bay."

"But you didn't actually see Thomas Darcy?"

"Oh yes, I did. He was sitting in a car parked along Kennedy Drive, reading a map. He didn't see me, I don't think, but I saw him. I might not have recognized him, because he'd grown a beard, but I saw his distinctive hands on the map, and after all, he was on my mind, since John had just told me that he was going to meet him."

"What kind of car was he in?"

"It was not the one John had described. This one was small, white, ordinary. New-looking."

A typical rental car, Kate thought, writing the description on her pad.

"I suggest, Dr. Sawyer," said Hawkin evenly, "that it is fortunate for you that Thomas Darcy did not notice you."

Sawyer held up his left hand, rubbed his thumb on the indentation carved there by his ring, which now lay in an envelope in the property clerk's basement room, and shook his head slowly. "Poor, poor Beatrice. A queen among women. She saw him. She must have."

"Not that day. Earlier, when he drove his own car out from Texas, then she saw him. The rest was Thomas Darcy's guilty imagination, reading too much into her words."

"Did she suffer?"

"I don't think so. The same as John, a hard, fast blow to the skull, immediate unconsciousness, and then death."

"Poor child. So pointless. Will she have a funeral?"

Hawkin was taken aback at this unexpected question. "I really don't know. It depends on whether or not someone claims the body. The city doesn't pay for elaborate funerals."

"She had no family left. I will perform the ceremony."

"We'll have to see about that."

"I can raise whatever money is required, Inspector Hawkin. And although I suppose my license has expired, back in another lifetime I was once an ordained priest."

♦

Late that night, Kate went up to the sixth-floor jail and stood outside David Sawyer's cell. He was on his knees on the hard floor, his hands loosely clasped, and he looked up when she appeared. A smile came into his eyes and his face, and he got to his feet.

"I'm sorry to interrupt you," she said.

"Dear Kate. What a pleasure to say your name, Inspector Martinelli. Names are one of the few pleasures I have longed for. I was not praying. I don't seem to be able to pray, but going through the motions is calming. What can I do for you?"

"I just wanted to say thank you, for today. I know what it cost you. Or at least I can begin to guess."

"Had the payment been made a month ago, a life would have been saved. No cost would be too great, were it to change that."

"I've often thought how nice it would be if we could know the future," Kate said, and realized with surprise that she was now comforting him. The thought reached him at the same time, and he gave her a crooked smile. Then he did a strange thing: He put his right hand out through the bars and, with his fingers resting in the hair above her temple, he traced a cross with his thumb onto the skin of her forehead.

"*Absolvo te*, Kate Martinelli," he said. "What you and your partner did was both necessary and right. No apology is due." For a moment, he rested his entire hand, warm and heavy, on the top of her head, then retrieved it and stepped back from the bars. "Good night, Kate Martinelli. I hope you sleep well."

◆

TWENTY-SEVEN

◆

By nature he was the sort of man who has that
vanity which is the opposite of pride; that vanity
which is very near to humility.

Kate was involved in the final stages of the case and even testified during the trial of Thomas Darcy, but her heart was not in
it, and the case seemed remarkably distant and flat in the wake
of the revelations of David Sawyer's statement.

Once they had the name, the case quickly became water-
tight: plane tickets, a gasoline station receipt, and a hotel clerk
with a good memory placed him in San Francisco the week his
brother was killed. The identity of the John Doe in the park
was confirmed as that of Alexander John Darcy through the
partial fingerprint raised by forensics and the dental X ray sent
by his Fort Worth dentist. By the time Thomas Darcy was

faced with Beatrice, he had become slightly more wily, but he had still used a credit card to hire a car; the newsagent in Fort Worth testified that Darcy had received the Wednesday San Francisco paper with the interview of Beatrice on the day after it had appeared; and Darcy was remembered by the sales clerk in a Pacifica hardware store where he had bought a pair of narrow, strong wire cutters. He even took the wire cutters home with him to Texas, where they were found in an odds-and-ends drawer in his kitchen. Forensic analysis proved that the clippers had been used on the cut ring found near Beatrice's body, a ring remembered well by many, including the owners of Sentient Beans, who testified at Darcy's trial, as well. The partial fingerprint lifted from the side of the ring had enough points of similarity to clinch the case.

For his brother's death, he was found guilty of the lesser charge of manslaughter, but for the killing of Beatrice Jankowski, the charge of first-degree murder persisted to the final verdict.

He was never tried for the death of his brother's dog Theophilus, although traces of canine blood were identified in the crevice between the sole and upper on the right boot of a pair in his closet.

Before all that, though, on the day Thomas Darcy was arrested in Fort Worth, Kate went to the jail and personally supervised the release of David Sawyer. She waited outside while his orange jail clothes were taken from him and his jeans and shirt, duffel coat and knit cap, the worn boots with the dust of Barstow still on them, the knapsack with two books and a jug of stale water, and the worn gold wedding ring were all returned to him. When he came out into the hallway, he was met by the sight of Inspector Kate Martinelli, propping herself up against a carved hiking stick nearly a foot taller than she.

He stopped.

"I thought you might want your stick back," she said.

He did not answer and made no move to take the staff; he said only, "Is there some place we can go for coffee?"

She carried the awkward pole through the halls, into the elevator, out the doors, and down the street, finally threading it through the door of the coffee shop to lean it against the greasy wall in back of her chair, all the time wondering if he was going to leave the damned thing with her and what on earth she would do with it.

The waitress came by with her pad, looking as tired and disheveled as the chipped name tag pinned crookedly to her limp nylon uniform.

"Just coffee, thanks," Kate said.

Sawyer looked into her dark eyes and smiled. "I, too, would like a cup of coffee, please, Elizabeth. Would you also be so kind as to give me some cream and some sugar to go in it?"

The woman blinked, and Kate was aware of an odd gush of pleasure at Sawyer's undisguised enjoyment of the words he was pronouncing. He seemed to taste them before he let them go, and she thought she was catching a glimpse of what Professor Whitlaw had meant when she described his power as a public speaker.

Their coffee came quickly. Sawyer opened two envelopes of sugar, stirred them and a large dollop of cream into the thick once-white mug, and put the spoon down on the table.

"Beatrice's funeral is this afternoon," he said.

"I planned on going. Al, too."

"I asked Philip Gardner to take the service."

"Your license being expired," she said with a smile.

"I did not feel I had the right to the cassock."

It suddenly struck Kate that he was not wearing his wedding ring, either. She set her cup down with a bang. "Now look, David, you can't go around taking all the world's sins on your shoulders. You didn't kill her; Thomas Darcy did. You're less to blame than the newspaper reporter."

"I only intend to shoulder my own sins, Kate, I assure you."

"Then why—"

He put up a hand. "Please, Kate. This is something I must wrestle with alone, although I do truly appreciate your willingness to help me."

"Where will you go? Do you have a place to stay?"

"Eve wishes me to go to the house she is borrowing, after the funeral. In fact, she has asked me to go with her to England, assuming she can persuade the authorities to issue a passport to a man with no identification papers."

"And will you?"

Sawyer let his eyes drift away from Kate until he was focusing on the wall behind her. For a very long time, he studied the piece of carved wood that stood there, and slowly, slowly his face began to relax, to lose the taut, pinched look it had taken on with the news of Beatrice's death. Eventually he tore his gaze away from the staff and looked back at Kate, but he did not answer her question. Instead, he asked, "Will your friend come to the funeral, as well?"

"My friend?" Do you mean Lee? I hadn't thought to ask her. It's difficult for her to get around. She's in a wheelchair."

"I know. Still, she might find it a good experience."

"Lee has been to a depressing number of funerals over the last few years," she said flatly. He nodded his understanding, finished his coffee, and stood up. Kate went to the cash register to pay their bill, and when she turned back to the room, she saw that Sawyer was standing outside the door. The staff was still leaning against the wall. She retrieved it, followed him outside, and stood beside him, looking at the familiar dingy street.

He was watching a filthy, decrepit, toothless individual pick fastidiously through a garbage can on the other side of the street. Kate waited to hear some apt quotation about the human condition, but when he spoke, it was in his own words, about his own condition. "Everything I told you, with the exception of seeing Thomas Darcy in a car reading a map, would be discounted as hearsay evidence, come the trial, would it not?"

"Some of it would, yes."

"Most everything, I think. You do not need my testimony."

"That depends on what forensics finds. If he covered his tracks carefully, we'll be up shit creek."

"With my scant evidence your only paddle."

"That's about it."

"Well. I don't imagine a defense counsel would permit it to get by without considerable battering. We shall just have to trust that more concrete evidence will be forthcoming.

"Thank you for your friendship, Kate Martinelli," he said abruptly. "I shall see you at the church this afternoon."

"Wait—David. Do you want your walking stick?"

He looked at it, then looked at her, and a smile came onto his face: a sweet smile, a dazzling smile—an Erasmus smile.

"Yes. Yes, I suppose I do," he said, and reached out his hand for it. He cupped his palm briefly over the smooth place on top of the carved head and then ran his hand down the shaft to the other worn patch just below shoulder height, and then he turned and walked away.

◆

To her surprise, when Kate got back to her desk, she found herself phoning Lee to ask if she wanted to go to the funeral of this homeless woman whom Lee had never met. To her greater surprise, Lee said yes.

◆

255

Half a dozen photographers lounged around the steps to the church, but Kate had expected them, so she continued on around the block to a delivery entrance. The mortician's van was parked there, and she pulled up behind it, extricated Lee and her chair from the car, and they entered the church through the side entrance.

There was a surprisingly large congregation. Kate recognized many of the faces in the pews from the investigation, most of them street people, a few store owners in Beatrice's home area of the Haight. Krishna and Leila from Sentient Beans were sitting in the front row; the three veterans, with the damaged Tony in the middle, looking ready to bolt, sat in the last pew back. News reporters swelled the ranks and added contrast in the form of clean neckties and intact jackets. Al Hawkin sat almost directly across the church from them.

But no David Sawyer.

Kate took all this in as she was pushing Lee into a place along the side aisle. Then she took a seat beside her at the end of the pew.

She became aware of Philip Gardner's voice coming from the altar.

"We thank you for giving her to us," he was saying, "her family and friends, to know and love as a companion on our earthly pilgrimage. In your boundless compassion, console us who mourn."

A movement caught Kate's eye, one of the white-gowned deacons at Dean Gardner's side. It took a moment for her to realize it was David Sawyer. It took a while longer for her to recognize him, to her astonishment, as Brother Erasmus.

The service flowed past them. People stood up and read, haltingly or fluently. A hymn was sung, and another, and then Philip Gardner was raising his hands in blessing and declaring that the Lord would guide our feet into the way of peace, and it was over. The cassocks and surplices fluttered up the aisle, people began to shuffle in their wake, and then Sawyer, or perhaps Erasmus, was sitting in the pew ahead of Kate, with Lee's hand in his. The ring, Kate noticed, was back on his hand. She made the introductions, although they hardly seemed necessary.

"The wounded healer," he said quietly in response to Lee's name.

"I might say the same of you," Lee answered.

"Ah. Answer a fool according to his folly," he said with a grin.

"And are you? A fool, that is?" Lee leaned forward in the chair to study the old face opposite her. "Am I speaking with Brother Erasmus, or David Sawyer?"

"I am Fortune's fool," he admitted. "An old doting fool with one foot already in the grave. A lunatic, lean-witted fool. How well white hairs become a fool and jester."

"I think white hairs suit a fool very well. How does it go? 'This fellow's wise enough to play the fool.' "

The old man looked, of all things, embarrassed, and he seemed grateful for the interruption when Al Hawkin joined them. He stood up to shake Hawkin's hand.

"Is this the man that made the earth to tremble, that did shake kingdoms? Hast thou found me, O mine enemy?"

The detective laughed. "Never that. I just wanted to thank you for your help and wish you well."

"All's well that ends well." He turned to Kate, and she waited for his smile and his words, taken from someone else but made his own, and they came: "May the Lord bless you and keep you; may the Lord make his face to shine upon you, and grant you peace."

"I take it you're planning on going back onto the streets?" she asked.

"It is better never to begin a good work than, having begun it, to stop," he said quietly.

"You're getting old, David," she said bluntly. "It's a young man's life. Talk to Philip Gardner. You can do your good work at the seminary."

He nearly laughed. "Amongst all these stirs of discontented strife. O, let me lead an academic life!"

Kate had not heard Professor Whitlaw's approach until the English voice came from behind her, sounding both disappointed and sad.

"He was a scholar," she said, stressing the past tense, "and a ripe and good one."

Brother Erasmus focused his gaze over Kate's shoulder but only shook his head gently.

"Well," Kate said, "for God's sake, take care of yourself and don't do anything stupid like you tried that day with the young drunk. You could get hurt."

His face relaxed into amusement, and something more. They could see, shining clear as day, the regained source of his serenity. "The Lord is my light and my salvation," he said simply. "Whom shall I fear?"

◆

TWENTY-EIGHT

◆

*Yet the friends of St. Francis have really contrived
to leave behind a portrait, something almost
resembling a devout and affectionate caricature.*

Brother Erasmus, he who once was the Reverend Professor
David Matthew Sawyer, spent the next twelve days with his old
friend Eve Whitlaw at the house she had borrowed in Noe Valley. When Easter morning dawned, however, he was not at her
house; he was not even in San Francisco.

Neither Kate nor Al ever saw him after that. But among
the homeless, the marginal, the discarded citizens of a number
of large cities, the people of the street talk about Brother Erasmus. They say that he was a rich man who humbled himself,
and that he had a small black-and-white dog, a sort of familiar
spirit, who was killed by a demon man, who in turn was van-

quished by Erasmus. They say that he healed a sick boy; that he foretold the future; that he transported himself magically across the waters.

They say he is dead. They also say that he lives and walks the streets unrecognized. Some call him a saint. Others say he was a fool.

These things they say about the man who called himself Brother Erasmus.

And they are all true.